# WATERWEAVER

CHROMA: Book One

## MAYA GOULIARD

Second edition

ISBN: 978-1-967608-03-4 (paperback)
ISBN: 978-1-967608-02-7 (ebook)

Book Cover Design by Maya Gouliard.

First Printing 2024.
www.mayagouliard.com
Mayagouliard@gmail.com

**Calmillusion**
PRESS
INDEPENDENTLY PUBLISHED

# *Dedication*

There is something expected from a dedication that I am about to break, I believe. I debated, should I dedicate this to those I love? My children, my grandson, my husband? But this book wasn't for them, I wrote it for the broken-hearted mother I was when adjusting to my children growing up and leaving me. The sadness had consumed me, and I was in a dark place, that gave birth to THE WASTES that Lara lives in.

And so, I dedicate this book to the mothers looking at life after the kids fly away.

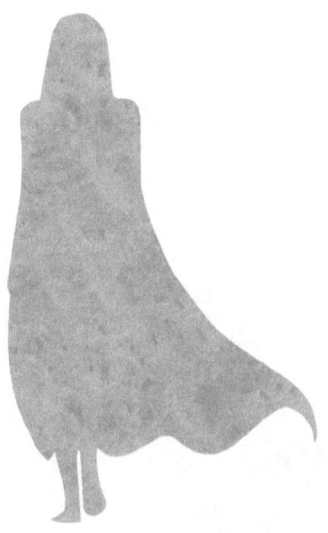

# Contents

# Acknowledgments

This book would not exist without all of the help I received from the random comments of strangers to the support from loved ones.

So, thank you to the bartender at the pizza joint I was working in when the idea first glimmered in my head for the encouragement.

Thank you to the servers at my fine dining restaurant job who asked how the project was coming along.

Thank you to the writing groups I joined for the support.

Thank you to my children who still are the joy of my life and inspiration, (even though they aren't kids anymore.)

Most of all, thank you to my husband, Jon, who puts up with all of the chaos I bring to his regimented days.

# A Note to the Reader:

In a magical realm based on color, it is important, I believe, to have a color map. However, I also believe it is important to save money when possible, so this book is in black and white.

Therefore, I encourage you to break out the crayons, markers, highlighters or paints and color in the map on the following page.

Thank you,
Maya

# REALMS OF CHROMA

RED - PIRON
ORANGE - LARAN
YELLOW - AMARA
GREEN - GREVENDALE
BLUE - AZURAL
PURPLE - MORCHAST
PINK - VAALEAN

# CHROMA

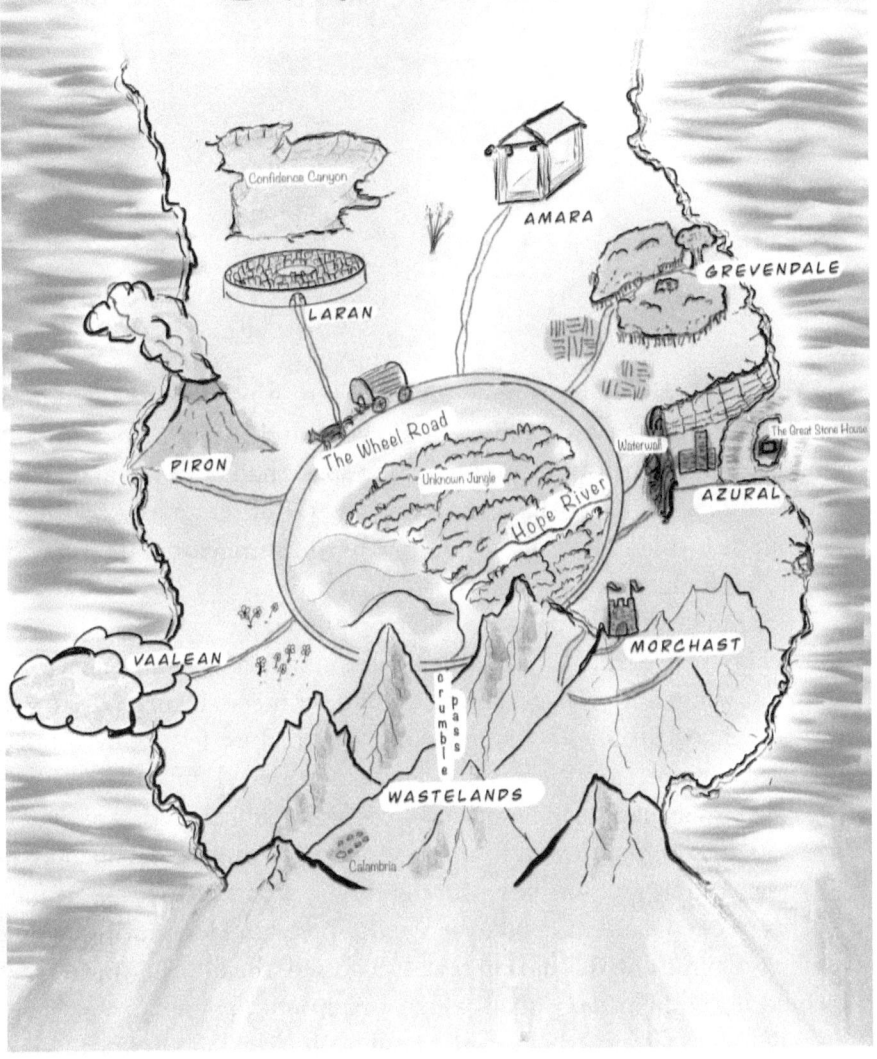

# Prologue

Everything was white, as it always had been. A pale light filtered through the egg's shell, casting a magical glow around the tiny creature nestled inside. The security and comfort of the space had been full and complete until moments ago, when suddenly the creature stirred, realizing the tightness of the little walls, feeling the need to stretch out the fuzzy limbs that had moments ago felt so right curled up close.

Scrabble and scrape. Chip and chip and chip.

Tiny claws, sharper than could be imagined, began tearing at the hard surrounding surface. The space had been comforting, but now it felt confined. As the shell's wall cracked, the creature felt re-invigorated by the excitement, and their energy level increased. Biting now, with teeth even sharper than their claws, at the pieces it had chipped away.

As the animal slowed from using all of its energy, an opening large enough to push its soft nose through finally appeared. Then, as the tips of its pointed ears came out, the slender body and long furry tail quickly followed, cracking the shell in half. Exhausted, the little newborn creature could do nothing more than lay on the ground, its breath wracking the small body as it sucked in the first taste of the frigid mountain air.

Laying there, it took in the outside world for the first time. Where before the light hitting the shell had given a lovely white glow inside, out here everything was different. Light bounced instead against dark grey clouds, casting a dull and dirty pallor. The ground was nothing but mud and dust, bleak and dirty. The creature didn't know what to expect but felt something was not right. No world should look this broken, feel this wrong.

Pushed on by instinct, the tiny, now very dirty fuzzball of a thing pushed up onto wobbling legs and looked for water and food. No small undertaking in the Wastes. But survival is a powerful motivator, and this little one came from a line of legends.

# Empty-nest

The wintry winds whipped against the closed shutters of the tiny cottage, throwing dirt and debris that clung to the already filthy eaves and outer walls, but those inside paid it no mind, for it was just the way of things here in the Wastes.

The interior of the small house depicted a more friendly environment. Warm golden firelight battled the darkness in the quaint room. A large family, at ease with each other, chatted and quarreled in the relaxed way of people who knew they cared for one another. This little home had been a haven to all of them, as the world collapsed around them.

Every emotion was bouncing throughout the cramped quarters. The oldest sister, Anna, took the lead in preparing her only brother, Peter, for his journey to Amara, the Yellow color realm. She covered her unease at his path ahead with knowing, and albeit bossy, advice. Her mind aflutter with all he must remember for his trip on the Wheel Road.

James, the father, spent most of his morning out in the yard caring for the remaining animals they had, a few chickens, and their nanny goat. When present, he had a wise voice in the confined area, often countering the oldest daughter's ideas with something a little less extreme. "No lad, you don't need that third blanket. It will be too much to carry."

The youngest sister, Sally, and her husband Fiero, brought the humor to the space, helping to balance everyone's stress at the prospect of another sibling heading out to the color realms. None of them had heard anything from the middle sister, Brie, who had left on her journey two years ago. That memory weighed heavily on the household as they were preparing to say goodbye again. They all understood there was a finality to this trip, they might never see him again. The youngest cracked jokes when she noted the mood turned and told stories of memories that highlighted the family's closeness.

The young man turned to his mother for items as he remembered he needed them, and she was already handing them to him. This past year, he was the only child remaining in the cottage and although they had always been close, there was now a comfortable way between them where they rarely needed to speak to know what the other was thinking. Mother handed him a handkerchief to tie around some trail-mix before the words even left his mouth.

Too soon, it was time for hugs and tears as the loved ones surrounded him at the door to say their final goodbyes in the cottage's warmth. Mother handed him his hooded cloak, and then Father opened the door. They all pushed into the stiff wind in the front yard.

Neighbors came out to wave a farewell goodbye, all aware that this might be the final time they saw him. Their close-knit community where everyone relied on their neighbors made the young man feel like family to all of them too. They watched from a distance as the family gave a last round of hugs and then Peter walked out of their front gate.

The youth's pack was full to the brim. He was prepared for the week's long journey to the Yellow Realm. He was on the quest of a lifetime, attempting to stonegraft. His story will be a wonder to hear, but this isn't his tale...

$$\gtrsim \gtrsim \gtrsim$$

Mother couldn't keep her tears back. She knew Pete would be fine. She was happy for him. She had said goodbye to her other three just like this. They had moved on and grown up. Each was amazing. She was proud of them all. But this was different. This was so final. He was the last to leave her — she had an empty nest. When he was no longer visible, she turned slowly and walked into the house, relieved that everyone else had stayed out in the yard.

Tears came quickly now, with no one to see them. She looked at the small, comfortable room. This was where she had nurtured their first steps, shared stories, mediated sibling fights, played, breathed, and simply been there as they grew. Her whole life had been about them. It was so quiet now. Tears continued to drip down to her chin.

She heard the family entering the front door and hastened out the back, she wasn't ready to talk to anyone. The yard was small but had everything they needed. She went and sat on her wooden bench that she and the kids had made years ago, her husband's goat coming up next to her.

Sheila was a great pet, but often Mother was jealous of the goat. Her husband doted on the goat and chatted with the goat, while his own wife sat alone inside sewing. She caught herself in the lie she was telling herself. Amazing how when one feels sad and depressed, you spin the entire world as doom and gloom. Her husband loved her very much. She knew this, but he did also adore this goat. Laughing, she patted Sheila on the head, and her heartache diminished just slightly.

She took a deep breath and looked up into the roiling black and grey clouds. The weather was always overcast, but with no rain. None since they had taken away the magic. Decades ago in her childhood, the Land of Chroma had been scoured for every magic stone that could be found. The Hunters had found every last one they could and left with them. The elemental magic of the stones had been taken along with them, and her home was left behind. The heaviness of the air was constant, and it added to her dark mood. She looked out into the distance.

Her home was now called the Wastelands, and it was called that for a reason - there was very little left. It looked like the color had leached from the landscape, and that was practically what had happened since the stones had all been collected. It was more difficult to start a fire, the sun no longer shone, the water was scarce, and even though the only color left seemed to be black, the dirt was dust, barely able to grow food.

Looking at the shadows creeping across the dull distance didn't help her emotional state. She was alone now. She had spent her whole adult life as a mother, raising her four children. That had been her entire focus, and now it was over. She choked back a sob and put her face into her hands, pressing her fingertips against her wet eyes. They felt warm to her, and she knew her face must be red from all the crying.

She still had two of her girls who were in town — but she caught herself. They weren't girls anymore; they had lives of their own. Anna was running the local inn and Sally had married during this past Yule festival. She was now busy planting her garden and renovating the shed with her husband for them to work on their leather trade.

She knew the girls loved her, but they didn't need her constantly like they used to. Sally, her youngest daughter, had not gone to sleep without her in the room until the age of nine or ten; needing her mom to be singing, telling stories, just being there.

Now, Sally only comes by once every few weeks. It hurt to see her, even though it was wonderful to see her.

If Mother wanted to see her oldest daughter, she had to go to the inn usually. Anna was always so happy to see her, but she didn't need her there to talk her through how to make bread anymore. She knew more about her craft now than she ever learned from her mom. They loved her, but the need was not the same.

At least she still could see them when she was compelled to fill the emptiness. Brie had left months before Sally's wedding, and they hadn't heard from her since. She had planned to head toward Orange, but no one knew if that was where she might have ended up. Brie had always been unsettled and restless, but she was also sturdy but flexible. When deciding on a color realm to travel to, she had a list of them, rather than just the one that Peter had chosen.

And now Peter was off. He was sturdy in a different way than Brie, a more complete way. Yellow was going to welcome him with open arms and be lucky to have him. After the few years of worrying about Brie, the prospect of Peter in the world was less scary for her. And ultimately, she knew that she and James had prepared all of them the best they knew how. Having been asked so often for parenting advice, she had condensed it down to two main points. Parents needed to know what their goals were. Hers were simple: she wanted them to know how to learn and to know who they were. She was confident that she had achieved that goal. All four of them were smart, unique, and comfortable being who they were.

She was so lucky that James had been so supportive of her and the children. His daily routine was much more structured than hers, but he understood her need to fidget and change. He worked as the town historian and records keeper, and although his days had been full of regularly scheduled tasks, his free time was always spent with the family.

Mother dried tears with her hands, then slowly stroked Sheila. The goat seemed to know that she needed some calming. After a few more minutes, she had pulled herself together enough to focus outside of herself, looking at the cracked dirt at her feet. Sheila's water bowl sat there empty.

"Are you thirsty, girl?" Mother took the bowl from the dusty ground and headed through her back gate to the stream that wound its way around the outskirts of the city. All the still-occupied homes in town were along this stream, for water was life in the Wastelands. She made her way across the loose black stones toward the stream.

When she was a little girl, she and her friends used to swim here. It had been more of a river, but over the years it had slowly shrunk and now it was little more than a few feet wide. Her favorite spot to gather water was just a few houses down where the rocks had a slight drop off — there, a tiny waterfall of about two feet, was the perfect place to fill up water containers. It also created the most soothing sound. She loved the water and missed swimming so much. When Anna had been a baby, she had often taken her swimming. Hours of splashing and playing in the water, an infectious smile and coos of delight. She would never have that time with her little ones again. She caught herself before she let the sadness engulf her.

With Sheila's water dish filled and her emotions mostly in check, she returned home.

James stood in the yard, staring off at the distant dark peaks of Mount Grist. Sheila was bumping against him, vying for attention, his body swaying with the force of it. He looked up when the gate squealed as she entered the back yard.

He watched her with intensity, trying to evaluate her state of mind, as she set the bowl down for Sheila.

"You alright Lara?"

She choked on her response, words not coming - instead, just a small squeak. She reached her hands out palm up and shrugged, it was a strained motion, and she could feel herself holding back as much as she could, her elbows tight by her sides trying to control the sorrow and keep it inside where she had a handle on it. Her face felt tense, her mouth in a tight smirk to the side, as though maybe the smile would keep the tears at bay. Her eyebrows shifted between a furrowed, concerned look and a quizzical one. She had known this would be difficult. It had been with all the others. But now they were all gone.

James quietly answered her silent response. "He's going to be fine. He's a smart one."

"I know," she squeaked out, "but that doesn't make it easier. I'm going to miss him. They are all gone now." Her last words faltered, and the tears began to flow. She stepped up to James and leaned her forehead on his shoulder.

He wasn't a hugger, but he was always there for her when she needed it. He encircled her with his arms and stood looking into the distance. She knew this was hard on him, too. She needed to stop making this life-changing moment all about herself, James had been by her side the whole time. With a quick final squeeze, she took a small step back from him, so she could look at his face.

"Well, here comes a new phase in our lives."

He nodded at her with a twinkle in his eye. "Just the two of us in the house should be fun." He smiled at her and her heart warmed.

"Agreed, but…" She still felt an ache at the loss of so many years filled with the children, her whole adult life. Taking a deep breath, she told him, "I just don't know what comes next for me."

"You can figure it out."

"I still have you at leas—" Lara's comment was broken off as Sheila stepped between them, her wide belly pushing Lara back another step. "Oh, for heaven's sake." Lara laughed and rolled her eyes as James squatted down to give Sheila all the adoration she expected of him.

# *Loved Ones*

The laundry had been hung on the line; the floors were swept. James had started a habit of doing more of the chores than he ever had back when the house was full - or maybe he had always been helping and there had just been so much more to do. She often caught herself thinking of things from only her own perspective and having to reassess. Even with his help, two people still made a mess. Dishes were in the sink, counters needed wiped, but it was just so much less. Things had changed in this quiet little house.

Over the last few decades, as the Hope River that ran behind her home had slowed to a stream, the town had voted to ration water. Lara's family ration was larger because of Sheila. She was the only nanny goat left in Calambria. What they took each day gave just enough water to keep Sheila healthy, get the dishes and clothes done, and then still have enough to take a damp towel to wash themselves. She often remembered the days of splashing in the tub out back as a little girl. Filled from the river the water splashing out the sides. Or even swimming in the river, hours of play and fun while Mom had washed their clothes in the shallows behind the house.

While she plaited her hair in the usual loose braid to the side, she looked at her fabric piled high on the kitchen table. In the month since Pete had left, she had learned how to quilt, learned how to paint, and tried to learn how to play the guitar. She had kept herself busy, but nothing really helped. The quiet was overwhelming. Days of running around after four little ones had honed her need for action. Reading by the fire or sitting with her cross-stitch just wasn't going to cut it.

She grabbed her shawl and gathering bag and headed out the door. She didn't really need anything, but the action of leaving the house felt good. It was supposed to be late Spring, but the sky was ever dull now with the thick, dark clouds obscuring the sun from view. There was a constant chill in the air. She pulled her shawl tighter around her and tied it securely. She had crocheted it herself years ago and it was exactly the size to fit her, the tight stitches keeping the wind at bay.

Looking at the little lane she lived in, she felt the sadness consume her still. The kids had run down this path laughing and squealing as they had come to the market with her. They would call from ahead for her to hurry up, Sally running back and forth between the big kids and mom, wanting to be with everyone at the same time. She had let them run, while she walked at her steady pace. Now she was not rushed along. Indeed, there was no pressing need to be anywhere.

Her depression brought the reality of the state of her surroundings into a clear, stark view. She saw the dirt caked on Nelson's windows. She saw the disrepair of the gate at the Franks' house. As a child, there had been a store in town with hardware to fix these things, but now the gate sat askew and propped open with a small boulder. All from a lack of supplies.

The houses were all small like hers, and she knew all the people who lived in them. As she continued down the lane, she noticed that although Abby's house was as dirty as the rest, there was a flicker of warm firelight through the windows. Life had become hard out here in the Wastes, but those who lived here were tough and kind. They were a community. She heaved a sigh and tried to shake her somber thoughts away.

She passed Granny Sanders' house on the right. As a child, Lara had visited Mrs. Sanders after school because she had the most beautiful flower gardens. Lara had loved attempting to catch the tiny yellow butterflies that had flocked to the buds. But now the yard was nothing but a shell of what once was. It almost looked haunted. The wooden fence was still standing, and the stone path still meandered toward the house. Now the large stones, the side of the house, and really everything else looked like they needed a good wash. But water was too precious for cleaning stones. Grass hadn't grown for years; the breeze carried grime that coated houses, windows, and gates.

Her homeland was now called the Wastes, a shadowland of what it had been in her youth. All the color had been sucked away, leeched from the ground and air till nothing was left but grays and blacks. It was dark, depressing and sad. There were so little of all the resources left. While the color realms grew and prospered, the Wastes had become this shadow of its former self.

Folks in these villages got by, but only by working together as a team. Helping each other, supporting each other, sharing what little everyone had. So, these communities were tight knit; more than just neighbors in proximity, they were neighbors in the best sense of the word. There for each other, whatever was needed.

Her place had always been with the children, she had taught many of the neighborhood kids once the school closed. But as the struggles got harder and the resources shrank, so did the number of children in Calambria. Families left town, hoping the color realms were better than here. Those that stayed were a hearty group, or possibly too frail to move on. And so, with the last of her children gone, and no new children in the village to use her skills, she was unsure of her place.

She headed into her friend Jada's house. Jada always was good at lifting her spirits. She was just kooky enough that many in town wondered about her. Jada had never really done things the way she was expected to. She had no children, and she had never been interested in marrying. "I don't need to be tied down for life!" She had told Lara when they were young. Lara understood that feeling, but she loved James and the kids so much, and her life had been so complete. She had loved running from task to task until she fell into bed. She had been so happy back then — she caught where her thoughts were turning and quickly shook her head. She didn't need to knock, Jada was always happy for her to walk right in.

This was Lara's home, away from home. Jada's house was not set up the way the other homes were. She had no kitchen table. Instead, she had a whole slew of instruments set up right in her living room. There was a circular carpet in the center of the room, worn down from years of people sitting on it as they listened, and wooden chairs with thin round rungs and no armrests. They were the kind of chair you didn't sit in to get comfortable and stay awhile, but rather to sit forward on the edge as you actively played your fiddle or flute. Lara loved it here, but she just enjoyed the atmosphere and people. She didn't play. Sometimes she would sing along if there was a group, but she had only ever sung alone to her kids at bedtime.

Jada was at her piano. It was her prized possession. Her grandfather had brought it, and a beautifully carved violin for her brother Stewart, to town when Jada was seven, and she had been pounding away on it ever since. She could play it so loudly the whole village could hear it, but she also could play the most entrancing quiet melodies that just made your heart ache. That is what she was playing now, and Lara could feel the ever-present ache in her heart swell up. It was always just under the surface. She felt like every moment she was at risk of breaking down. She missed them, she missed her life. She had been so happy.

Lara crumple to the floor and just cried as she listened. At home, she tried to keep it together. James was always trying to cheer her up. Here, she knew she was safe with her sad feelings. So, she let them out. The song went on, and she sat on the carpet with her face in her hands. She thought of the time Anna had first learned she could reach the piano keys and play along with Jada, the tiny chubby fingers reaching up and the adorable cherub face pounding on the lower octave keys. All of them laughing at the disconnect of the sound with her high squeals of delight.

She thought of the times Jada had welcomed all the children in town to come every Wednesday evening to do a sing-along with her. She remembered the moment that Pete had walked out the door because his sisters kept singing the same song over and over again, and that only reminded her of a few weeks ago when Pete had walked away from town, and her life as she had known it, had ended. She sat and cried.

She realized after a few minutes that the music had ended. Jada was sitting quietly, looking out her dirty windows at the distant, dark mountain peaks. Lara took a deep, calming breath as Jada crouched beside her and placed a hand on her shoulder. Jada reached out and offered her the glass of water she had been holding.

"Here, this will help." Jada said quietly.

Lara stared at the water. The glass was almost half full. She shook her head, there was no way she was going to drink Jada's ration of water. Jada just squeezed her shoulder and then placed the glass into her hands.

"I can't," but even as she said it, she realized she needed it, the words croaked out of her raw throat. It was rare for Lara to drink so much water in one sitting. She gave Jada a wilted smile, full of appreciation, but it was all she could muster. As she drank, the first touch of water hurt as it touched the angry skin in her throat. But as she took the second sip, the moisture had coated, and it went down smoothly. She closed her eyes and took the luxury of a gulp. The liquid flowed down cooling the heat that had grown in her as she had cried. The water gave her a feeling of washing away not only the physical pain but also a bit of sadness.

Jada smiled knowingly at Lara, and Lara laughed — a stilted, ironic laugh. "I just can't seem to keep it together. I am up and down with these emotions."

Jada stood up and rolled her ankles to work out the stiffness from crouching down for a bit. "No surprise there. Don't be hard on yourself. This is a difficult time. You will find your purpose for this next stage in life."

"Being a mom is just all I know. I was so good at it, dang it! Look at my kids, they are all amazing. I loved spending my days with them. I loved the difficult moments and solving their problems. Now, I have nothing. I sit all day looking at the shadows out my window and there is nothing around to cheer me." Lara craned her neck to look up at her friend. "I finished my chores for the day already!"

"You are a great mom, your kids are great, but that's not all that's in you. There is more for you: I am sure of it. You are destined for something else amazing. You just need to see it yourself. Find in yourself what you are capable of."

Lara laughed again. "Well, I am capable of heading to the town square for a few things." Ready to stand up Lara looked left and right and realized she had not thought through the idea of standing up when she had slumped into a heap in the center of the carpet. "I might not be capable of standing up though."

Jada came over and offered her forearm as leverage for Lara to heft herself up off the floor. "We aren't getting any younger, are we?" Lara said, her motion was stiff at first. She followed Jada's lead, slowly rotating her feet and bending her knees to get her body ready for her walk to the market. "Any chance you want to come along?"

Jada smiled. "I am always up for an adventure with you!"*

As usual, their first stop was at the inn to say a quick hello to Anna. Lara loved seeing her oldest daughter whenever she could. Jada pulled open the heavy door of the inn's tavern and they entered to see the usual bustle. The tavern was the only place in town you could come for a respite from the bleakness of living out here in the Wastes. Anna had taken over the Inn from Old Danny ten years ago and she had done a wonderful job of creating a homey, welcoming space to escape the troubles of daily life. People could find a good meal, or a hearty ale, a tasty dessert, or a warm bed- but more than anything, people found a smile and an ear to listen. Anna was a friend to everyone in town, and the very rare visitor to town.

Anna looked up to greet the new guests and her face lit up at the sight of Lara. She came over immediately and gave her a big hug, their usual greeting.

"Hi Mom. What are you up to today?" she asked.

"Just trying to keep busy."

"I know it is so hard for you, with Petey gone. I miss him too." Anna continued to speak as she walked to a nearby table and wiped it down with the dry rag in her hand. "How's Dad? He never comes to see me, and I never seem to get a break to stop by and see him."

"You know him, his work as town record keeper keeps him plenty busy. He spends a lot of the day sitting at his desk writing and thinking. Then he has his weekly meetings with Mayor Kelton, Farmer Oswald, and all those types of folks to get the information he needs to report on. And he also has his daily stop-ins to read to those who can't see so well, although if he doesn't have his glasses, he can't either. I think this afternoon he is going to Granny Winslow's. As long as his regular schedule isn't interrupted, and he has time with Sheila, he is content."

Jada snorted. "That goat of his cracks me up. I have never seen an animal connect with a human that way."

"He always has had some sort of animal following him around," Anna said as she walked behind the bar. "Would you two like to try the stew I made? Farmer Oswald brought me some okra and zucchini, and we still have a decent supply of dried mushrooms in the cellar."

Dried mushrooms have been a staple in the diet of Calambrians for the last few decades. Originally there had been so much water and the lush forests of the mountainside had been a breeding ground for mushrooms, with all of the undergrowth and decaying old wood. Her own children had spent days hunting mushrooms, coming back with baskets full.

But in the last ten years as the leaves had stopped growing on the trees in spring, and the ground had dried out, even the dead trees seemed to turn to dust rather than have the decency to decompose. With nothing in the ground to sustain them, fewer and fewer mushrooms had been found. As the supply had slowed the townspeople had decided to collect and dry as many as they could. There had been a whole year where people worked together scouring the mountainside. Nowadays, there were occasional pockets of fresh mushrooms found close to the river, but none up in the wasted away forests on the mountains anymore.

"No, save it for customers with something to trade. We were just stopping in to see you before we went to the market ourselves. You good?"

"Well, Old Danny came by this morning. You know how he is, always telling me how he used to do things. He has no clue how the shortages affect business. Today he went on and on about how the windows always used to be spotless and the menu had more options." Anna began scrubbing the same spot on the bar in an agitated manner. "I can't keep the windows clean anymore. The grime sticks to the glass right after I wash them. The storage cellar is getting pretty bare, and ingredients are harder and harder to come by. He gets so upset, and I am doing my best..." Lara grabbed Anna's hands to stop them from their frustrated motion and met her eyes.

Anna stilled at the connection. She breathed a few deep breaths with Lara and calmed down. Once Lara saw the tension leave her shoulders, she commented, "Old Danny has no idea of the way of things now. He's just tottering around remembering the good old days. We all wish it could be that way again, but you are doing an amazing job with the resources you are left with. The stew smells amazing, and this room is sparkling. Everyone knows that they can come here for a break, and you are the one who makes that possible. Keep on doing what you are. You are amazing."

Anna rolled her eyes but smiled an appreciative smile. "Thanks Mom, you always make me feel better."

"I am just telling it like it is. No one I know works as hard as you. Don't let someone who doesn't see it bother you. Know your worth, I do."

They all looked up when the door opened again, letting in the cold air and dust.

"Hi Ben, hi Griff," Anna called out in her customer service voice, at least one octave higher than she had been speaking a moment ago.

The two men looked grumpy and tired. They had obviously been out in the winds all day, their faces smudged with grime over their red chapped cheeks. They stumbled over to the bar and pulled out stools roughly, barely grunting a hello in response.

Lara felt for them. It must have been their turn to take on the job of keeping the towns fencing up, which was a real struggle. The winds started the process of pushing, but the ground over the past few years had become less stable. It was almost as if instead of dirt it was just dust, loose and impossible to drive a stake into. The fencing was falling over daily. For a while, the townspeople agreed to just let it slide. We could do without the fencing, and there were other concerns that came first, but then the wolves had gotten braver. Less food for them out in the wilderness had sent them sneaking into town at night.

The wolves had eaten three goats and five chickens in one week. That was when Sheila had started sleeping inside. Lara had not been happy about it, but James loved it. It was pretty cute how she laid snuggled on the floor next to his chair while he read at night though.

After that week, each resident able signed up for a day to work on the fences. It was tough work, and Lara remembered how hungry she was after that day's toiling. Seeing the state, they must have been up against it today.

Anna headed down the bar to stand in front of them. "I have some fresh soup with carrots from Dillon Oswald's farm today. Can I get each of you a bowl to warm you up? The bread will be going into the oven soon too."

Griff reached into his pocket and pulled out some change, then dropped it on the counter. "We only have enough for a shot of The Warmth each." He pushed the coins toward her as he gestured to the sole liquor bottle on the back bar. It was strong, and it was known to warm a person inside and out. For the short term.

"Warmth for the pain today, pain from the Warmth tomorrow," Jada sang quietly into Lara's ear.

"Shush Jada, we learned it the hard way back when we were young. Let them be. Plus, times are a lot harder now than they used to be."

Anna was pouring the shots of the clear liquor she distilled herself in the basement with a concerned look on her face. Lara recognized it as her, I gotta fix this problem' face.

"I am actually super glad you two came in. I was just trying to solve this problem I ran into. Now that the cellar is so empty, I am seeing how much better it would be to move the shelves to the far side, where the lighting is better. It is a job for a few people. I already tried to do it by myself. I don't have the money to pay anyone, but was wondering if you two might be up for a trade? I could cover your lunch here for a few weeks if you'd help me out?"

"I can help. How about you, Griff? Ben blurted.

"Eh, if you want to, I can help you."

"Wonderful," Anna's service voice punctuated. "Why don't you start with a bowl each while I finish up my bread. Then we can go down and I can show you what I am thinking?" She ladled out a bowl for each of them and then came back to stand in front of her mom.

"You really are a marvel, Honey." Lara said, misty eyed at her daughter's kindness.

"Oh, Mom, don't make a big deal about it. At times like these, we all must do what we can." Anna paused, and the three of them looked surreptitiously at the men eating. Pounding her hands on the bar, Anna pushed back from them and spoke, "I have to get back to work. My bread dough should be done rising, and I should get the loaves into the oven."

Jada chimed in at the mention of the bread. "Might have to stop by for a loaf on the way home, nothing like a fresh, warm loaf of your bread, Anna."

"Then maybe we will see you later, Hun." Lara turned and headed to the door. "Love you, bye."

"Love you too, and Mom…" Lara turned back to look at her, "thank you." A smile touched Lara's lips. With her heart filled, she exited the inn, feeling lighter than she had.

# The Water Well

Their next stop was the town square. Most mornings everyone gathers here for trading and bartering. If you needed something this was the place to go. Only a few tables were set up around the central fountain and they quickly found Farmer Oswald's table.

"Hey there!" He called to them as they walked up.

"Hey, Dillon!" Jada shouted back across the square.

"Hey there Farmer Oswald, how's the day going!" Lara said, voice raised. Dillon had been friends with Jada and Lara since childhood. The three of them playing make believe games in the school yard at lunch, imagining faraway places. Reliving traveling tales, they had heard Jada's grandfather from his travels around Chroma, or retelling fairy stories of the Guardian Dragons and their magic. When her children had been introduced to him as Farmer Oswald, the name had stuck in her head, and she still called him that. It used to bug him, which had been fun, but now it was just who he was.

Farming has become a science in Calambria over the last few decades. With each year changing how crops grew: changing how many nutrients were in the ground and how much water was available, Farmer Oswald had experimented, tested, failed and succeeded. The crops he grew now were so different from their childhood of carrots, onions, wheat and potatoes. Now he grew okra, eggplant, corn and this wild cross of wheat and rye.

Looking at the table, Lara scrunched her nose. "So much okra," she complained lightheartedly, "and I don't see any squash."

Dillon laughed. It was a running joke with them about the okra. The first time he had grown it, about ten years ago, they had invited the whole family over for dinner. Lara, James and their four kids at the time ages between nine and eighteen, had joined Dillon, and his girls around the table in the old farmhouse. The dinner had been lamb and okra and all of Lara's children had loved the okra. James had loved the okra. When Lara had taken her first bite, the texture of it had overwhelmed her, it was different than any food she had eaten, and not in a good way. She had said as civilly as she could, "Let's just say, I don't love it." And now it was always offered to her. Her daughter Sally had once even wrapped some up as a Christmas gift for her.

Dillon reached down and pulled out a small cloth bag he had under the table. "I already set aside a portion for you." Lara took the bag and peeking inside let out a squeal of delight. The bag was full of chickpeas. This would feed her and James for a week.

She held the small bag tight to her chest with both hands and her smile reached her cheeks as she looked at Farmer Oswald with over exaggerated adoration. "Who's my hero?"

Jada laughed at the reminder of childhood play. "Who's the hero?" She laughed and placed her arms akimbo on her hips. "Today's hero is…" she broke off and all three of them chimed in…

"Dun, dun, duuuuunnnnn…"

Jada swept her arms in a wide circular motion to bring them around and cut them off together, "Farmer Dillon Oswald!"

All three mature adults broke down in laughter, and Lara noticed a bit more of her sadness lightening. Friendship was a balm for her soul.

A sudden shout from behind them brought their lighthearted laughter to a quick end. Turning they saw a crowd of about eight surrounding the well.

Rushing over Lara looked at the faces and knew it was bad. Jada's brother Stewart was standing at his usual table next to the well. It was his job to tally when the townsfolk took water. There had not been any problems for the community, but everyone felt better that they knew who got how much. Stewart was a big man, he towered over the nearest adult by a whole head, but he was the kindest man in town. He spent his days cranking the well's water bucket up and down, refilling everyone's supply.

He loved it because he loved making people happy. Jada and he had been raised to bring joy into the world. He always had a ready smile and a hug for everyone.

But not now. His face was stone. Lara had never seen him look so worried.

Lara heard whispers around her. No one wanted to say it aloud. Words like, *empty, water, what can we do,* swirled around her.

Everyone watched as the bucket was slowly cranked up with the hand crank. The sound in the town square was completely silent aside from the squeak as Stewart's hand reached the bottom of the circular motion. The rope attached to the bucket slowly wrapped around the metal rod, and everyone watched with bated breath.

Creak, creak, creak. The handle of the bucket peeked through the darkness. Creak. And the intake of breath was palpable. Everyone stood in stunned silence. The bucket was empty.

The well was dry.

〉〉〉

The entire village was there. Lara sat in her usual row of the Town Hall meetings with her daughters and James, directly behind Jada and her brother Stewart. This room had been built with the intention of holding all the villagers for meetings such as this. Little did they know that so quickly things would change. The empty space echoed with the voices of those present. Lara was again reminded of her childhood when the room was standing room only shoulder to shoulder when meetings like this had taken place. Now everyone had a chair, and still half the room was left empty behind them.

Too many had been forced to leave since the stones had sucked all the resources away. Supposedly, the color realms had been set up as protection for the stones and to keep them from dangerous people. Keep the power controlled, so that everyone was safe. But the people in those far off realms didn't think about the Wastes. They didn't come out here and see how everything was slowly decaying and being sucked away into nothingness.

The mayor was a woman with short, curly black hair and a sharp nose. Lara had known Diane her whole life. They weren't friends, but

Lara trusted her to make the right choices for the town. She was smart and analytical. She would have options for the villagers to discuss, she always did.

"We don't have a lot of choices," Mayor Kelton began. "I don't want to scare you, but we should all be scared. The well is completely dry. It hasn't rained since that drizzle we had seven months ago. The Hope Riverbed has only a tiny stream of water, and I fear it will just continue to shrink. We need water."

Lara heard Sally, under her breath, whisper out, "duh" and turned and patted her daughter on the knee.

Sally rolled her eyes, and Lara smirked at her. She had such a little temper on her, quick to rise and easily calmed.

Everyone already knew all of this, but to hear the mayor say it put Lara on edge. She heard people call out questions as the mayor stood patiently waiting for the townsfolk to settle before continuing.

"So, what's the answer?"

"Are we all gonna have to pack up and move to the color realms like the others who have left us?"

"Yeah, where would we even go? Would we have to say goodbye to all our friends and neighbors, or all try to go to the same place?"

"Right, and would any of the Color Realms take all of us?"

Lara got more upset the more she heard. How dare the Stonegrafted pull all the resources away from honest, working people? Why couldn't her village, her home, just be like it used to be?

When the magical color stones had been found and collected during her mother's childhood, they had been taken to separate corners of Chroma. Each community guarding their colors magical stones, and the resources connected to them, in different ways. Although only rumors, the people of Calabria had heard that all the Realms followed a few similar practices. Lara thought about what she had heard over the years.

All the Realms had trials that had to be passed for the right to try to stonegraft. Stonegrafting was the process of connecting with a stone and becoming a magic weaver, and it was rare. Once connected to the stone, the magic was part of that person. They could control the resources of the color with the stones' help. But no one in their small, removed community had any details about the realms, about the process of stonegrafting, or about what the trials entailed. It had become a coming-of-age milestone. When children were old enough, they decided if they would stay in town or go attempt the trials. She thought of Pete and Brie and the adventures they had left for.

The room began to quiet, and Lara looked back up as Mayor Kelton continued. "Someone has to bring back a blue stone."

It was obvious that everyone else in town was as surprised by this statement as Lara was. Comments came all at once, "But that's impossible. It's hard to earn a stone!" "Would they even let one of us attempt the trials?" "Is that really the only option?" "Who would even go?"

Mayor Kelton raised her hands and patiently waited for everyone to quiet down. "It is the only option. We can ration more harshly, and all limit our use even more, but we have been doing that for the last few decades. The Color Realms have slowly seeped us of all of our resources. If we just sit here and ration, we are just sitting here waiting until it is too late. Our water supply will run out if we don't bring a blue stone's magic back to our corner of the world. As far as we know the trials are open to anyone who can prove they want it. Someone here must be willing to go and try."

There was a general hubbub around her, but Lara wasn't listening. Her thoughts were super focused on what she knew about the blue stone. It would work. The blue waterweavers were said to have complete power over water. No one in their village had seen it themselves, but they had all heard the stories from the few travelers they had spoken to. The color weavers controlled the resources. The water weavers controlled the water.

She heard Mayor Kelton raise her voice over the mumbling crowd. "The blue stone represents order, responsibility, and trustworthiness. Someone here must be strong enough in these to be willing to try?"

These were characteristics Lara knew too well. It had been a core piece of what she felt was important to teach her own children as they grew up. Under her breath, she turned to Sally and said conspiratorially, "After raising and teaching you lot, maybe I should do it."

"Yes! You'd be perfect." Sally turned to Anna. "Mom says she should go."

"Wait, I wasn't…" but Lara was interrupted as Anna turned from the conversation she had been having to her left.

Her eyes pierced into Lara. Anna was her oldest child and seemed to know her better than anyone in the world. She held her hand up as if to slow Lara's thoughts. Slowly she tipped her head to the right, still holding tight eye contact. Lara found herself almost mesmerized and turned her head, too. Then Anna snapped out of it and stood up. It didn't take long for the townsfolk to quiet down.

Everyone knew Anna. She fed them, listened to them, cared for them. She waited until the last of the smaller conversations tittered out. "My mom has offered to go, and I think she could do it. I think she can bring the water back."

Lara's eyes shot open wide. She stared at Anna, then Sally, then twisted to look at James. He had a similar look of shock on his face. She turned to look at Sally and Anna again. Her look of reproach turning to a quizzical look with her eyebrows rising in question. Sally reached out and squeezed her hand. "You can do this!"

Lara looked around the room. She knew everyone here. They were her family, her friends, her community. They were near and dear to her. She loved them all. "Maybe someone else would be better?" She went over a list in her head of possibilities. Looking around the room at them, slowly each got crossed off the list. Everyone in town had a place to keep the community running, or people to take care of, or were injured or too old to make the journey. "I think I need some air…" and she stood up and stumbled out into the town square.

# Decisions

The fresh chilly air stung her throat but felt good after the meeting room. Her mind raced to catch up with her raging emotions. Why had she even said anything to Sally? They made comments under their breath to each other all the time, poking fun at the world around them. Painting the world with their own ridiculous comments helped them keep the darkness surrounding them at bay.

But this comment had backfired. She had meant for it to be an offhanded remark about her years as a mother, and suddenly the whole town thought she should go on some Colorweaver Journey? It felt like a joke.

But it hadn't been. The look in Anna's eyes had been more serious than she had seen her in a while. And Anna knew how to look serious. Of all of Lara's children, Anna was the one who thought things through, making lists and plans and figuring things out. Anna didn't make jokes the way Sally did with her and James and the other kids. She would laugh at a good joke, but she wasn't one to tell them.

And here Anna was telling the whole town that Lara should go to Azural and stonegraft. Did she really believe that Lara could actually travel all the way to the Blue Realm of Azural when she hadn't ever been past the edge of town?

Then, that she could pass the blue trials to earn a right to connect to the magical stone?

And then, after earning the right to try, that the magic of the water stone would choose Lara and connect with her?

It was not so simple as just picking up the water magic like the vegetables at the market, to bring back to Calambria so they could have water again. It felt like a joke, but Anna had been so serious.

Lara walked over to the old fountain in the center of the square. She kicked a few ground in pebbles with her foot until she broke one free. It was a nice, shiny black round one. Dusting it off, she stood in front of the short stone wall holding the wish dragon statue. It hadn't been a fountain since she was a little girl, but the kids still made wishes into the base. Pebbles had built up until almost the entire base that used to hold rippling pools of water was now filled with dirty rocks.

Lara held the stone in her right hand, rubbing it between her thumb and the first two fingers. She dusted it and then began to shine it. The repeated motion of her fingers calmed her, and she focused on the stone. It had no color. Nothing around here did anymore. Just dirt and mud, dust and grime. Darkness. Bleakness. The Wastes. Eventually the stone shone, but it was still black, like the dark skies and everyone's moods right now. Without water, things would just fall apart faster.

Lara closed her eyes and pictured the stone in her hand trying to imagine it as a blue stone instead. Water here in Calambria again, the dragon above her spitting water out into the waiting basin below. When she had a vision of it, with her eyes still closed, she recited the old nursery rhyme:

"Wish dragon, wish dragon, listen to me,
wish dragon, wish dragon, here is my plea,
Guardian by day, and guardian by night,
Listen and answer, with all of your might."

She paused, focusing on her wish, letting the powerful idea build inside her. Her neighbors and family gathered here on a sunny day, the sky bright blue overhead. The sound of the splash as the fountain water hit the basin.

She poured all of her energy into the simple words.

"Help us save our town."

She tossed the stone into the basin and was pulled out of her imagination when she heard the pebble hit rocks rather than water. She opened her eyes and slumped to sit on the edge of the short wall. Her knees were at the perfect height for her to rest her forehead on and she sat quietly for a moment looking at the dirty pebbles between her feet, until she felt James sit beside her.

"Remember when Brie came here and asked the wish dragon for a little sister?" He asked.

"Well, we all love Sally very much," Lara laughed.

"Maybe they will answer this wish too? What are you thinking?"

"That it is impossible for me to even consider. That I haven't ever even gone all the way to the Wheel Road, let alone to another Realm. That there must be someone more qualified than me to take this on. That I was done raising the kids and would finally have a break. That you might get lonely without me." She paused, and he just sat quietly and waited.

She took a deep breath and continued. "That we might have to move if we don't have water. That Granny Sanders wouldn't be able to make the trip to the Wheel Road at all. That everyone we know needs this to happen. That if I don't even try, then how do I really know I can't?" She paused again. "That…, oh, I just don't know…"

James finished for her, saying what was circling in the back of her mind, but she was too scared to say aloud. "That you, of all people, have followed the blue Tenets your whole adult life as a mother. Responsibility flows through your veins, Lara. That you are bored sitting in that now quiet house quilting every day. That the kids being gone is tearing you up inside and you need this adventure as much as we need you to go on it."

Lara had never felt so seen and loved.

# Obligations

Lara walked up to the door of Sally and Fiero's workshop. The smell of the leather and whatever it was they used to work it always made her feel warm and cozy. The shed was a welcome, cheerful space; it blocked out the icy winds and miserable setting.

Sally looked up and rushed over to her mother. "Mom, I have been wondering about you all day," she exclaimed. She embraced her and Lara returned the hug, holding it longer than usual. She physically felt the tension in her chest lighten.

"I'm okay. Dad and I have been talking. He thinks I should do it. He says I have been moping around long enough and that I always am happier when I am actively solving some problem." Lara let out a sarcastic laugh. "I guess the problems are few and far between now that all of you have moved out."

Fiero laughed from the other side of the workbench. "Come on Mom, you know Sally is still plenty of trouble. Why, just last week, she urged you to come over here to smell the fireplace because she believed there was a terrible smell that I was missing."

Lara smiled and looked at Sally. "Fiero's right. If I go, who will smell stuff for you?"

Sally rolled her eyes at the two of them. "I will just have Anna come help me. She would probably be nicer to me, anyway." She paused for a second, hands on her hips, "Actually, she would just tell me from the first that she was sure Fiero was right and not to worry about it."

Sally pulled her mom over to the bench at the side of the workshop. It was worn wood, and they had sat there together for many conversations. Sally turned toward Lara, pulling her leg under her so she could face sideways comfortably. "Mom, I've been thinking about it all night and morning. From what we have heard, the blue tenets are," Sally counted them off, raising her fingers, "reliability, order, intelligence and calm. Who better than you? You raised us four and kept your head through the chaos - calm. You were always there for us and still are - reliable. We always knew we could count on you to keep things straight - order. Few parents were as honest with their kids as you and dad. I think you could do this."

"But we don't even know what happens in the color realms, so few have come back after they have left us. No one from the Wastes has earned a stone as far as we know." Lara had thought all night herself and had a list a mile long of why this might never work. "What if I can't do it?" She whispered.

"What if you don't even try?" Sally answered quietly. "Then we are doomed for sure. There is no more water, Mom. It's just getting worse every week. The winds get stronger and colder. The sky is darker and drearier. Something has to be done. We need to try something to get blue skies and fresh water flowing."

"Maybe you should go," Lara said. She kept a straight face for a beat and then all three of them started laughing. Her entire childhood Lara had told Sally that she would fit nowhere but the warm colors. She was a little firecracker of energy, always happy and exuberant. She brought a light into a space, but she was the furthest thing from calm that anyone could imagine.

When they had all calmed down a bit, Sally said, "We have something for you, Mom." Fiero brought over a beautiful leather pack. Lara reached out and touched the soft, supple leather. It was a light brown and looked like a new piece, rare around here since the wolves' attacks had decimated the goats and cows in their village. Most of the items that Sally and Fiero worked on were recycled from other pieces. This must have been saved for something special.

"Oh." Lara could barely speak, her words choking in her mouth. Tears touched her eyes as she saw the design carved into the flap of the pack. It was a map of Chroma with The Wheel Road. At the South edge of the map between the flower fields of Pink and mountains of Purple a small heart sat right where their hometown was. Around the wheel Sally had carved symbols to represent the color realms. Lara stared at the waves that showed Azural. The Blue Realm didn't look very far away when she looked at this little map on the pack.

Her pack, she thought. She looked up at Sally and realized she was crying again. She had worried so much about whether she could even earn a stone, but now she wondered if the hardest part of this whole thing might just be walking out of town.

James was cooking dinner when Lara got home. She talked with Anna that afternoon and Jada too. Everyone said what Sally had. Anna had handed her the bread she had baked and some trail-mix she had made for Lara's journey. She had already decided that Lara was going. "You know it, or you will soon. Just take the trail-mix Mom," she had said with tears in her eyes. "I'm going to miss you. Don't make me worry you aren't eating too."

"It smells delicious." Lara said as she came in.

James looked at her with a bit of suspicion in his eyes, "It's just sautéed veggies you got from Farmer Oswald the other day."

"I know. I will miss it while I am gone."

He nodded his head. "When will you leave?"

"I don't know. I suppose I should go soon?"

"The water is a drizzle out back. I think you should go in the morning." He shook his head. "You know to be careful, don't trust everyone, walk slowly through Crumble Pass, don't forget to eat, you always forget to eat." He brought two bowls over to the table and handed her a spoon.

"Anna gave me some trail-mix and bread for the trip."

He smiled. "Our kids are pretty amazing, and we had a small hand in that. If we can get those four hellions raised, then we can do anything. I know you can do this."

Lara warmed at his comment. He knew her better than anyone. The kids knew her, but they loved her differently. She would always be something to them that was just a little unreal. Lara liked to believe there was magic in being a mother.

But a wife? James had seen the best and worst of her. He knew her better than she knew herself. She trusted him more than anyone. He believed she could do this. She took a sip of his delicious soup and began thinking of what she needed to add to her beautiful new leather pack.

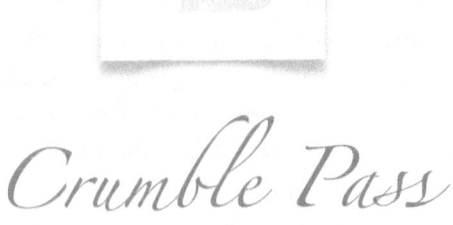

# Crumble Pass

Lara did her best to not think too much about the actual end goal. Focused on what she needed for the journey, she had packed up her satchel with items she could trade along the way. She had just gone through this with Pete, so she already knew what was needed. Her map, her favorite warm cloak. There were a few things she packed Pete hadn't needed being a boy. And then there were the memories. She carefully rolled up the painting that James had made of the family when the kids were little. She packed up her journal and favorite pencil and sharpening knife.

They had sent Pete off with their good hunting knife, but the mayor had come by and given her a few things for the trip. A knife with a leather belt holder, a bedroll that included a soft mat and a warm quilt, a soft leather water pouch, and more food for the trip. Everyone in town had pitched in, she said.

And so, not long after she had waved goodbye to her son, she was out the door and down the path out of town herself.

The path led North from their village to the Crumble Pass. The stream trickled by to her left, all that was left of what used to fill this cavern with rushing water. What the old riverbed had left underfoot was treacherous to walk on and she had to pay close attention to her footing. The ground was cracked earth and brittle black stones, and she would slip into the jagged larger rocks on either side if she wasn't extremely careful.

She had not traveled this way since she was about twelve and had visited the village next to theirs where her aunt had lived. That village was no longer there, everyone having left for the color realms. The path had changed so much she barely recognized it. There used to be a hard dirt walkway next to the river between these two rocky cliffs that had been overgrown with wildflowers and tall grasses. All of that beauty was gone. The only thing left were the dirty rocks and dust beneath her feet that had broken off of the cliffs as they became more and more fragile, all of their essence being sapped away, pulled toward the magical stones on the far sides of the continent.

As she looked at her footing, she thought of how terrible everything was. The color realms had stolen the resources her community needed to live. They had the power all centered together, taken away from her and her loved ones. What a mess the world was. All she wanted was to be close to her family again. She wanted to spend time with Anna as she was baking for the inn, to sit in the yard with Sally as she tanned the leather. But there was little leather to work with, thanks to the Stonegrafters. And she missed her daughter Brie so much. It had been years since she had hugged her, and now it would be years before she saw Pete again. This ridiculous broken world had broken up her family.

She slipped and realized she was stomping a bit too roughly from her anger and slowed her pace. Best to keep an even temper and focus on staying safe.

She stopped at midday to have a bite to eat. She was warm from her walking, so she laid her black cloak out on a larger rock and sat on top of it, pulling out some jerky and her water flask.

As she sat there, she thought about Blue. She had heard that it was a magical realm full of water. That the skies were as blue as a sunny day from her childhood. That their society was focused on the main principles - the Tenets of Blue. She had heard many stories about Chroma from her childhood and was a bit intrigued to see for herself what was out in the world. This path wasn't too impressive so far, though. She looked back toward her village and then down the pass toward her destination. Just gloom and dirt.

She was about to take another sip of her water when she noticed small gray ears peek out from behind a rock. Next, she saw big round gray eyes rise over the edge and look intently at her food.

"You must be so hungry. There is nothing around here to eat, is there? Want some?" Lara slowly reached out as far as she could and placed a bit of the trail mix on the path. Then she pretended not to care about the animal at all, simply taking a sip of her water.

The animal slowly crept from its place behind the rock. Lara had never seen an animal like this. Its slender body was about a foot long with a fur that looked just long enough to cause trouble as it was all clumped together and matted from the dirt. It reminded Lara a bit of a fox, but its furry tail was so long, at least twice the length of any fox she had seen. The tail flicked from side to side in an agitated way, and Lara knew to keep still.

She was entranced by the tiny thing right away. As it cautiously approached the food, its pointed muzzle pushed at the pile. Its nose twitched from side to side: the motion of the soft white whiskers on either side exaggerating the slight motion. Slowly, it opened its mouth, and Lara froze at her first sight of this tiny creature's teeth. Double rows of sharp jagged teeth glinted for just a moment before it quickly slipped a bite into its mouth.

After the animal had relaxed a bit and set itself down to eat fully, Lara asked it, "Is it yummy? I bet you could use some water too?" She looked around for a place on the rock that might hold water. There was a small dip in a boulder close to where the scruffy little fluff ball was, so Lara stood slowly and walked a cautious step or two closer. She knelt down and poured a splash of water onto the rock. It pooled up, and she slowly stepped back to have a seat.

The animal looked at her. Its wise eyes startled Lara even more than the teeth had, there was intelligence there, like it was taking stock of her, not just reacting. Then it walked over to sip from the pooled water. After a full drink, it sat on its hind legs and perched, studying Lara as she looked at it.

Lara was conflicted in her feelings, there was an essence of calm she felt from it, but the image of those teeth still lingered in her mind. Its eyes were a very light gray, like pools of water reflecting the gray sky. The fur on its body was gray and matted, and Lara couldn't tell how much of the color was just dirt and grime. The animal sat back on its haunches turning its long body into almost a little round ball, the tail curling around the body in a wide arc until the creature grabbed the tip of it and held its front paws together gazing fondly at the trail mix bag next to Lara on the stone.

"Oh ho. You want more?" Lara laughed and sat more in front of her, but this time not reaching far away.

The little animal came right up to her and began eating, abandoning the fear it had shown at first. She sat quietly there as it ate. When it had finished up the last of its trail mix pile, she said, "Well, it was lovely to meet you, but I must be on my way. I am hoping to reach the Wheel Road before dark. It would not be comfortable sleeping on these rocks, you know."

She stood up slowly so as not to startle the animal and wrapped her cloak around her shoulders. The chill had set back in now that she had been still for a while. She headed down the path.

Turning back to say goodbye, she was surprised to see that the little thing was right behind her. "Are you joining me? Not much food around here, huh? Well, I am happy for the company."

The second half of the day went by so much more quickly as she talked with this little one about her thoughts. By the time the sun had dipped behind the mountain peaks and the sky had darkened to dusk, it had already learned so much about her. She shared about her years as a child growing up in the bustling village, to her years of raising four kids with little resources as the area slowly lost its vitality, to her current trip toward Blue to do whatever she could to save her village from being deserted.

It was a good listener. Ears perked up and giving her every sign through turns of the head to the side and occasional nods that it was fully understanding what she said. The thing that really got her was the eyes though. They appeared so intelligent, she could almost believe it really was invested in her stories and felt her emotions with her.

They finally reached where the Crumble Pass ended, and Lara could see the open space of the Wheel Road ahead. As the cliffs on either side gave way, she was reminded that the world around her was really going to change as she traveled. No more was she surrounded by the dirty grays of home.

The riverbed continued on to the north, but ahead of her, about fifteen feet up, was a strong wooden bridge that had stood the tests of time. It spanned across the original riverbed of the Hope River as if the water still flowed. The bridge had been worked on recently. She saw repairs of lighter wood planks in some places. Travelers who cared about the safety of the bridge but had not imagined traveling toward Calambria.

Above her, Lara saw the beginnings of the path that had originally led home. There on the East side of the bridge was the wooden signpost that read Calambria, carved in a lovely script. But it was worn down from time, barely legible, and the dirt path only lasted a few steps before erosion had completely pulled the ledge from the mountainside. From Lara's point of view the rubble of the old path mixed with the stones of the riverbed, and she was unable to tell where one started or ended.

Lara scrabbled up the edge of the riverbed trying to reach what was left of the path. When she had made it about halfway up, the dirt fell away under her hands and feet, and she slipped to the bottom bruising her backside and bumping her head. As she stood, she noticed a tear in her cloak and regretted not packing her sewing stuff. Laughing at herself she realized a little tear was not her problem here, it was getting up the side of this cliff.

She looked again at the steep incline. Studying it to see if there was any other way up. Her new little friend sat beside her for awhile, then suddenly in a burst, set forth and dug sharp claws that Lara hadn't even noticed before deep into the dirt in the cliff, climbing up and as it reached the top peeking over at Lara as if to say, "come on then."

Lara laughed and flexed her fingers. This time she dug deep into the dirt, taking her time to really sink in each finger and foot hold before she reached up a bit higher. When she finally reached the solid footing of the path, she was sore from the tightening of muscles and winded from the effort. On each side of her, tall trees with thick trunks reached out to the sky. The brown of the bridge and trees shocked Lara a bit. Everything looked so different in these umber shades.

Ahead of her was a wide path of hard dirt that reached out to the right and left. "Well, we've made it to the Wheel Road. It's beginning to get quite dark, so I think I will set up a little camp here and start down road tomorrow. Want to help me out? First, we need to start a little fire, so let's collect a bit of kindling."

She searched the little wooded area and found many small broken off sticks. As she began piling them on the ground by her pack, she found that her little friend was helping. It came running up with a stick in its mouth and dropped it into the pile she had been making. "Why thank you. What should I call you? If we are to be friends, you need a name."

She thought about it throughout the making of the fire and their dinner of more trail-mix and jerky. "How about... Minx? No, that's too close to another animal. Ragamuffin, because of your sorry state? I could call you Muffin?" She shook her head, a little frustrated. "Sorry, I'll keep thinking about it. Something will come up and stick. For now, I need to get this fire going. To be honest with you, I am nervous about the wolves tonight." She added wood to the flames.

A short while later, the fire was roaring nicely. She sat near it sharing her story with her new companion when she heard the first howl not far away. She pulled her knife out and stood with her back to the fire. There, just past the tree line, a smaller wolf came toward her, pacing back and forth, as if to test her. She knew the best thing was to trust in her fire and stay calm. She had done fence duty herself when she was younger and had been up close with wolves.

In her experience, they rarely came too close to the fires. As expected, this young wolf hung back from the flames. But then Lara witnessed something she had never seen before. The tiny creature leapt up, moving confidently toward the wolf. Lara's first instinct, driven by fear, brought her two steps forward with her knife up. Suddenly she stopped short as the wolf bowed its head and lowered its front paws, slowly touching its nose to the ground at the mud-caked paws of Lara's little friend.

The wolf stayed there for a moment and then slowly rose back up. It looked directly at Lara with tearful eyes, brimming with emotion. Lara had never looked so deeply into a wolf's eyes, her confusion likely obvious. The wolf blinked once, looked back at their tiny friend and then turned and raced away. Lara heard it howling out, as if sending a message to the whole world, in a way she could only describe as joyous.

"What was that, little one?" Do all wolves react to you that way? Who are you?" Lara sat back at the fire and studied the animal. It simply pranced back to the fire and sat near her cracking open a nut it must have collected while hunting for wood. She couldn't place it specifically in any family, it was too long and skinny to be a squirrel. It's nose too rounded to be a fox, the tail too long to be any. As she studied it, the animal finished enjoying the nut and turned to look at her. Again, she was floored by the intelligence in its eyes. "Well," Lara sighed, "I, for one, feel much safer suddenly."

Feeling much more comfortable, Lara laid out her bedroll and set her pack under the top for a pillow. She cuddled under her quilt. Looking at the flames, she smiled, "Tomorrow we head out on the road. I am glad we aren't heading West, so we won't have to pass by Red. I have heard they have roads of fire. Common', you are welcome to curl up by the fire too. You helped me make it after all." The little one bounded over and curled up next to her. She reached out to pet it slowly and was blown away by an immediate psychic connection. Her mind reeled an intake of images, emotions and thoughts that were not her own. This was no ordinary little furry forest creature!

Lara immediately felt a connection with the animal that was consuming. She wondered at how comfortable and safe the animal felt nestled next to her. It went beyond just thinking the animal looked like he trusted her. But she also knew it. Because she felt it. The animal trusted her, and she knew it. The comfort the animal felt was so powerful that it rubbed off on her and mixed with her exhaustion from the long day's journey of tight careful steps. Her body finally relaxed, and she fell asleep.

# Brown Travelers

When she woke up the next morning, she immediately knew the needs of her little friend. The animal was no longer lying asleep. In fact, Lara couldn't see him, but she knew right away that he was climbing the tree to her left and finding acorns. She felt his satisfaction as he cracked one open and ate it. She had never heard of something like this happening before and wondered at it. The little creature came scurrying down the trunk and sat looking at her with cheeks full of nuts. They puffed out and Lara laughed at how adorable he was. She felt a rush of happiness coming from the little guy that layered on top of hers. "My little friend. I have never seen anyone quite as amazing as you." She sensed his pleasure at this. "We still need to find a name for you, but we can think about it on our way. We must keep moving."

Before packing up she looked at the map Sally had etched into her pack. The animal perched up on her shoulder, looking at the map also, "You see, we are traveling to Azural. It will take at least four days' journey. We should be able to see the towers of Morchast on our second day." She turned that thought over in her head. She hoped she would see the towers of Purple, for she had heard that they were fearsome and imposing, but she had also heard they were magical and inspiring.

They traveled most of the morning without seeing anyone. She wasn't surprised. They were still traveling next to the Wastelands and few people needed to be in this area anymore. But a few hours after they had some lunch, she felt her fluffy companion's attention perk up. His curiosity heightened. Not long after that, she began to hear the sounds of carts wheels trundling along behind them. She had known eventually she would meet up with some brown travelers. She was excited about it, for she had always been amazed by their lifestyle.

While most people had decided to leave the Wastes for the different color realms, some had chosen a life on the road, making a living by trading between the color realms. They wore browns to signify that they did not belong to any of the color realms, instead they were of the dirt road, and proud of it. They traveled around the land on a circular path they had named The Wheel after their transportation. Their caravans circled the land, then left the Wheel Road to follow narrower Spokes Roads toward the Color Realms. They were the connection in a world that was broken.

She was caught off guard as her new little friend scurried right up her cloak and inside it to hide away. She felt a caution from him, not fear so much as the need to be careful. He was burrowed on her shoulder next to her pack strap, so she imagined anyone who saw the bump would not notice it as anything more than her belongings, but she pulled her loose braid over to that side also, just in case.

She turned to see the first cart rolling closer. There were two people dressed in long brown robes sitting on the front bench. They called out a friendly greeting and Lara waved a hello in response. Their fully grey hair told Lara they were at least ten years older than her. The woman sat comfortably on the front of the cart while carving a piece of wood, expertly navigating the sharp knife even with the bumps in the road. Beyond them, she saw that there were two more carts, all of them were closed in with rounded tops and intricate, artistic, wooden carvings.

The first cart passed her by, and as the second cart came closer, Lara saw a young girl, probably about twelve, at the reins. She looked extremely happy to see Lara there and waved enthusiastically, her brown ponytail bouncing along with the cart's motions. She opened a small window behind her and called inside. An older smiling face with the same dark brown curls peeked out and Lara saw her say something to the girl. The young girl immediately pulled on the reins, probably a bit too quickly, and the horse and cart came to an abrupt stop not far from Lara.

The woman and two even younger versions of the girl driving came around from the back of the cart. "Good day! My name is Nessa."

"I'm Kate!" the young driver piped in, speaking loudly over her two younger sisters, who also shouted out their introductions.

Years of experience with young children had Lara ready, and she quickly responded, "Hello Nessa, my name is Lara. So nice to meet you." Lara faced the young ladies in turn, giving them a quick little curtsy, "Good day Kate. Hello Jenn, and hello to you, Miss. Betty." The girls beamed at the royal treatment.

Nessa stepped forward. "We don't see many travelers walking the Wheel Road - forgive me for this - at your age. May I ask where you are headed? Maybe we can give you a ride? At least for part of your journey?"

Lara smiled. "I appreciate the help, as it will speed up my trip. I am traveling to Azural to attempt the blue trials. We are almost out of water in Calambria, my village. We need the magic back or will all have to resettle."

Nessa gave a slow, sorrowful nod. "I know too well the challenges. The home I grew up in is no longer an option, but no way in seven hells would I go join a color. They are the ones who created this mess in the first place."

Lara nodded in agreement. "Taking all of our resources and leaving so many with nothing. It has been so difficult, and as each year goes by, it's just getting worse."

"Well, we can't just make them change, but I have a new life that makes me happy." Nessa gestured toward the three girls, who were over feeding the horse carrots. The carrots were bright orange and longer than Lara's hand, with vivid green fronds. Lara was entranced by the hues. "I have my family here, my home there," she pointed to the cart, "and a community of loved ones. It looks different from when I lived in a house, but it honestly is much the same."

"I would be happy to join you for a bit of my journey, if you and the girls don't mind."

"Not at all. The girls love company, and so do I. Come along, I will show you my home." Nessa led her around to the back of the cart. "Kate, get us moving again, please. You are still at the reins until dinner."

As they rounded the back of Nessa's cart, Lara was greeted with a friendly wave and warm smile from a larger man sitting on the front of the third cart. Lara craned her neck to see if there were any more carts on the road, but saw it was just these three.

The back of the family's cart had a round wooden door with a beautifully carved wheel centered with the spokes radiating out to the sides. The two sides were framed by tree trunks growing from the base of the cart, with branches reaching out over the top of the circular door. Lara was fascinated by the detail in the wood. She saw a fox at the base of a tree, an owl in the branches of one. The longer she looked, the more she saw.

Nessa pulled the handles, the round door was hinged and opened on each side. Lara's view was pulled from the artwork on the exterior, to the cozy interior of the cabin. There were two wooden plank steps that reached out from the back and the younger two girls clambered up them, half crawling to reach the first step. Nessa hitched up her skirt and pulled herself up and then offered Lara her hand.

The interior of the cart was simple and well organized, leaving much more space than Lara thought possible. To the right side was a bench with woven multi-color blankets covering it. To the left was a counter that reached all along the cart from front to back. Lots of cabinets were along the wall above and below this counter and Lara realized that the storage was more than she had back at home. The counter was covered in more fresh fruit than Lara had seen in ages. There were apples, berries, and bananas. Her mouth watered immediately. Nessa was a great hostess and quickly offered Lara her choice. Lara almost cried, taking a bright red apple in her hands. It smelled delicious.

She took a bite, and it was juicy and everything she had remembered and imagined. She suddenly felt a pang of jealousy. At first, she was confused by the emotion until she realized it was her tiny stowaway friend. Nessa was settling the young girls back down for their afternoon naps in the front of the cart, so Lara bit off a piece of the apple and handed it to him under her cloak. Her feelings of gratitude to Nessa for the treat were mirrored in this creature's gratitude to her.

Once the girls were settled, Nessa came and sat with Lara. The cart trundled along at a steady pace and the swaying was surprisingly relaxing. Lara found herself chatting comfortably with Nessa for the afternoon. They had a lot in common, and Lara spoke of her four children. She shared some of her favorite stories.

"So, you are a mom like me, and now you are going to attempt to stonegraft Blue?" Nessa sounded amazed. "I have only seen youth go attempt the trials. It would be pretty amazing if you could connect with one of the stones and harness that magic. I've thought about it myself sometimes, but they were just dreams, I never would actually go do it."

Lara couldn't hold back, her mind was full of a thousand questions, they all slipped out in rapid succession. "What do you know about them? We are so far away from all the color realms in my village that we only get the most generic stories. We had a youth who failed the first round of trials at Green return and told us of food that people didn't even have to till the soil or give water to grow and how everyone wore green and how different everyone behaved. Said he never even got to meet one of the Color Weavers, but he saw them in action, and he had never seen anything as vivid and beautiful as the green floating through the air." Lara paused, realizing she had just gone on a mile a minute. "Sorry, I just have so many unanswered questions."

"Oh, I understand. It must seem so strange to hear about when you've never seen it. The magic is really beautiful. I have seen it many times, and each time everyone around just stops as if almost..." She paused with a far away look in her eye, then laughed with a start "entranced. Not in a dangerous way, but it really is amazing."

Nessa explained, "Each land is so different. The stones' magics are powered based on the emotion each color connects with, so all seven realms have grown around a different set of principles. I don't like the system. I don't like the way it encourages everyone to be the same, homogeneous. I love encouraging freedom and individuality in my girls. Every time we approach a realm down their spoke-road I get upset all over again. I don't like how they hoard the power and the resources. I have been so angry for so long about the broken world that they ignore while they sit in their realms, or like in Blue, behind their waterwall. I don't even know if they have a clue what goes on in the Wastes."

Nessa shook her head, then continued, "Anyway, Blue is all about order. I imagine they have clear guidelines for how to enter the trials and what is expected. Most travelers I have met from Blue are peaceful and calm, and very clean, of course — they are the land of water. I imagine the first thing they do with new visitors is get them a nice bath."

Lara looked sheepishly down at her clothes and imagined the state she must be. "Oh dear."

"Darling, you aren't alone. Look at the dust built up on my skirts alone. We may have plenty of drinking water, but I ration it for the cleaning." Nessa shook her skirt hem, it was beautifully decorated with a dark brown cross-stitched geometric design, and brown dirt wisps circled into the air, she laughed a booming laugh, and the girls turned over a bit, catching herself she quieted and shushed them back to calm.

Lara chatted amiably with Nessa throughout the afternoon. Although they lived in very different circumstances now, they had both grown up in smaller villages when the land had still thrived. They both had a comfortable way of dealing with multiple children around. Lara had seen many styles of parenting, and loved that Nessa let her children be rambunctious, but still kept an eye out. She spoke with the girls in a firm but respectful voice when they crossed a line, for example, when they jumped off the higher bed onto the lower one. "Girls, that's enough. You know not to do that." Then conspiratorially to Lara, "they are showing off for you."

"I can see that. It is so good to be around these littles. I loved my years running after my own." Lara felt a familiar pang of loss, but realized she was able to let it pass quickly rather than wallow in it.

Just around the time she began to feel the emptiness of hunger and was also alerted to her little friend's hunger, the cart pulled over to the side of the road and stopped.

Nessa jumped up and opened the door, and the little girls were out before it was even opened the whole way. Nessa smiled a knowing smile and turned to Lara. "Ah, to have the energy of youth. We have stopped to make camp for the night, come and meet the rest of our traveling party."

The couple from the front cart met them outside, along with a larger man who looked to be the same age as Nessa. He came up and grabbed Nessa in a bear hug. "Have you found a new friend, Nessie?" His voice boomed, and he set Nessa down and turned to Lara. "I'm Tallon. These two are Theo and Sara. We are about to make camp. We can chat in a bit over the fire."

After a quick hello, everyone got to work. They worked as a well-oiled machine. Everyone knew their job and although Lara tried to help by collecting some firewood, the children had it done lickety split. Within half an hour, they were all sitting on wooden folding chairs around a cook pot over a roaring fire. Lara was included as if she had always been with them. These people were used to travelers joining them and enjoyed it. "Keeps the conversation stimulating," laughed Theo. "Otherwise, we would only be sharing stories we all already knew."

Her little friend had snuck off as she sat at the fire to chat. She had felt his pent-up energy growing as he cuddled beneath her cloak, but also his trepidation at meeting more people. He had quietly crept through the undergrowth until he felt free from the eyes of the group.

They were all interested in her town's well running dry, because Sara, Tallon, and Nessa had all come from similar towns and knew of the loss. When she finished with the basics of her story, she had questions for them, too. "Why did you choose to travel The Wheel instead of just move to one of the color realms?" Lara posed the question to all of them.

"Damn Stonegrafters! They are the cause of all of this in the first place." Tallon's jovial attitude changed so quickly, it surprised Lara. "Why would I go grovel to follow their rules and lead, when I can travel the open road and be free? I have everything I need here. In fact, a lot of those realms are lacking stuff we get from traveling. For example, we get all the spices from Orange, and all the veggies from Green, so our stew is some of the best anyone can eat." Lara could smell the truth of that, as the stew bubbled in front of them.

The others in the group nodded. Sara spoke in a quiet, soothing voice, "I think this is the consensus of us Wheel and Spoke travelers. We may have lost our original houses, but now we carry them with us. If we run into trouble, for example, if we need water like you... then we just head to Azural and trade for some. The house comes along, the kids come along. Our new village is intact. We are just on the move."

"Change is hard." Lara said. "I respect your decisions, but I don't see how many of our grannies could live like this. I worry about them. I'll do what I can to see about earning the blue stone so I can save them, and my home, as it is now."

Nessa turned to Tallon and placed a hand on his shoulder. "We all harbor a lot of anger about what happened to those who couldn't make it from our villages. Tallon and I lost many loved ones when our village wasted away. I may not want to live under the Stonegrafted, but I support you in doing what you can to save your village."

Sara's quiet voice whispered across the fire. "There are no easy answers. Theo, why don't you tell her your story of leaving home?"

Theo looked at them all in turn, then focused on Lara. "The world is broken, and I don't know how to fix it. The stones are the source of life's resources. They are the holders of the magic that used to grow the fields of flowers behind my home and the rain showers of spring. I grew up in what is now the yellow realm. Our fields of flowers slowly lost the pinks and purples and reds and became a sea of yellow. The world changed from what I had known. By the time I was old enough, it was obvious I was not a fit for Yellow."

Lara said, "My son left home a few months ago to head to Yellow. I try to envision him there. Your description of fields of yellow flowers is a great image for me. Thank you. So, you left. Did you immediately start traveling the Wheel?"

"No, initially I thought I'd travel to Piron, the red realm, and become a flameweaver. I thought I would show my family they could be proud of me, that I had a place. I thought I would show the world that I was powerful and capable."

Theos eyes glazed over and he looked up at the branches overhead, continuing, "But Red was not the place for me either. I struggled to keep up with their expectations from the moment I arrived. Just the fact that most of them carry swords was overwhelming to me, I was going through culture shock."

Sara patted his knee and pulled from his dreamlike thoughts he turned to her, his thinning grey curls swung as he turned to look at her. "I had only ever known the way I was raised in Yellow and although I knew I didn't fit in at home, I quickly found that I didn't fit in at Red either. The expectations were so cut and dry. It was clear quickly." He barked out an ironic laugh, "I failed their first trial, which was literally as simple as learning the beginning sword forms and was sent packing. I didn't feel comfortable staying in Red to work some menial job, and I was too proud at the time to go back home to Yellow.

"So, I kept my pack on my back and started walking the Wheel Road. I found others like me, and we began to travel together. The early days on the Wheel Road were a bit different from nowadays." Sara and he both let out a short laugh. "Luckily I found Sara, and we have been on the road together ever since." He put his arm around her and pulled her close and she set her forehead on his shoulder for a moment, her silver hair falling to cover her face.

"Did you ever go back to Yellow? See your family?"

"It took me a long time, but when Sara and I had two little ones, I began to see my brother in their faces, and it sparked memories of our time growing up together. I missed him and wanted him to meet the kiddos. Sara helped me work up the courage to stop by for a visit. It was awkward, but I am glad we did. He had always been comfortable there. Turns out he was missing me, too. And we have kept in touch ever since. He is one of the Teachers in Amara now. (That is what we call the Yellow colorweavers, Teachers). He raised his kids there, and we visit once every few years. But it is always a bit strange, and I always feel like an outsider, even though aside from this wagon it was the only home I had."

Nessa chimed in here, "We have seen a lot of people over the years fall out of society for many reasons. So many are scared they won't be welcomed back to the only homes they have known. Who knows Lara, maybe you can earn a blue stone and go back home. And while you are at it, maybe you can figure out how to put the world back together, too?"

They sat quietly for a bit, eating and looking into the fire. Eventually, the little girls came skipping over from their play and ate, too. The mood lifted with the laughter of the girls. Children were so wonderful to have around. As she watched them, she suddenly had a momentary flash of an image cross her mind. It felt like a memory, but nothing she had ever experienced. The image had come from high in a tree with a view of a tall ring of mountains. She couldn't understand it and wondered if her imagination had created it. Then she felt an instant of pure joy, and realized she was experiencing something through this connection to the little creature. He was climbing up and down the trees and looking at the land around them.

The images fizzled and her attention snapped back to the children in front of her. She wondered if her furry companion might enjoy running around with them. But she could feel how happy he was exploring the new area. The wonder of seeing a different world from the top of the tallest tree. He seemed content to stay away from people generally.

The talk turned to the plans for the next day. Theo shared with Lara, "In the morning we turn down the spoke to Purple. You are welcome to join us, but it will take up at least two weeks of traveling and trading there. Purple is the most remote of the realms and takes the longest to get to from the Wheel."

"I think I will just continue on my walk then. I should get to Blue in a few days that way, don't you think?" Everyone agreed, and they passed the rest of the evening in happy conversation, telling their favorite stories to Lara, everyone else pitching in and speaking on top of the original storyteller since they all knew what happened. It was a lovely evening, and Lara knew she had made some real friends here. They even set up a little tent for her that they had for visitors with a soft bedroll raised up off the ground, a lantern, and even a soft pillow.

Once everyone had said their good nights and she was settled in the tent, she felt the little animal's quizzical confusion. She peeked out of the tent, and as she opened the flap, a grey streak rushed in, joyously chittering. She didn't know what he was saying, but she felt all the excitement of the adventure coming across from their psychic link. She even saw a quick slip of an image from high in the trees. This link between them was getting stronger every day.

He placed his paw on her forearm. She looked into his eyes and said quietly, "We have had quite the day, haven't we? I guess you are on this adventure with me now. I really need to name you." His tail twitched, and he sat back on his haunches looking adorable, but muddy. Her arm had a tiny paw print where he had touched her. It had five distinct tiny claw marks. "It took me months to decide on names for my four children, and honestly, I had help from James. For now, I will call you Five. That's better than Ragamuffin, at least."

They settled down and, with trust in the safety of a group and a full belly from the delicious stew, slept well.

# Purple

Five was bouncing down the path ahead of her as she walked at a brisk pace. Nessa had brewed her the most delicious concoction this morning called coffee, and she felt an energetic pep added to her motions. Although it had been lovely getting to know the Brown travelers, it had cemented in her mind what was at stake for her own village. Her friends and family were counting on her to do her best to bring them water. She didn't know how long they had before the water completely stopped flowing, so she needed to keep on task.

She could feel Five's exhilaration at the journey, and found that she shared the feeling. Everywhere they looked, there were new things to see. They started the morning with the familiar dark black and gray mountains to the right and she hoped eventually they would soon get a peek at her first color realm. Near the start of her day, a rocky cliff directly next to the road, rose on her right. It was quite tall and blocked off the view of the distance, so she focused on the path in front of her.

Around lunch time they sat down for a respite and bite to eat, and she noticed that there in the grass at her feet were violets. She had loved violets as a child. They had grown everywhere back then, along with the bright yellow dandelions, and she used to collect as many as she could hold in her tiny hands for her mother every time she was out. She remembered her mother accepting them as though they were a grand bouquet and wrapping them with tiny bits of colorful ribbons and placing them with honor in tiny glasses on the kitchen table.

She picked one reverently and showed it to Five. Five came forward and smelled it, curiosity emanating from him. He looked at Lara and then, before she understood what he intended, he took the violet from her and promptly ate it. She knew violets were safe to eat, for she and her mother had put them in salads when she was young, but she had expected him to look at it, not eat it. Giggling, she reached out and patted his tiny fox-like head. He smoothed his fluffy pointed ears back flat against the top of his head and looked at her with his large eyes. She noticed they reflected back specks of the purple from this lovely setting.

Seeing the deep purple violets excited her to move forward, so she didn't sit long. They were back on the road after a quick bite to eat. By mid-afternoon, the rocky cliff gave way to an open space that again showed her mountains in the distance, however these mountains were quite different from the ones out her kitchen window. She was overpowered by the sight. Color filled the horizon. High purple peaks in the distance were surrounded by a light purple haze of mist around them. She saw the outline of distant parapets and towers and knew that she was seeing her first glimpse of Morchast, the Purple Color Realm.

She knew very little about the colors, but Tallon had told her that Purple was the most remote, and that it had the smallest population of the realms. She had even heard that there were fewer purple stones than the other colors, but she wasn't sure how much of that was true. She didn't even know how many stones existed. But it was obvious that the purple stones were here. The ground reaching up into the mountains almost looked purple. It was filled with so many wildflowers in various hues, light violet to deep velvet shades. It was beautiful, and she stopped short and just stared.

Five jumped up on her shoulder and curled around her neck. She felt his awe at the scene mix with and intensify her own. After so long in the bleak wastelands, this was a sight for her sore eyes. The magic was real. She could get to Blue, find a way to earn a stone, and save her home.

After a while, she moved on but kept staring at the color to her right. She was drawn in and began wondering what it was like in Morchast. Who were the people there? She wasn't even sure what Purple's magic was. The mystery of it pulled at her and she found that she almost wanted to turn around and head straight there to find the answers. She caught herself, speaking out loud, "How would that help those back home?"

Five, still wrapped around her shoulder, craned his neck and looked at her. She felt his comforting reassurance that she could forgive herself for the questions. She wondered at the complexity of the feeling. This connection to the animal was stronger than she had initially thought, but it also felt so natural.

Five rode along on her shoulder for a while, but his pent-up energy got the best of him, and he jumped off her and started ahead again. Bounding forward, stopping to look back at her, picking up stones on the road and smelling them, then as she got close enough running ahead again. He was adorable, and she found herself as interested in watching him explore as she was looking at Purple.

As they were rounding a corner, a young man wearing a blue tunic came from the other direction. Five froze in the center of the cart path. Lara, feeling his surprise, called out to him and he scampered over to her and climbed up under her cloak. For a moment Lara felt as if the ground had rumbled beneath her, but chalked it up to the force of him hurtling into her arms. The youth had seen Five and was now looking at Lara with a bit of wonder on his face.

"Hello," Lara called, raising a hand in a light wave.

The youth practically danced toward them, and she could see that he was about her son Pete's age, so under twenty. He was probably on his way to try for a color like so many at this age. She wondered which one.

"Hi." His bright eyes looked more interested in the bump where Five was than her. "I've never seen an animal like that before. Is it a pet?"

"He found me as I was walking and he just kind of joined me. I call him Five." Lara tried to send calming emotions toward the little guy and said, "He might come out in a minute, you just startled him. I'm Lara."

"I'm Zane. I'm on my way to Pink." His voice was melodious, and Lara felt at ease with him.

"I'm going to go out on a limb and guess you're coming from Azural?"

"Yup, my clothes gave it away, huh? I've lived there my whole life. My dad works at the aquarium and my mom is a stone layer. They both came to Azural from their small village to attempt the trials, but you know, not everyone succeeds. Even though they didn't Stonegraft, they found a place there. Me not so much. I am looking for my place in the world, and I think it is pink." He smiled at that and repeated it, this time singing, reminding her of Jada. "I think it is pink. I like that. I turned seventeen yesterday, so I finally get to leave and go prove myself. I have been waiting for this ever since I was thirteen and knew I wasn't meant to be in Azural. Where are you headed?"

"Actually, I am on my way to Blue."

He looked at her a bit more closely. She could tell he was taking in her worn clothes in shades of gray and dingy black. She assumed it was obvious to anyone who saw that she was from the Wastelands. "Do you have a child at Blue? I might know them and could tell you where to find them? I know most of the blue trial candidates."

Lara realized he hadn't even considered that she intended to join the trial candidates herself. "No, my youngest child left for Yellow about a month ago, and one of my daughters went to Orange, I believe, about two years ago now. I'm actually heading to Azural to attempt the blue trials myself."

Zane barked out a quick laugh and then seemed to realize that it was rude. "Sorry, I just have never seen anyone your age just starting the trials. I mean, a lot of the Stonegrafters are your age and older even, but just starting the trials now, that is interesting." The words cut into Lara's psyche and left her hurt. Her fears of if she was capable of this slammed forward.

He was looking at her and shaking his head, laughing when Five scrabbled around her arm and out from underneath her cloak to perch on her shoulder. He started chittering at Zane angrily. She felt righteous indignation from him and realized he was defending her. She suddenly realized that she was letting her fears drive her and her friend could feel it.

She knew what she was doing was strange, possibly never been done before. She also knew that just because it was done a certain way didn't mean it was the only way, or that it was the right way. These color realms had been slowly destroying her land and the lands of others like Nessa and most of the Brown traders. It had also torn apart families, like this young man's parents who traveled to the color realms to attempt the trials and just ended up staying. And now he was leaving them just like Brie and Pete had left Calambria. She was so tired of these problems.

"Thank you for the insight into what I am up against," Lara said, "but if it is to be that difficult, I suppose I had better get a move on and get started."

Zane raised his hands, waving them in apology, as much toward Five as to her. "I meant no offense. Just because it hasn't been done before doesn't mean it can't be done! And with this little guy to protect you, I imagine you will get on well enough at Blue. But he's going to need a good bath before they let him join you at the Great Stone House. Good luck Lara, I best be on my way too. I think I have about a week's journey ahead of me. You, on the other hand, should reach The Azural Spoke by tomorrow morning."

Lara waved goodbye and wished him well. Five calmed down quickly when he was out of sight. "Well, it looks like I have a little champion in you, huh? Champ might be a better name. Do you like it?" He ran ahead with no indication he cared one whit for the name.

$$\gtrless \gtrless \gtrless$$

She tried multiple names throughout the afternoon. Calling out to him when it was time for a rest, "Hey, Zippy! What do you think of that name?"

No response.

She knew it was time to stop when she was trying names like Flufferbottom and Nutso. She resorted to falling back on Five for the time being. He at least looked at her when she used it.

The afternoon's walk was passed in land much more familiar to her, for the little purple flowers had disappeared and the color had seeped away. Again, they were back in the Wastes. This was the land left behind between Purple and Blue. She knew she was moving closer. Lara imagined that there were other small villages like her own in these dark shadowed lands, people struggling to get through with little resources left to use.

As the sky began to dim, and twilight made her vision blur, everything softening, Lara saw up ahead a large stone monolith standing beside the cart path. As she came closer, she could see the path to Azural appear. The way to Blue would be down that road.

When she finally reached the large stone, it was already dark. She needed to eat dinner still, so decided to make camp and get some rest. Tomorrow would be the real beginning of her adventure. Although she had worried about a bit of trouble on the road, that was mostly around in the Northwest of the Wheel by Red and Orange, where tempers were more volatile. Her journey here had been safe.

Lara had met new friends in the Traders, had seen the edge of her first color realm, but tomorrow she would enter one for real. She knew nothing about what to expect, aside from the tiniest hints. She knew the cities were large. Her village had always been smaller, but had shrunk in size as people had emigrated to the color realms. All the realms had been large cities before the stonegrafters moved in. She remembered Jada's grandfather had bought the piano in what was now Green. But she also knew that they were magical realms now. Everyone had heard stories about the wondrous sights in the realms. She heard that the Orange realm had floating rocks that people jumped across to reach tall peaks in the sky. She had heard that Pink was nothing but fluff and pillows and that no one did any work there. She had heard impossible things. And now she was about to see for herself.

She had a lot of trouble sleeping that night. The dust from her travels had gotten into her hair and she felt itchy. Her little friend also showed the wear from the dirt on the road. She could see the gray dust from the Wastes layered underneath the brown dirt from the Wheel Road on his fur. "Don't worry. As soon as we get to Blue, we will have time to clean up. I have never felt so dirty. The road seems to stick to us as we travel." He had his back to her as she was trying to pat the dust off of him, but she could feel his excitement. He really seemed to understand what she said.

She wondered if she might find out more about her new friend at Blue. She imagined they had amazing libraries. Back home, most families had treasured books and shared them with each other. Her home library had two large bound books of fairy stories, a book on vegetables and stews, and her prized possession had been an encyclopedia set. The schools had closed a long time ago in her village and all children studied at home. She had encouraged them to look through the encyclopedia and ask questions. When she didn't know the answers, she would try to send them to someone who might. The kids loved cute animals, so she thought she had learned about all the creatures, but this little guy had not been in her books.

Azural held answers to so many questions, and also solutions to so many problems. She was antsy to arrive. As she fidgeted and couldn't lie still, she found that her little friend began mirroring her actions and she could feel him get antsy too. "Sorry, I think you feel my emotion as much as I feel yours, maybe?" She settled herself and tried calming her breath and thinking of more names. "Skipper...Ace...Puff..." she paused after each to see if he responded.

She was getting pretty sleepy as the names came out, she began thinking about how he mirrored her emotions, so name ideas became word association, "Mirror...Reflection...Fleck...," she was startled wide awake when he perked up at that and sat on her chest looking at her. His eyes shimmered and caught the faint light, but they looked straight at her. "You like Fleck?" He reached out and put his two little hands on her cheeks and pushed his tiny, soft (and very dirty) forehead into hers. The strength of it surprised her. "Alright then, Fleck it is. Short for Reflection, my little emotional mirror. I'm glad we have that settled. Shall we go to sleep now, my friend? We have a big day tomorrow."

Relieved to have that question off of her mind, she found herself awake the next morning, not even realizing she had slipped to sleep so fast.

After packing up in the morning, they headed down The Blue Spoke Road toward Azural. The skies were a familiar gray when they awoke, but the clouds moved quickly over her head toward the West. It was as if they were being pushed away from the center of Azural.

An hour into her walk, she saw her first peek at the sky behind a break in the clouds. It was a startling shock of pure blue color. She stopped still and just stared. She felt an immediate sense of wonder and had a flashback of her childhood looking up at clouds in the blue skies.

As a girl, the Wastes hadn't been all gray skies and shadows. She had seen rolling clouds with peeks of blue just like this throughout most of her childhood. She tried to remember when the last of the blue sky had been over her village. It had been before her children were born. They had never seen this vibrancy. But they had loved to find shapes in the shadows of the clouds. They had laid on blankets in the yard seeing dragons and fairies.

She again caught herself as she felt the pain of the loss of those hectic days full of stories and errands and endless questions. Fleck jumped up on her shoulder and placed a paw on her cheek. He, too, looked up at the blue in wonder. It reflected in his pale gray eyes, making them look blue themselves.

As they traveled throughout the morning, the blue patches in the sky became more regular. There were also spots of blue showing up in the environment on the surrounding ground. A bush with bright blueberries that Fleck had scurried to so quickly and started ravenously eating that by the time Lara arrived, his cheeks were plumped out full on each side, dyed blue from the berries. He had reached out sheepishly, offering Lara a few berries, and his paws had turned blue from the juices, too. They saw a pair of blue birds flittering by calling out a trilling tune to each other.

Just before midday, they began to hear the roar of water. She knew they had to pass through a waterfall to enter Azural proper, so she imagined that they must be getting close if they could hear it. She was surprised to find that they traveled much longer to reach it than she imagined was possible, the noise was so loud it was deceiving.

While the sky was more and more blue, she found that as she looked into the distance, it also looked blue. At first, she thought the blue sky went on into the distance, but as they got closer, she realized that there was an actual wall of blue looming in the distance. And as she got even closer, she saw that the wall was water. There was a waterfall coming from the sky with no land or rock to fall from. Off to the distant left she saw a cliff face and in front of her on this side there was another cliff. The rock was a deep grey/blue slate that looked impossible to climb, a slick surface. The waterfall fell next to it on its own. This was the work of magic, for sure. A color-weaver had shut off the entrance to their city with this wall of water.

Around mid-afternoon she came upon a cart coming towards her from Azural, the horse fresh, obviously just starting the journey. There were two friendly waves from the people on the front seat as they passed by. A bit farther down, she saw a gathering of wagons and carts to the right of the road. It looked like a small village, with the Brown rolling homes parked as if they were houses in a row. There was a separate fenced in area where all the horses were grazing, and a separate open building with a high wooden roof on tall thick wooden posts. It looked to Lara as though there were at least twenty carts in the tiny village.

This must be the trading post for Azural. The trading must have happened earlier in the day, because now she saw the people, all dressed in brown, amiably talking to each other and children running and playing. When any of them caught her eye, they gave a friendly wave, and she waved back. There was no point in calling out hellos, because the waterwall drowned out all sounds. However, her experience with Nessa was confirmed. These Brown traders were a welcoming, down-to-earth group.

She was now close enough to the waterfall to see that the water came down with such force that it created the most breathtaking and dangerous, churning waters below. There was a moat that reached from cliff to cliff. The only way across was a bridge that led directly into the waterfall next to the cliff on this side. The spoke road leading right up to it.

Lara stopped where the dust path ended just before the wooden bridge. She took a deep breath and steadied herself. The air was refreshing, and it felt as if she had taken a cool drink as her throat coated from the mist in the air. She was definitely entering a new world. She would step through this water and on the other side she would set off to save her family, her friends and her home. They needed this water, and there was obviously plenty to spare.

With Fleck peeking at the water from his spot on her right shoulder, she could feel his excitement. Or maybe it was her own. They stepped onto the bridge.

She had to watch her step because the boards of the bridge became more and more slick. As she looked up, she saw that the wall reached up in the sky beyond where she could see, and she wondered where the source of this water was. How could it just keep falling from nowhere?

The power of the falling water scared Lara. The thunderous sound, mixed with the tempest of water hitting the moat made it obvious that the stream of water coming down had enough force to knock someone under the water. She wondered if she would even be able to walk through it.

As they came up to the edge of the falling water, she realized that the section of the waterfall in front of her disappeared and an open room sat beneath the raging water. She could not fathom how it was possible, but the powerful cascade just stopped and instead a thin trickle of water was all that was left between her and the next space on the center of the bridge.

Gearing up, she stepped through the water screen. After wiping the water from her eyes she found herself in a narrow room with thin water screens behind her and in front of her. Immediately, the sounds of the water were muffled out to a dull background noise, as if a door was shut to a storm. To her right was the shale of the cliff and to her left the roaring thickness of the waterwall, but ahead of her a smooth thin screen of water like the one she had just walked through.

She forced herself to look up at the raging waterfall above her. From this angle, it was an odd sight. The water bubbled and roiled about, but it streamed off toward the sides rather than falling onto her head. She thought for a quick moment about what might happen if the magic were to fail. That spurred her to move forward.

# Under the Waterwall

The room under the water wall was empty aside from one person who stood at a podium with a quill and paper. He was wearing a bright blue tunic and matching leggings with two bands of deep blue around his right upper arm.

"Welcome to Azural." He started in a bored voice. "Please state your name and business."

"Lara. I am here to attempt the trials."

He looked up, startled. "I'm sorry, what?"

She guessed she had his attention now. She took a breath and repeated herself, trying to put more authority behind it. "My name is Lara, and I am here to attempt to stonegraft blue. Could you please give me directions to The Great Stone House?"

He still looked flummoxed. "But whatever do you mean?"

Her annoyance came quickly after her long journey, and Fleck, ever turning into her true champion, jumped forward, began chittering at him as he had at Zane.

The man looked from Lara to Fleck and back again a few times. "I think you had better wait here." And he stepped out of the wall toward town.

Lara looked at Fleck with a mix of frustration and amusement in her eyes. "They don't know what to make of us, I guess. Let's clean up a bit. May as well make use of all of this water here." She walked back to the stream of water she had first walked through and just stood there with the water streaming down her. Fleck did the same.

She closed her eyes and concentrated on the feel of the water from her scalp to her toes. She opened her eyes and watched as the dirt moved away in the puddles beneath them. When the water ran clear, she stepped back into the room.

Fleck jumped forward a few bounces and shook off droplets of water going in all directions. She felt his satisfaction at getting the grime off. It was dark in this water room, but as Fleck bounded back over to her, she could tell right away that he had cleaned up quite a bit. "Why Fleck, you aren't gray at all, you're white!" His fur was clumped together, still wet, but he was all clean.

She waited for a few more minutes but became impatient. Why must she wait here? She sidled up to the far wall and peeked through. After a moment of letting the water run down her face, she looked and saw the backs of four smartly dressed guards lining the path toward town. They wore jackets, tailored to their shape with two navy bands on the right upper arm just like the original man.

Between the shoulders of two directly in front of her, she saw the man she had spoken to was returning with two serious looking folks dressed in the same blue. However, both of these had three dark blue bands. "I guess we are moving up the ranks, Fleck." She moved back a few steps and stood as though she hadn't just been about to step right through.

$$ \text{ʓ ʓ ʓ} $$

The newest two entering looked like they were important, and they knew it. All three entered through the water with their left arm raised at an angle, the forearm touching their forehead, palm facing out. Lara noticed that this kept the water from getting into their eyes as they passed through the wall.

They stood at the podium and the shorter of the two, a woman in her mid thirties, Lara guessed, stated just as the original two banded man, "Welcome to Azural. Please state your name and business."

"Lara, I am here to attempt to stonegraft a blue stone."

"See! I told you," The younger two-banded man whispered very loudly.

Both of the others gave him a stare that was so forceful he stepped backward and quieted down.

When they turned back to her, she found the glare still on their faces. The older woman spoke to her with a wary voice, "We don't get a lot of outsiders here at Azural. Most understand what our waterwall means. We, of course, accept youth that are meant to be here, but you are obviously not on your quest to find your way in life."

"Well," Lara stammered, "I... realize I am no youth, but I am on a quest." Her voice getting stronger as she realized they just needed to understand. "My home is in the Wastes, and we have almost run out of water. It is really important that I find a waterweaver to come help us, or we will have to all leave the only home we have ever known. I came for help."

She noticed the young man standing back at his podium snicker a bit and, confused, looked at the two higher ups.

They had turned to each other, and she could only pick up snippets, "really, the Wastes," "above our banding" and "let them deal with her." There was a nod between them, and they turned back to face her. The glare was less aggressive, the strain from a few moments ago gone from their faces and bodies. She got the impression they were happy to realize she was someone else's problem.

"We will be taking you into the Parliamentary Building. They will deal with you there."

"This way," and they stepped through the water, arms back on their foreheads.

Lara followed suit and placing her left forearm to her forehead, stepped through. It worked like a charm. She stepped through and on the other side, she gave her arm a quick shake and the droplets sparkled in front of her as the blue sky reflected on them. Her eyes were clear to see, but poor Fleck had not prepared and was shaking his face, the water from his fur getting all over her face. "We are going to have to work on that," she whispered to him.

The four guards had moved formation and were now standing two on each side facing the path. Lara tried to smile at them. They did their best to look at attention, but Lara felt their eyes follow her as she walked past them.

The wooden bridge continued on the far side of the water wall and led them across the moat to a well-manicured path of steppingstones. Lara noticed a strange blue tint to them; unlike any stone she had seen before. The two led her down this path, away from the roar of the falling water. As they got farther away, she began to hear them speaking to each other quietly, but again, she could only catch small bits of the conversation. "Shauna will be upset...doesn't like surprises...never seen...only youth..." The taller man, who was probably about Lara's age looked over his shoulder at her and quieted his companion down, realizing they were far enough from the churning waters and that she could probably hear them now.

They came up to a tall stone wall with an arch opening and as they passed through, Lara was inundated by the sounds of a large city. She had never visited one, but she had heard from her mother about her trips before the land was broken. She had known to expect sounds, but she was not prepared for the feel of the noise. It wasn't like she could cover her ears and remove the noise. There was a buzz in the air that came from the energy of so many people in one place. She counted more people in her current view than were in her whole village.

The city loomed in front of her, the buildings growing taller and taller as they met in the center. Indeed, she was certain there were a few buildings that were almost as tall as the waterwall. In the distance, she saw the expanse of the ocean. Azural was set in a cove, with tall cliffs on either side, with ocean in front of her and the waterwall behind her. It was entirely enclosed: a blue enclave.

Once they had passed through the wall, they were on a path of large stones. These also had a hint of blue. These were laid close together, leaving no room for anything to grow between them. Everything was neat, tidy, and orderly. There were no roads that she could see. In fact, she didn't see any carts either. Instead, she was led to a canal and the three of them got into a boat. The water flowed in one direction, pulling them along toward the center of town.

As they moved farther toward the tall buildings in the distance, she saw a complex network of bridges and waterways with small boats that ferried people around. The current in each flowing in a certain direction. As she passed under a bridge, she saw a larger boat full of children in light blue school uniforms flowing in the water over a stone bridge. The kids squealed in delight as it went down the far side of the bridge. She felt that same excitement as her boat flowed over another waterway, the current pulling the small boat up and over another canal. She felt her tummy jump as the boat slid a little more quickly back down on the other side.

All around her, she saw people going about their days. She saw bakeries and clothing shops. Everything was familiar, but nothing was the same. The most overpowering thing after the hustle and bustle was the color. There was blue everywhere. The water was blue, the clothes people wore were blue, the sky was a clear blue without a single cloud, even the buildings were blue. There were a multitude of shades and hues, so it wasn't like everything blurred together, but it was like nothing she had seen. It had a strange calming effect on her, even with all the people and happenings around her.

Lara marveled at all of the water. Everywhere she turned she saw fountains and art made of water. There was more than enough to share. All she would have to do was explain her situation and get some help. The water was plentiful enough.

The boat slowed as it pulled up to a dock at the side of the canal. The woman with her reached out and swiftly grabbed a post, pulling the small boat to a complete stop.

They were in front of the largest building Lara had ever seen and looked to be the most imposing in Azural. The base was as wide as six of the other buildings in the area, with about four stories, while the center reached far into the blue sky. The windows reflected the bright sky in a slightly warped way, creating a kind of dissonance that really vibed with how Lara was feeling. She craned her neck to see the top of the building but was abruptly pushed from behind by her escorts.

A man stood at the entrance in much the same way the man at the podium had under the waterwall. Another gatekeeper. He also had two bands along his right upper arm, but he was older and had kinder eyes. He addressed the two with her with deference but smiled at Lara in greeting.

Her two escorts gave him a brusk nod and walked straight past without a word to him. Under the water sheet entrance, they continued walking without a hitch, while Lara had to slow her pace as she set her hand up again, trying to learn the correct placement of it to keep her eyes dry. She didn't get it right this time.

Trying to dry her eyes off with the cuff of her tattered black sleeve, she was abruptly aware of how out of place she looked. Everyone around her was pristinely kept in bright blue shades and hues. She didn't see a hole or tear in a single piece, let alone a stain. And they were so clean. She, on the other hand, was still in her muddy boots from the travel on the road, along with the fact that all of her clothes were not just dirty from sleeping on the ground but had been mended multiple times. Indeed, her cape had a whole square of fabric to patch the largest tear. But they had learned to make clothes last in the Wastes. Indeed, her favorite pastime and the skill she was often most proud of was the hand stitching over a roughly worn area to give it more strength. She self-consciously reached for the tear she had gotten climbing up the loose stones at the beginning of her journey, even more aware it hadn't been repaired.

She was led into a room off to the side of the main hall with fewer people bustling about. This room had a large table, and she was asked to sit in the only chair on one side, while the other side had multiple chairs. Sitting down, she counted seven chairs across from her. There was also a small table off to the side with a single chair at it. Her two escorts disappeared, and she was left alone.

Fleck peeked out at her neck, darting his head from left to right, his ears and whiskers tickling her cheek.

"It's alright. I imagine we just need to explain ourselves. They must not get many visitors. And I can understand why, that waterwall was fairly intimidating." She could sense that Fleck didn't like being closed in and realized that he had likely never been in a building before. She tried to calm herself to help ease his discomfort. "You might want to keep hidden for now, though. Why don't you curl up in my pack?" She motioned to her pack on her lap, and he dove in, curling up into an adorable fluffy ball.

Lara closed the flap over his head and rubbed her fingers along the map that Sally had burned into the leather, her fingers lingering on home. She marveled at how far she had traveled already. She hoped they were all doing alright back there. How long did they have?

A motion at the entrance brought her out of her thoughts into the present. A woman, likely ten years older than Lara, entered with a notebook and a small pouch. She smiled at Lara and sat at the small table in the corner. This woman had two bands on her right arm. As she sat down, she pulled out a few writing implements and what looked like a sharpening knife. After she was all set up, she looked around the room and nodded to herself. "I'm going to go get a glass of water. Would you like one?"

"Oh, yes!" Lara said. As soon as she said it, she worried that she sounded too eager. "Please."

The woman was gone and back very quickly with two glasses of the most crystal-clear water Lara had ever seen. She set a glass in front of Lara and pulled out the chair across from her, sitting down with an ease that made Lara relax just a bit more.

Lara held the glass up to eye level and just wondered at it, "This looks so amazing. Where I come from, we never get a full glass of water, just sips throughout the day, and usually we use it for cooking, so we get our nutrients in with our hydration."

"Go ahead and drink up. There's a ton more here."

Lara lifted the glass to her face. She could smell the water. There was a crisp, mineral bite, but more than anything, she could feel the moisture in her nostrils. She took a sip, and it hit her throat. Fresh, smooth, clean. She took another sip and let it sit in her mouth for a moment. She could feel the moisture coat the inside of her mouth and became hyper-aware of how dry it had been just a moment ago. How dry it had been for years.

She swallowed a full gulp down, aware of the water touching her throat, cooling it.

She then proceeded to chug the whole glass. Immediately, her stomach sloshed around, making her a bit queasy, but her mind seemed to almost instantly have a fog lift.

"My name is Kierra. I take notes at all the meetings and important events here at Azural's Parliamentary Building. There are going to be a few of our senators coming in to ask some questions and I will be sitting over there, at that little table writing everything down."

"That sounds so similar to what my husband James does back home. But of course, on a much smaller scale. Everything here is so much bigger than back home. You must write ten times as much as him in a day."

"There are only a few people here who know how to keep up. I taught myself a shorthand that allows me to get everything said on paper. I only have to write a dash to represent whole words, and then I rewrite it afterward in long hand for the court library."

"I taught my kids to write, but I don't think I have ever heard of a shorthand. That is amazing. Maybe I should have learned that instead, and I could have saved time with my kids." Lara laughed.

"How many kids do you have?"

"Four, but they are all grown now. Do you have kids?"

"I raised two. Both work here in the APB, that's the Azural Parliamentary Building. I love getting to see them every day."

Lara sighed. "I feel the same way about the two that stayed back home. I see them regularly, but I also am very proud of the other two who have left to find their way in the world. It is hard, because I miss them, but it's their life, not mine. What jobs do your kids do?"

"My oldest runs the water shoots out back. He was always interested in them. As a kid, he would come to work with me and ask to ride them up and down till the woman who used to run them just took him under her wing and taught him everything about it. My youngest is a bookkeeper. He loves numbers and works with tallying all day long."

"Guess he sort of took after you then?" Lara commented.

Kierra came up short. "Wow, I guess you could say that. I always looked more at the differences, but you're right, we do have quite a bit in common." Kierra laughed and then looking toward the door, commented quietly, "Do your best to remain calm and just be honest with the council. They just want some answers, so your best bet is to give it to them straight. I better get over to my seat."

"Thank you, Kierra, it was nice to meet you. And thank you for the water." Lara smiled and was warmed by the smile she got in return.

Kierra sat down and began sharpening one of her pencils with the knife in quick, sharp motions. Lara found it entrancing for a few moments, convinced she would slice her own finger off if she attempted it.

The mood in the room shifted immediately as six somber people walked in. They were all wearing blue jackets, similar to the people she had seen before, but they were more refined. Each had individual tailoring and, more importantly Lara noticed, they all had four or five bands. She was definitely moving up the ranks.

They settled into their comfortable chairs and all began studying her. She was immediately uncomfortable. She found herself squirming in her chair, trying to settle the nervousness. As they studied her, she pictured how she must look to them. Her face was dirty, probably streaked from the water washing dust from her hair, her clothes stained and torn. She tightened her hands, wringing them in worry and noticed not only her white knuckles, but the dirt under her nails, and quickly pulled them under the table, hugging her pack, and Fleck inside for grounding.

# Senators

After what Lara thought might have been minutes, but was more likely just moments, a seventh man entered the room. He wore five bands on his right shoulder, but his garment wasn't as closely tailored to his torso the way these others were. He wore a loose robe, Lara thought it looked comfortable. As he took the seat closest to the door on Lara's far left, the people seated across from her all greeted him respectfully.

"Good afternoon, Chairperson Gliron."

And he greeted them back in unison, "Good afternoon, everyone. Now let's get started, shall we? What has pulled me away from my fishing with Lucas to this dank chamber on this lovely afternoon?"

As he settled in his seat, he took a look at Lara across from him, smiled, and then looked over at the small table behind him. "Kierra, are you ready to begin?"

"Yes, sir," Kierra said, grabbing one of her pencils, the tip sharp and glinting in the light.

"Calling to order on the Fifty-second Day of Spring, a most beautiful day for fishing, I might add, this Questioning." He turned to Lara. "Can you please tell us your name for the record?"

"Lara Soleil."

"Thank you, and why are you here in Azural?"

Lara was a bit taken aback by the question. Why would they care why she was here? "I have come to visit the Great Stone House to try for a stone. We desperately need water back home in my hometown of Calambria."

A man on her far right spoke with force, snapping Lara's attention and head to the other direction. "Didn't you have any youth to come try? There is no way you were the one to send for the stone trials." He sounded distrustful, and Lara began to wilt under his icy blue-eyed stare. She took a deep breath and turned to face forward again, responding to the question so that all of them could hear her.

"Our town population is small now. Probably only twenty percent is left from when I was a child. People have moved on to find a more secure home." Lara explained. "You know how hard it can be in the Wastes."

All of those across from her started turning to each other, mumbling. She tried to hear what they were saying, but couldn't pick out words, as they all were in conversation. The only one left out of the pairs of conversations was Chairperson Gliron. He studied her with his head tipped to the side.

"Attention everyone." They all hushed immediately. "Let's continue with the questioning so we can finish up. The fish were biting, and I would rather be there than here. Lara, most of us here in Azural do not believe the rumors that the Wastes are a real thing. You expect us to believe that your home is just a wasteland without resources? I am a native of Azural and indeed lived here as a child when it was still called Petra Bay. There is no way that in the forty years since the waterwall went up, that the world has crumbled away to a Wasteland."

"Exactly!" This from the man on the far right again. "There is no way the Wastes even exist. This woman is obviously lying, and we need to keep her away from the Stone House. Our youth are there, and they don't need to be introduced to these kinds of lies. She must have ulterior motives." Turning to face Lara, he said. "Where are you really from? Yellow? I know they have wanted to 'research,'" his voice grated out the word as if it tasted sour in his mouth, "how we run our government and stone trials. Indeed, we turned that man Phillips away not two months ago. Maybe she is undercover to try to sneak past us." His lovely face contorted into an angry expression and Lara couldn't help but wonder at how ugly hate was.

"Right," snickered the woman next to him. She was plump and wore more jewelry than Lara had ever seen, the lapis blue stones on her necklace sparkling in the light, almost dancing as her bosom rose and fell with her laughter, "This costume you have on is obviously fake. How pitiful that you would think we might believe that this is what people would wear in these 'so called' wastelands."

Lara was at a loss for words. They didn't even believe that the Wastes were real? They actually considered she was a spy, rather than here to help her family?

A woman seated directly across from Lara cleared her throat quietly. "Chairman Gliron, may I ask a question of our guest?" She gave a pointed look at the man and woman on the far side of the table, reproaching them for their lack of etiquette.

"Of course, I call on Senator Sabine Giesen." He nodded to her. She was younger than Lara, dressed pristinely with little jewelry, but her clothes were obviously expensive with velvet on her cuffs and collar and light clear blue gems for buttons that caught the light. She had four dark blue bands around her upper arm, also in the velvet material. Lara thought it looked very refined.

"Thank you, Chairperson Gliron. Lara, we do not get many guests here in Azural, indeed most outsiders are youth coming to join the Great Stone House. Even our traders wait outside for us to join them at their paddock. It is unprecedented for us to have a woman your age even enter our city, let alone tell us she wants to try for a stone. Can you please give us a bit more detail about where you are from? It is extremely hard for us to believe that things are so very bad beyond our waterwall."

Lara took a deep breath and addressed Senator Giesen directly. "When I was a child, I remember blue skies like you have here everyday back home. That is a joy my own children did not have. Over the last forty years, the skies have grown darker and darker. The land too has lost its color. All you need to do is look around to see the changes that the blue stones have wrought even here in Azural." Turning to Chairperson Gliron, Lara questioned, "Was the world here so very blue when you were young? Has it not changed more than you could have imagined?" At his nod, she continued.

"With each of those magical stones unearthed and brought to a color realm far from our home, the resources have dried up. As you look here and see all the amazing feats of water canals, beautiful blue clothing, especially the waterwall in all of its glory, how can you not see that the magic is glowing here? It is fortified and layered and practically humming in the air. When I breathe here, I can taste the water in the air." Lara took a deep breath. "All of that magic came from somewhere else. It was stolen from the land and the land misses it. I just —"

Lara was cut off by the man at the end of the table. "I knew it! She just wants to come and take one of our stones! She isn't here to become one of our waterweavers. She is here for herself."

"Senator Rombauer, you need to be called on if you want to speak." Chairperson Gliron chided. "We have protocol, and you know it."

"Permission to speak, Chairperson Gliron?" Rombauer said in an icy tone.

"Yes, the Chair calls on Senator Noren Rombauer to ask a question of our guest." He enunciated the last few words.

"Thank you, Chairman. Were you to succeed in becoming a waterweaver, what would your next step be?"

Lara answered as honestly as she could. "I realize it is very difficult to earn a stone. I am hoping, one way or another, to bring a bit of the magic back to our corner of the world. I am hoping that by returning a blue stone to Calambria that we will get water again, that our well will no longer be dry and that our community can stay in our homes."

"See!" Rombauer said triumphantly. "She is only here to try to take a stone away."

"Chairperson Gliron?" A young man, he looked to be the youngest of them, likely only in his twenties. "Permission to ask a question?"

"The Chair calls on Senator Bariano."

"Lara, we have very clear rules here in Azural about expectations of our waterweavers. Even if you were to earn a stone, no waterweaver leaves Azural. Indeed, no citizen has left unless they are a youth trying for another stone, and they go through our youth preparation courses to be sure that they are making the right choice. Do you understand?"

"You seriously all believe it is for the best to live behind that waterwall and anyone on the other side is not your problem?" Lara was a bit shocked by this.

"We take care of ours. They can take care of theirs." The young Senator Bariano said this with such clarity, as if it were the most obvious fact.

Lara began to take this in. How in the world was she supposed to get help if no one was even allowed to leave Azural? Even if she got a stone, they wouldn't trust her to pass the waterwall? It seemed extremely unlikely that if this was the consensus of thought that she would ever convince a current waterweaver to come with her. Had the world broken so far that no one even realized it was broken?

All of these people happily plugging along in their magical blue world full of water, they could not even begin to imagine that things were so bad, as they were in the Wastes. Lara's reality was a foreign made-up story to them.

The man across from her, who had been quiet until now, cut into her thoughts, "With your permission, Chair?"

Gliron responded with, "The Chair calls on Senator Mersault."

"I think we should just kick her out. It is obvious we can't trust her. Her goals are against Azural, and the Tenets of Blue."

The last woman to speak was sitting directly next to Chairperson Gliron. She raised her hand slightly for his attention and he said, "The Chair calls on Senator Bieler."

"Blue's Tenets are Honesty, Order, Intelligence, Responsibility and Peace. I believe this woman can prove her self worth, or not, in her attempt to earn these bands. We can help her understand why we have our rules in place. I realize she is older than many who have come to Azural for the Stone House trials, but I do not see a reason why we should keep her from trying. We have all been through them and know that the classes and trials are not only there to find those worthy of attempting stonegrafting, but also to teach about our ways and the truths of Blue. Let her learn about us more, and she will be able to see why the Waterweavers must stay here. We have already seen honesty from her. Maybe she will grow to love it here and find her own place in Azural."

A sing-songy voice called out to her right, "Chairman Gliron?"

"The Chair calls on Senator Doria."

"Lara, my dear." The woman with all the jewelry seemed to look down on Lara as she spoke, even though they were all sitting at the same level. "You understand now what our expectations are in Azural?"

Lara held back the bite from her words. She did not appreciate being spoken to like she was stupid. "Yes, ma'am."

"Oh, that's sweet, but you can address me as Senator Doria." Lara looked at her for a beat and realized she was waiting for Lara to correct her mistake.

"Yes, Senator Doria."

"It seems to me that The Great Stone House will solve this problem for us." Lara readjusted herself in her seat. She didn't much like being referred to as a 'problem.' "We trust in its ability to weed out the issues, the people who don't fit our expectations. I say let her go and attempt the trials. It was no easy feat for those of us sitting here to earn our four or five bands. Let the Stone House decide."

Chairperson Gliron nodded and took a few quiet moments to gather his thoughts. Lara already found that she respected this man. He obviously held the respect of the people in this room, even with their varying opinions. She wondered if he was the one to decide her fate. She hoped so.

Chairperson Gliron answered her question without it being asked. "Lara, all decisions made in Azural are made by the vote of the Senators present. So, we will be putting this up to a vote. I will clarify what it is we are voting on for the record." He turned and smiled at Kierra, who waved her pencil in response. Lara noticed that she was on her third pencil, two more dull laid next to her paper. "The vote is whether to allow Lara Soleil to continue on her journey to The Great Stone House, or to escort her to the waterwall to leave Azural."

# Put to a Vote

Lara was buzzing from the shock that her whole journey could end right here. She studied those sitting across from her and realized they were so different from her. How could they even begin to understand her need? She held back the temptation to plead her case with them, realizing that each time she tried to convince them, they would pull further from supporting her. Her only chance to move on was if they believed she might just decide to stay in Azural.

"Senator Rombauer?"

"Send her away."

"Senator Doria?"

"Let her try. She will find it is not so simple to just waltz in here and get a stone. Let her find it out and take that knowledge with her as she leaves."

"Senator Giesen?"

"Let her go to the Great Stone House. The trials are made to test people, let them see into her heart."

"Senator Mersault?"

"I don't think we should waste the time of our waterweavers or subject our youth to her outsider thinking. Send her away."

"Senator Bariano?"

Lara looked at the younger man. He studied her for a minute. "I think we should send her away. It is obvious to me that she does not respect or understand our Tenets and ways."

"Senator Bieler?"

"As I said before, let her try for the stone. I have often wondered if I had waited until I was older, if I might have succeeded in stonegrafting. In my youth, I didn't look at the world as I do now. I am actually very interested in how a woman with life experience might fare at the Stone House."

With a laugh Chairperson Gliron said, "The Chair calls on Chairperson Gliron as the tiebreaker vote. Well, I would very much like to get back to my pond, so I will make this quick. I appreciate this woman's honesty with us, and I vote to let her continue on to the Stone House. Let her be Shauna and Axel's," here he paused and looked down the table, punctuating his next word, "'problem.' I trust them to know the best next steps." He stood up, gave a short nod to Lara. "Nice to meet you, but I am going to run back to my husband and our picnic by the pond. The fish were biting, and I am in a hurry to return."

"Thank you," Lara said, meeting his kind eyes and trying to send all of her appreciation through the look. He smiled in return and spun around, loose robes flowing around him, and was out the door.

The rest of the Senators didn't care to hang around either and while she got a kind smile from Senators Sabine and Giesen on their ways out the door, she found herself alone in the room with Kierra less than a minute after the vote.

Kierra was making a few last-minute marks on her paper, and when she looked up, Lara noticed a small shift in how her eyes focused. As if she had just realized they were alone. "Oh, goodness. They all just left you, didn't they?" Shaking her head, she stood up. "Well, let's find you an escort to the Stone House, Lara."

At that moment, it sunk in that Lara was back on her path. She realized she had a huge unplanned hurdle in her way of getting back out of Azural, but she would deal with that when she got there. She stood and shouldered her pack gently, not wanting to disrupt Fleck too much, but she could feel him awakening at the motion. *Let's get to the Stone house,* she thought. And Fleck sent a content sleepy response of agreement.

She found herself with the same two sentries who had led her to the Parliament building, and she could tell that neither was very happy about the Senators' decision. But they kept it to themselves. It wasn't their place to decide these things.

Back in the boat, they passed out of the center of downtown past more shops and homes and then on toward the Ocean. Just moments after passing through the buildings, the small boat entered larger open water. Lara changed her focus from the open view, taking everything in and instead focused on what was directly in front of them.

This was definitely The Great Stone House. An island sat in the center of this large open still water. From afar she saw the hustle and bustle of boats entering and leaving the docks along the west edge of the island. Rising above everything in the center of the land was an enormous building. The lower floors were hidden from view by walled gardens that surrounded it, but small windows lined the upper floors. As they came closer, she saw that the outskirts of the island had paths leading into meticulous stone gardens, benches, fountains, and ponds.

Her two escorts stood and grabbed hold of a post, and the ride came to an immediate halt. They tied up the boat, jumped out, and began down the paths toward the center of the island. Lara quickly jumped out to follow them.

On their walk, she saw fish in the ponds and heard the quiet sounds of water gurgling as it bubbled over pebbles. She realized then that the loud buzz of the city was left behind them. The Stone House was its own space. She still felt a vibration, but this was different. It wasn't from the people; it was from something else.

# Order

Shauna was unsettled, and she didn't like the feeling one bit. Fighting the urge to crumple up the paper in her hand, she carefully lined up two corners and pulled her fingers along the edge to give it a nice crisp fold. The satisfaction from the sound had her fold it in half one more time. Then she placed it in her pocket.

All the weavers would get messages from their connections in town, and everyone would be meeting up to discuss it soon. She was in no state to interact with them yet.

As soon as she had read the note from Rombauer, she had walked briskly to her favorite garden, if you could call it that. Of all the gardens on the island, this was the only one without any plants. The high stone walls created an echo chamber that only held the sounds from inside itself. She had found out in her first few months here, decades ago, that this was her place. Her rooms, even now as a Weaver, allowed in sound, albeit muffled, of laughter and screams from the students at The Great Stone House. She did her best to keep things together, but there were often times she needed to come here to get control of her emotions back.

The floor of this garden was also stone, but the gardeners had carved thin, deep grooves in a pattern that circled out from the center in an orderly way, with angled pathways. In the center, a small fountain bubbled up, creating the only sound in the space. The grooves made a star shape around the water, but as the grooves moved out the shape morphed into a complex maze heading back and forth and included sharp angles. Shauna let just a tendril of her power loose from her right hand, the blue light faint enough you could barely see it. She used it to cup a handful of water from the fountain and placed it into the groove at the beginning of the pattern. Slowly and carefully, she moved the water along the path with her magic, following and focusing. She needed to get control before she headed to talk with the others.

When she reached the end of the path, she took a breath in, filling the upper half of her chest with air. She could feel the familiar tension in her shoulders, a known side effect of keeping control when the world around her was off kilter. If Rombauer was right, she was in for a lot of trouble.

The handful of water sat in the grooves where her weaver magic held it at the end of the maze. She allowed herself the indulgence in this private place to vent a bit of her frustration, pulling it up to float in front of her and then pushing hard with a quick and solid force toward the fountain in the center. It gave a satisfying splash as it joined the rest of the water.

She carefully opened the door in the wall and then closed it and locked it behind her. Once she had become headmaster, she had added the lock onto this door to keep at least one space that she could escape to.

The path outside her garden had high bushes on either side. As she walked briskly along toward The Great Stone House, she ticked off the issues that must be addressed.

This woman Lara, wanted to take a stone away. Not allowed. She said she was from the Wastes. They don't even exist. She was hoping to be a student here, but Rombauer said in his note that she was an older woman.

Shauna just hoped that the other waterweavers saw what she did. This was trouble and the woman should be sent away.

As she entered the meeting room, she counted, and all eleven of the others were already there. She refused to register how the demeanor of the other weavers changed when seeing her. They had always bristled a bit when she was around. She was used to it. The chaos of the space, however, added to her ill ease.

"Let's all get seated. We have a lot to discuss," she said, heading to her seat. She knew from experience that it was best to lead by example. The rest were much quicker to follow her words, if she did it first.

Once everyone was seated, she opened the conversation. "I am sure you have all heard about the outsider on her way over here. The Senators at the Questioning have decided to leave the decision up to us. Well, I believe it is obvious. She wants to take a stone weaver and, therefore, a stone away from Azural. This is not allowed, so we should clearly send her back to where she came from."

She looked at Fallon sitting next to her. He was the newest weaver, and although they had very little in common, he was generally the first to agree with her. "It is our responsibility to keep Azural and the stones safe; and I was told she claims to be from the Wastes?" Fallon said.

This raised a lot of rumbling discussion among the Weavers, and although Shauna agreed that this was ridiculous, she did not like the disorder. "We don't need to even discuss that; we all know that the rumors of a wasteland beyond our borders are ludicrous. I remember when the waterwall went up, there is no way that the land could be that depleted in just a generation. We have already had an issue with spies from Yellow trying to get into our Realm. This is most likely another tactic."

Shauna looked around the circle to gauge how the others were reacting. Many looked like they were in agreement, but then she reached Axel. She was not surprised to see that he had the look of someone about to step in and take over. He took his time, but when he cleared his throat, everyone quieted and looked his way.

Axel had given his seat up as headmaster to Shauna almost ten years ago, but as the founder of Azural and The Great Stone House, he would always hold sway. His body might be frail, and his steps might be slow, but one only had to look into his eyes to see that he was still quick witted, and his years of wisdom often inspired the rest of the Weavers in this circle. Shauna deferred to him with a nod.

"I think this is a lot of hullabaloo for a single person. It isn't like she can just take a stone and walk out of here. The stone only grafts to those who are ready and worthy. You all know this. Many of you spent years getting through the trials and we all have friends who attempted the grafting and didn't succeed. The stones know. Let us trust in the virtues of Blue here."

Shauna felt the change in the others, and tried to bring the conversation back in the direction she had planned. "What about her claims to be from the Wastes?" Shauna asked.

"The tenet of honesty will catch her then. You all went through these classes and trials. Once we interact with her, we will know more. You can get a better look in class. If she even makes it through the gatekeeping trial. This all might be moot. Let's see what happens this evening. If she succeeds in joining the house, let her succeed or fail based on the same expectations of all the other students."

Shauna felt he had made his decision, and when Axel weighed in, it was often final. No one was quick to go against him, they all revered him too much. With one last thought, she added, "What about her age? All of our students are 20-30 years younger than her."

"The first decade I created the Great Stone House, we had a lot of older students. There has never been an age requirement here." He looked deeply into Shauna's eyes, and she could tell he was reading her by the quick sapping of her energy. She wished she could get a read on him as easily, but he was quite talented at blocking his thoughts from the other waterweavers, keeping to himself. A skill she was jealous of. "Don't worry Shauna. You can trust in the rules of The House."

Of course, he was right. The rules would keep this woman in line, but she just knew that her peace and order was about to get turned upside down. If she was lucky, the woman would fail this afternoon and head back through the waterwall to wherever she had come from.

# Initiates Test

Lara followed the two down a path to the left of the main house to a side building. It was long and narrow, with windows all along the walls. The glass doors led into a large open room with a view, through clear, wide windows, of the ocean to the East and gardens every other direction.

"Wait here with the rest of the initiates." The woman sentry told her gruffly, and they headed up to the front where a small group of smartly dressed Blue leaders stood. There were six of them up there in total, and Lara counted three and four bands on each of their arms. Her two traveling companions joined them, and they grouped up to listen to the sentries. She saw them pointing in her direction, followed by looks from all the leaders, a few with startled reactions, and then nods all around.

There were about thirty people milling around her, most in blue, but there were some dressed in other colors. None wore the grays and blacks that Lara wore. She felt a need to find some space for herself and maneuvered through all of those standing and chatting toward the windows hoping for her first good view of the ocean.

Everyone in this room must have been between the ages of seventeen and twenty-five. One more example to her of how out of place she was. It was no wonder she was getting sideways glances from everyone in there. Her clothing made it obvious that she wasn't a Blue leader, and she definitely wasn't under twenty, considering three of her children were over twenty now. That was impossible. She laughed to herself, and she felt Fleck send a warm, happy vibe at her humor from his place in her pack. He seemed to have a knack for when to keep out of sight.

One of the leaders up front, a young woman likely in her early thirties with her blond hair slicked back into a tight ponytail, walked calmly to the back corner of the room where Lara only just noticed an older man sitting with his legs crossed on a mat next to a lovely indoor waterfall. His eyes were closed, but Lara thought him to be closer to her age than anyone else in this room. His salt and pepper dark hair was unruly, curls cut short enough to stay out of his face, but still long enough to bounce as he nodded slowly to whatever the woman had told him, his eyes still closed. The woman straightened and pulled the bottom of her jacket to remove any creases from bending over. If Lara hadn't been staring, she might not have noticed her quick eye movement to check on Lara, but their eyes locked and the woman quickly looked away.

Feeling ill at ease from all the attention, Lara turned to look out the window, and for the first time saw the sea. She had never seen it before, and she was sucked in by it. There was an amazing feeling of constant motion, but at the same time, a stillness from this distance. She saw rolling waves pull toward her and the pattern of it calmed her.

"Welcome initiates!" The six leaders had lined up at the front of the room, and the one with blond ponytail spoke with a strong, clear voice. "Blue welcomes you. All of you have dreams of stonegrafting, and maybe some of you will even get the chance to try for it, but few stones exist. There is a way, and we follow the path laid out by Axel, the first waterweaver. To reach the final stage and attempt stonegrafting, you must pass and complete the trials."

A hubbub went through the crowd as they excitedly chatted with those next to them. The woman raised her hands and waited patiently as they quieted and calmed down. "The first test is to begin now." At that Lara raised her eyebrows, and many in the room gasped and reacted with nervous tension.

"It is simple. There are five tenets, or values, of Blue, but at its core is that of calm. We will ask you all to sit here quietly and calm yourself. If you speak, fidget, or otherwise show that you are not calm, you will be tapped on the shoulder by one of the six of us and asked to leave. This is our gatekeeper trial. If you cannot sit quietly here through the test, you are not ready to enter the Stone House. You may attempt it as many times as you like. I see many familiar faces," she added with a smile.

"We will give each of you two minutes to settle in and then will begin."

Lara looked around the room. The young people were fidgeting, settling. A few looked like they were trying to center themselves. They reminded her of a large group of birds shaking their feathers and moving about as they settled down to the nest.

She found a seat on the bench near where she stood and settled herself. She wasn't worried. She, too, had been fidgety as a youth. When she was young, she had gotten into trouble all the time for not staying in one place. As she had matured, her restless nature had switched to other aspects of her life. She still changed from one pastime to another, but the immediate squirming was no longer an issue for her. She had learned to be at peace.

She had also learned quickly with her young ones that they will mirror your energy. If you want them to fall asleep, it was best to have them see you calming your breath and closing your eyes. She had spent many evenings sitting with her children, quietly breathing to help them drift to sleep. From those experiences, she knew that it also ended up calming her down.

And so, she closed her eyes and just breathed. She focused on the breaths going in and out. She let her thoughts take them where they may, but she did her best to relax into them rather than get caught up in them. Just as if she needed to fool the kids that she was calm, she could fool these leaders. She sat and thought about whether she was fooling them or if she really was showing them what they wanted. She thought about how it didn't really matter. What mattered was that she went into that Great Stone House. That was her next step.

Breath in, she could smell the salt of the ocean. Breath out, she relaxed her shoulders, which were weary from the trip. Breath in, she could also smell the fishiness of the sea, breath out. She was hungry. Breath in, she could hear others shuffling past and out of the room. Breath out, she was still here. She let her thoughts pass the time. She thought about the large town she had just passed through and wondered if they might have that coffee stuff Nessa had given her the other morning.

She let her mind wander to Fleck and found that he was also breathing deeply, but in actual sleep. The city must have been exhausting for the little guy who had ever only known nature.

She couldn't say how much time passed, but she was brought out of her quiet state with an announcement from the front. "We have finished."

She opened her eyes to find that the evening had come upon them, the skies outside dark. Only six of them remained. It had been quite a while, and Lara wasn't really surprised that it had been difficult for the youth to sit through it for so long. "Congratulations, you may follow us through these doors."

She let the younger kids line up ahead of her. Three of them were wearing light blue, so they must have lived in Azural, however there was a young boy in green, and the other young girl was wearing orange. Seeing the two other colors was a bit jarring within all the blue. They looked as out of place as Lara thought she might.

As Lara stood, she stretched out and took a few smaller slow steps, her ankles and knees stiff from being still for an extended time. After the fifth step, they were back to themselves, and she walked briskly to line up and walk out the door.

# The Great Stone House

The entryway to The Great Stone House was great indeed. Lara had never been in a building this large, let alone a room this size. The meeting house back home could fit in this single space alone three times over. The room was made of a light gray-blue stone from the large blocks on the floor to the high walls. The ceiling was painted a blue so pale it was almost white.

Along the walls were five pennant banners that Lara judged to be at least fifteen feet long and ten feet across. Each one featured with a tenet of Blue: Honesty; Responsibility; Peace; Order; and Intelligence. Lara marveled at the artistry of the words. They were embroidered, but each word stood a foot tall. She could just see the stitches from the distance she stood below as they caught the light while she moved across the room. Under the beautiful script was a symbol that represented each tenet. All were water, but each had a unique image. Lara was reminded how water was so changing, from storms to peaceful ponds.

It was very quiet in the hall and their footsteps echoed loudly. She heard one of the girls in blue ask about it and they were told that it was dinner time so most of the students were in the main dining hall to the left. However, their group was ushered through the doors to the right into a more private dining space. The room was much less imposing than the large entry hall, and Lara immediately felt her nerves relaxed.

She was amazed by the intricate patterns on the carpet. It was covered in waves that looked as though they were moving. They were so realistic. The seats at the table were covered in soft blue velvet in deep hues that looked like they were inviting you to sit in them.

Their guides stood by the door and Lara looked at them to see if they had any queues for them, but they just stood at attention. She took it upon herself to find a seat on the far side of the table so that she faced the entrance. She did not enjoy having her back to an open room. As she set her pack on the floor beneath her chair, the rest followed suit and found seats. Lara sighed as she sank into the comfortable chair; this was a far cry from Jada's wooden chairs back home. She smiled at the young man who sat in the chair next to her. He smiled timidly back. He was the young boy dressed in green, his pack set in his lap.

"Hello," Lara began, quietly nodding to him.

He reacted a bit nervously but nodded back with a faint smile.

She turned to the rest of the table saying "Hello," a bit louder to the table at large. They also nodded. No one responded past the nod, so she decided to keep quiet and wait along with them.

Not a moment later, a man about ten years older than Lara walked in. His hair was mostly grey and cut short. He was obviously the most high-ranking person they had seen so far. He had five bands on his arm. She was happy because she hoped he would have answers. She was tired of just following along with all the quiet.

He had a seat at the head of the table and took a moment to look each of them in the eye. When Lara looked at him, she noticed his moment of surprise and she realized she was getting used to it. She smiled to give him a sign that she totally understood his reaction. Yes, I know I am older than everyone else here. Now let's get on with things her smile said.

"My name is Detmer, and I will be your main liaison in your blue trials. Think of me as your advisor. Any questions will come to me. We have many people in The Stone House, all trying to achieve the same goal. Only a few ever actually meet this goal, but every day you spend here will raise you in our ranks. I see that we have three who are not from Blue, so I will give you a quick crash course in Azural ways.

Our tenets are simple. We value serenity and peace, honesty and trustworthiness, intelligence, order, and responsibility. Each of our trials is designed to prove that you are worthy of earning a ring in the tenets.

Those who have earned all five rings may try to stonegraft. There are currently twelve waterweavers. We have five stones in reserve. It is not simple to earn these stones. Many have tried. But even if you fail to earn the stone, you will earn a place in Azural."

Lara was shocked by this news. There were only twelve Blue stonegrafters? Why would five stones sit unused? She looked at Detmer, more aware of the five bands on his arm, as he continued talking. Was he one of the Waterweavers? Could he possibly hold the magic she needed to help her home?

"You will be served dinner and then escorted to your rooms. Each initiate is given a small room of their own." He reached into his pocket and started a slow walk around the table, placing a key to the right of each of the new students. "As long as you continue with forward progress, you are welcome to stay at The Stone House. We will all meet tomorrow morning in the Great Hall, and I will take you to your first classroom, which will be your home room. We will begin every day in that room, and you will stay as a group throughout the day, attending courses designed to prepare you in our tenets for the stonegrafting, or for a career and life in Azural."

Lara picked up the key placed beside her. It was a heavy metal, twisted round with the tines of the key looking like waves cresting. Lara was entranced by the workmanship. The top of the key had been tamped down to thin metal with a number drummed into the top. Detmer continued, "I will be meeting with each of you individually regularly to answer questions and discuss your journey through the trials. I look forward to learning more about each of you."

He stood and walked calmly out the door without even a goodbye.

"Wow! We lucked out getting Detmer," this came from the young woman in blue near the head of the table. Her large dark eyes matched her shining long black hair, which fell in tight braids that were held back from her face with a lovely thick blue ribbon. "He is the only mentor with five rings! Most of the five rings who haven't stonegrafted hold high places as senators."

The tall young man in blue shared, "I heard he never even attempted the stonegrafting."

The other girl in blue scoffed, her demeanor tight and controlled, and said, "There is no way. Everyone wants to at least try to stonegraft. He probably failed and just doesn't talk about it."

Dinner came in served by people dressed in blue, but she saw that none of them had any bands on their shoulders. Lara thanked the man who set the plate in front of her, and she received the usual look of surprise. But the look quickly gave way into a grin and a pat on the shoulder. "Good luck," the man whispered. Lara grinned back, warmed by the interaction.

The plate in front of her was unlike any she had ever experienced. There was salad, but the hue of the lettuce was a shade closer to blue than she was used to. Everything was strangely tinted. She began to take in her surroundings with a bit more clarity. Everything was blue, or at least a shade closer to it. Indeed, the only items she saw that weren't had entered with her and the other two from outside Azural. The magic of the blue stones looked to have seeped into every item around them.

She looked back at her plate and felt like she might as well be wearing James' reading glasses with blue glass in them. The world was so changed. Her first few bites were timid in the face of the color changes, but she found that everything tasted wonderful and as it should to her mind, if not her eyes. She was immediately aware of the difference water can make to a crisp lettuce. Her bite crunched, and she felt the moisture in the lettuce line under the roof of her mouth leaving it cooler than before. And she was ever so hungry, not just from her trip, but from years of light, malnourishing meals.

She ate for a few minutes in silence, contemplating what had happened. Even after the hurdle at the Parliamentary building with the Senators, she was here, in the Stone House, so much closer to her goals. Somewhere in this building there were color weavers and magic stones. Even though she now knew getting a stone or a waterweaver past the waterwall was going to be a big problem. One way or another, she was going to find a way to bring water back to her home.

After eating for only a few minutes, she found herself full. She was not accustomed to large meals. With a full stomach and a more hopeful outlook, her spirits lifted, and she looked at the others eating with her.

The young man to her left from Green sat with hunched shoulders, his scraggly, curly brown hair covering his eyes as though a shield from outside attention. He looked with concentrated intent on his food, so she moved on to the young woman across from her. She was wearing blue and had the look of someone who knew she was where she was meant to be. She sat rigidly in her seat as though she was in command. She noticed Lara's attention and nodded.

Lara took the opening. "I'm Lara. From the Wastes obviously," she motioned with her left hand to her drab clothing.

"I'm Stella. From Blue obviously," she mimicked Lara's motion to her clothes with exaggeration, giving Lara the impression she was poking fun at her. She felt her defenses go up and a stir from Fleck as he reacted to her emotions. "That's Brandon," she motioned to the young man to her right.

The young man looked up at the mention of his name. Friendly deep brown eyes met hers and Lara immediately felt the difference in his demeanor from Stella's. "Hey. I'm Brandon. Nice to meet you. Where did you travel from?"

"My home village is called Calambria. It's on the far side of Purple in the shadowlands."

"Was it a long journey? I haven't been anywhere but Azural, never been beyond the waterwall even. I had heard the shadowlands weren't real, but I guess maybe they are?" He spoke in a friendly conversational tone, and Lara got the impression that he was genuinely interested.

"Oh, they are real. I've been living there, so I should know. It took me a little over three days, but I was lucky and rode part of the way with some Brown traders."

This brought the young girl from Orange into the conversation. She spoke quickly, almost stumbling across the words. "I rode with some Brown traders too! They were very friendly. I can't believe they live in those little carts, though. Back in Laran, our homes have open windows, we don't even use glass. I felt so claustrophobic sitting in that cart. After the first hour or so, I asked to sit out on the front. My name's Delly." She raised her hand in a wave to them and Lara noticed small, healed scars all over her hands and arm.

"Hi Delly, nice to meet you. It must have been a long trip from Laran." Lara said.

"Oh, yes, but I have traveled the Wheel & Spokes before. My mom liked to go on adventures with us as kids. We got to visit most of the color realms. I've now been everywhere except Purple and Red. Mom thought Red was too dangerous for little kids, and," Delly raised a hand to her mouth like it was a secret even though it was shared with the whole table and said conspiratorially, "Purple was too remote and strange for her liking."

"When we walked by Purple on the way here it was beautiful, a purple mist over distant mountains, the peaks of the towers barely visible. I'd like to go there some day." Lara said. Surprised by the revelation herself as she shared, "I'd like to visit all the lands myself."

"Not me! I love Blue, I wouldn't want to be anywhere but here, but I'd love to hear about the other realms." This was the girl who had spoken up first at the head of the table, her dark braids falling sleekly over her right shoulder as she leaned forward to face the rest of the group. "My name is Iris, by the way."

Lara smiled. "Hi Iris, it is wonderful to know where you belong. So, we have, Stella," Lara nodded as she looked around the table, "Delly, Iris," she moved to her side of the table, "Brandon and..." she paused, looking at the young man in green next to her.

"I'm Van." He said quietly.

"And Van." Lara finished with a smile. "It's nice to meet all of you.

"If you don't mind me asking," this came from Brandon, "I've never heard of anyone your age coming to the Stone House..."

Stella jumped on this. "It is very strange. Are you sure you are even allowed to attempt the stone trials at your age?"

Lara bit back her first response, which would have been to tell this girl to mind her manners. But she didn't do such a good job of holding her emotions in check, and Fleck had no problem speaking up for her. He bounded up to the table and began chittering in his usual heroic way.

Everyone was startled and handled it in different ways. Stella jumped out of her chair and stood behind it, Delly had her hands up to her cheeks clearly enamored with Fleck, Iris just looked with surprise from Fleck to Stella to Lara and back again, Brandon had stood up and looked comically on guard with hands raised. But most interestingly, Van looked up, his hair out of his eyes for the first time, and he looked overjoyed. "It's a Pelanor! It's just a baby, but that's a Pelanor, isn't it?!" Fleck turned around to study Van, and Van looked from him to Lara expectantly.

Before Lara could answer that she had no idea. The others at the table were sharing their disagreement.

"No way, man," Brandon laughed. He was seating himself back down, showing no signs of embarrassment over his initial reaction to Fleck.

While Stella speaking loudly over him, trying to take command of the conversation, stated, "Pelanors are not real. They are just a fairy tale. We all know this." She gave Van a disapproving look.

Lara raised her shoulders as she tried to scoop Fleck up and calm him, but he didn't want to budge. He seemed very interested in what Van was saying. "I have no clue." She answered Van. "He found me on the walk here and hasn't left my side since." She took a calming breath.

Van looked at her in awe. His eyes were a topaz golden color, and they shone bright with his interest. "So, you connected with him?"

Lara immediately turned and gave Van all of her attention. "Yes! Yes, we connected. I didn't even know what was happening at first. I barely understand what is going on now. Can you explain what you know?"

"This is ridiculous. There is no way that little animal is a Pelanor!" Stella practically shouted. She was obviously upset, although Lara could not really understand why. Lara found herself getting a bit heated in response and caught herself. She knew better than to be drawn into teenager drama. She was reminded of her many interactions with her own daughters at this age, where emotions ran high and there often was no real problem to be found. Best to take a beat and let emotions cool.

Van was still not backing down. "Oh no, they are real. And this guy is," but as he looked at her, he faltered a bit under her aloof gaze, stumbling over his words, and finished a bit more quietly, "uh, he is one of them, I'm sure of it."

"It looks like it's just a squirrel to me," Stella commented, and Fleck spun around and gave a hilarious intake of breath, as if he was affronted by the thought.

Everyone but Stella laughed at it. "Well," Lara said to Van, "I think you and I should talk more about this later, but for now," she brandished her key, "I'm ready to find out what these rooms they offered look like, and mostly that bed." She stood and picked up her bag. Fleck leapt quickly from the table to her shoulder and then scrabbled beneath her cloak to his favorite spot just next to her pack strap. "It was great meeting you. I'll see you all in the Great Hall tomorrow morning," and she headed to the door to find someone to take her to her room.

She was more exhausted than she was comfortable sharing with these young kids. A good night's rest might let her contemplate all the new information swimming around in her head, from the mystery of Fleck to the problem of getting water out of Azural. Yes, a good night's sleep was sometimes the best answer to any problem.

As she left the room, she realized she had no idea where to go from here. The kind man who had delivered her dinner walked past with empty plates he had cleared from their table.

"Excuse me," Lara said.

"How can I help you?" He asked.

"I was hoping you could point the way to our rooms?"

"I can do better than that. I can walk you there. Give me one moment to drop these off and I will be back in a jiffy." He walked with crisp, fast steps across the hall and disappeared into a doorway.

Lara took this time to look more closely at the hanging banners. The Order banner showed water moving through channels similar to those in the downtown area of Azural. The Calm banner showed a still pond surrounded by simple stones. The responsibility banner showed a river carrying a single leaf down its path. The Honesty banner showed many small tributaries pulling together to create a larger river. The Intelligence banner showed a tall waterfall falling into churning water.

Lara tried to make sense of the images and was again floored by the many faces of the water. She heard the door rattle open, and the man walked up to her with a smile on his face. "This way," and he walked toward the arch to the right.

"Do you know your room number?" He asked. She fished the key Detmer had given her. It had the number 145 engraved on the end.

"Oh, that's good news, fewer stairs. The first floor has more noise coming from the windows, but I think it is worth it to avoid all the trudging up and down. My name's Jasper."

"Oh, sorry! Where are my manners? My name's Lara." He stopped short in front of her and turned.

"No need to apologize. We are all so curious. It must be a grand story you have, showing up at The Great Hall in your state." He caught himself, putting his hand over his mouth. "Oh, no! That sounded all wrong. Sorry. Now, I am the one who forgot their manners. It just felt so nice to be talking to an adult that didn't look at me like I wasn't present."

Lara realized this place was even more foreign to her than she initially thought. "I am so out of place. I get it completely. It's really nice to talk with you too. I've only been in Azural for a few hours, and I really needed someone to talk to me normally."

He smiled. "Down to earth. I can do that. I can't believe I am talking to someone from outside the waterwall. I have so many questions. My mother's side of the family lived in a town outside Azural, and we haven't spoken to any of them since the wall went up. Cousins, aunts and uncles. No idea what has happened to any of them."

"So, you are as trapped in here as I feel?" Lara asked.

"I wouldn't say we feel trapped. It is just the way of things." He said, he started back down the hall. She noticed the room numbers posted neatly along the wall. 101, 103, 105.

Lara tried to answer his question about his family outside of Azural. "How they are doing really depends where they live. The color realms all seem to be thriving, but all the land left beyond their borders is reaching dire straights. I came here because our home has almost completely run out of water. I hope your family is in a color realm."

As they passed room 139, she saw the hall was ending soon. "I do too. My sister left Azural in our twenties, and she hasn't come back. I like to imagine she found the other family members and is settled with them. She didn't come back, so that feels like a good sign." He stopped in front of her room. "Here you go. I am really glad to have you here. Good luck!"

"Thanks Jasper." Lara said and unlocked the door to her new room.

Inside she saw a single bed, with what looked like a very fluffy pillow. Lara forced herself to turn from the comfortable bed to look at the rest of the room. There was a small desk and a wardrobe. She went over and opened the wardrobe and sucked in a breath at her uniform. It was such a beautiful blue, and as she reached out to feel the fabric, she was amazed at how thick it was, or maybe her own clothing had thinned over the years of use.

The uniform included tight leggings, a jacket with shining dark blue buttons and a beautifully embroidered crest with a wave on the front left. The jacket reached mid-thigh, and there was a mid-calf length cloak with a large soft cowl that pinned to the lapel. There were also stockings and soft blue leather boots inside. She was amazed to see that the sizes were correct, and wondered if that was the magic, or more likely Jasper and his friends had years of experience sizing people up. She pictured them hustling to set up the rooms before the new students moved from the dinner hall to their bedrooms.

Then she noticed a narrow door to the side of the wardrobe. She opened it and was awestruck. It was a bathroom. She had her own private space, with a sink, toilet, tub, and above the tub was a pipe with levers. Lara moved over to test the lever and was immediately splashed in the face with a jet of water. She quickly turned the lever back. Shaking the water off her face she called Fleck, but he was already there, splashing in the puddle of water that sat in the tub.

After some time under the jet of water, Lara moved back into the small room and unpacked her belongings. She moved to the desk and pulled out her painting from James. Fleck came up and looked at it with her. "This is the family, Fleck. James painted it a few years back when even Anna still lived with us." She pointed at each child telling Fleck stories about them.

After all of her precious items from home were set on the desk, she looked around her new living quarters. She felt further from the family seeing the items so out of place in this new room. Feeling herself so out of place in this new Realm.

The room was sparse, but Lara was used to that. What she wasn't used to was how comfortable the bed was. As soon as she laid down and her head sank into that pillow, she barely acknowledged Fleck curling up beside her before they were both sound asleep.

# *Potential*

Axel stood at the front of the empty classroom for a moment. He had been sitting in behind every introductory class at The Great Stone House since it was built, some sixty years ago. Each morning was a slow process to get moving, the pains of age slowing him. He remembered with fondness the years when he used to only complain about a sore knee. Now the knee pain was a comfortable reminder of all the years he had survived since then. He was eighty-three. He held a wistful moment, remembering trekking through the central mountains with his friends. They had all been so young and energetic. He tried to picture what they might all look like now. How many were still even alive?

A flash of Carlie's soft dark brown curls bouncing high above her head as she had jumped off the rock outcropping into the pond below. The image froze with her high in the air, eyes sparkling with excitement as she looked at him. Suddenly, as he knew it always did, her cheeks dropped, and her eyes turned to disappointment. Disappointment in him and he was whisked away to the last time he had seen her, almost sixty years ago, walking down the path away from Azural. The pang of mistakes made, lost friendships and regret turned him away from this line of thinking, and he focused again on the room in front of him.

He always looked forward to this appointment in his schedule because he could see the potential future waterweavers. This past few years he was looking for something specific, and he had yet to find it. Generally, he entered the room early, his movement slow now that his body had aged. He took deliberate steps, not wanting anyone around to see the careful steps as a sign of his constant pain but rather believe it to be patience.

He took his seat in the back corner of the room. It was a comfortable overstuffed contraption that was wonderful to sit down on, but always difficult to climb back out of. Detmer had placed it here, wanting to give Axel comfort, so Axel didn't want to complain.

He relaxed back into the chair and watched the youth funnel into the room after Detmer. Each week, new students were added to the ranks of The House. Most didn't last past the first year, but he enjoyed seeing them at the very start. He liked telling Detmer who he thought had potential and being right long before anyone had a chance to really get to know the youth.

The emotions in the room were always rampant. Young people always felt things so strongly, the apprehension, the excitement. He was looking for those who walked in the door with clear Blue feelings, strong from the outset. That was the key to those who would make it through Blue's rings.

A young girl with a dark complexion and shining black hair held to the side in a tight braid pulled the door open and Axel looked up with interest. He could feel her honesty across the distance. She was sincere in her thoughts and emotions. There was potential there.

Following her in was a young girl with fire orange hair — he felt all sorts of emotions from her. She was happy to be here, excited, more at peace inside than she looked on the outside. She might reach the second ring, but she was no waterweaver.

Two young men followed behind. The first was definitely from Azural. He showed the outward peace and order of those raised in Blue, but Axel looked deeper. The young man was intelligent, another one to watch, but Axel didn't see a color weaver jumping to come out. The other was not from Blue, most likely Green or Yellow, Axel guessed. He had a reliable nature that Axel thought might find him a good place here.

Axel stopped short. The woman entering was not young. So, this was the infamous Lara. Her emotions hit him hard. She was carrying a burden of responsibility. She was here for others as much as herself. She was intelligent, and he could feel her putting in an effort to keep her inner peace and balance. She held the door for a young woman who gave her a smile, then looked away and smirked. The older woman smiled the knowing smile of a mother, not offended by the youth's attitude, but patient with it. Axel felt her emotions from across the room. Detmer was right. He would likely need to speak with this woman. He needed to get to know her better. She might be the one to help him. He sat through the short class, letting his plan come together.

When Lara had entered the room behind Brandon and Van, she had suddenly felt emotionally drained, like she wanted to cry and laugh at the same time. She had taken her seat quickly in the center of the room, breathing deeply to calm her nerves. She snapped to attention when she heard Detmer begin.

"This will be our home room each morning, so starting tomorrow, you can all just meet me here. Today, you will be introduced to the House, and tomorrow, you will begin your courses."

Lara knew that learning is a process of relations. With each tidbit of information you gain, you open up doors to even more knowledge. Lara had learned to value all of her experiences. She knew that even the littlest thing could be useful. Although her end goal was to save her home, she was really enjoying the prospect of learning along the way.

They were seated in individual wooden desks, and she was reminded of her childhood years with Jada and Dillon, before the small schoolhouse had closed down back home.

A dour-looking woman entered the room, replacing Detmer at the head of the class. Her white shoulder length hair was pulled back in a loose bun at the base of her neck, and Lara wondered how the woman kept the hair around her face so neat and tidy, whenever Lara tried to do this with her hair, flyaways tickled her ears and face, and she looked messy. This woman stood there erect and quiet, not a strand of hair out of place.

When everyone had settled and quieted, she began in a formal, practiced tone. "Congratulations, and welcome to The Stone House. My name is Shauna, and I am the headmistress here. All questions should be brought to your mentor, but I have final say in all things here at The Stone House."

She looked slowly around the room, meeting eyes with each student in turn. When she laid eyes on Lara, Lara felt the look penetrate her. She hadn't realized it until this moment, but Shauna was a colorweaver. She felt the power from the gaze and leaned into it. She focused on her calm breathing and concentrated on why she was here. She couldn't let this woman end her journey. She felt her responsibility to her town on her shoulders and focused herself. She felt like the look lasted longer for her but wasn't sure if it was her imagination. When they broke eye contact, her mind felt fatigued. And in the next instant, Shauna was focused on the next student.

With the connection broken, Lara immediately focused on the fact that there was a colorweaver right here. This woman had the magic and wherewithal to save her home. Could Lara just ask her to go? Could she skip the path of her going through the trials and just bring a colorweaver to Calambria? Could she convince them to leave the realm? Would they be allowed to leave?

Shauna's look around the room at the recruits was over so quickly that Lara wondered if she had looked at everyone the same way. Time was such a fickle thing, what you did in a moment could make it stretch or fly past.

She prattled on as if it were rote, "What Blue represents is the most important information you can get to start this path through the rings at the Stone House. Whether you achieve great heights and become a waterweaver or whether you earn not a single ring and go live a life in Azural proper, you will benefit from understanding what Blue is all about. These principles come from the emotional connection to the blue stone's magic. They have been studied, researched and felt by colorweavers starting with Axel to now."

Lara was off put by the tone of her voice. It sounded to Lara's ears like practiced chiding of the youth in the room, almost demeaning. "Each class will hold crucial information for you about the stone, the emotion, and the realm. Do not take your studies lightly."

After a short pause, her voice changed. She was off script; this was not part of her usual speech. "I realize that many of you are familiar with the rules of The Stone house, but for those who are complete outsiders," she gave Lara a sneering look, "I will begin with the basics. Everyone needs to understand and follow the rules here."

Shauna walked slowly back and forth in front of the class as she began to state the rules of the House. Her steps were rigid, and Lara began to get the feeling that Shauna did not make many missteps.

"There are five trials to pass before you earn the right to try for a blue stone. These trials are built to show that you hold the talents and true understanding of our five Blue Tenets: order, peace, intelligence, responsibility, and honesty. Each trial can be attempted when you have been invited by the Lead Tenet Waterweaver, who will be overseeing your class work. Once a trial has been passed, you earn a ring. You may have seen the circles around the shoulders of Azurans," she motioned to Detmer's shoulder, "these represent the trials passed.

Shauna did not have any rings on her shoulder. She wore a flowing blue blouse with soft, draped sleeves that fell loose about her fingertips. Lara watched as Shauna continued, "Those of us who have earned our stones no longer wear the rings," she began slowly folding the hem at her wrist. "Instead, we wear these, the mark of the blue stone." Around the elbow Lara saw small narrow edges of blue tattooed into Shauna's skin. With the next folding of the material, the blue lines became thicker and started to look like waves upon the sea. With the final fold, Shauna had her shoulder revealed and Lara saw her first stone. The size of an acorn, embedded right on the side of Shauna's shoulder at the top of her arm. It was a brighter blue than she could have imagined. The variegated top was filled with all shades of blue, making it look like light hitting a rippled water surface. Lara was entranced by the stone. She found herself getting lost in it but was startled out of it when Shauna suddenly dropped her sleeve back over it.

Lara wondered if they might get their first look at magic, but soon saw that Shauna was not interested in that. She instead prattled on in her serious voice about the expectations that students of the Stone House behave in a certain way and respect the rules of the House. "Once you have earned your ring, you will receive a new uniform to show your status, and you will no longer need to attend those courses so that you may spend more time on the tenets you need more effort with."

Shauna had reached one of her turns and gave a swift spin and began walking back in the other direction. "The House runs smoothly because we understand that Order is the best way to run efficiently. The schedule at the Stone House is very important. Do not take it lightly. The bell system is here to help us all successfully stick to the routine. There are the main bells and the lighter bells. The main bells will ring to notify you of wake up, breakfast, morning classes start and end, lunch, afternoon courses beginning and endings, free time and dinner, then room time and finally lights out. You will find as you become comfortable with the routine, you may not even need the bells' reminders. We will continue to work on your routines in our classes in Order starting tomorrow when you begin your regular courses."

As she spoke about the daily schedule, Lara was surprised to learn that it was very strict, that fell under the tenet "order" she imagined. Lara was a bit disappointed. She had thought that meeting a colorweaver would be something impressive and amazing. She had expected to be blown away by the personality and power of the one wielding this magic. She spent most of the rest of the class sorting through her realization that the magic weavers were just people.

On the way out of class, Delly fell in beside Lara as they walked toward the cafeteria for lunch. With it still weighing on her mind, Lara asked, "I was surprised that we didn't get a chance to see any magic. Have you ever seen a color weaver in action?"

"Oh yes. The orange color weavers are always throwing their magic around. I've seen them ever since I was a baby. We even have a daily fair and a few of them do performances for people. Super fun, but I get the feeling that Blue is more," Delly paused and said the last word, enunciating each syllable as if it was a new concept to her, "respectable."

"The world really has been divided."

Iris came up behind them and pushed excitedly between, slipping an arm into each of their elbows. "Did you two see Axel? I have never been that close to him!"

Lara was confused and saw the quizzical look mirrored on Delly's face. "What?" Delly exclaimed, "Do you mean that old man in the back of the room was The Axel?" She stopped and looked like she wanted to turn back, but Iris pulled them both along.

"Come on, he didn't want to talk to us, or he would have. You don't just go talking to one of the Finders." Delly gave a disappointed sigh. "Dang it, I can't believe I was that close and didn't even realize it was him."

"I didn't notice him either." Lara commented, a bit amazed.

"Well, no worries. Most people don't ever get to speak with him, and I am sure we will all see him again. Anyway, I am supposed to meet my parents for a few minutes this afternoon. Want to join me and get that tour of Azural? From the sounds of what Headmistress Shauna just shared, after today, our schedules are going to be so tight it might be our last chance for a while. Am I right that we all meet with Detmer later this afternoon?"

Lara felt a touch of unease at the thought of heading back to town, but her curiosity was also present. When she met Delly's twinkling eyes, she laughed, and they both gave an excited "Yes!"

# Visit to Town

Even as a child, when her town was full and prospering, she had never experienced crowds like what surrounded them on the streets of Azural. Everyone wore shades of blue and she felt much less conspicuous now that she was also in her blue school tunic. The cape folded over her shoulders and slid down her back, looking very official. She almost felt like one of the kids, but as she looked down at her braid, she couldn't help but notice her gray hairs glinting in the sunlight.

The crowds streamed along the paths, sweeping the girls along with them. Lara glanced up at the building's upper levels. They shined against the blue sky, reflecting it back just a shade darker with a glint of sunlight bouncing down occasionally. However, the dizzying effect mixed with the concern of bumping into someone brought her attention back to her own level.

Iris led the way and called back to them, "I know you aren't used to these crowds Lara, but it's not far now." Lara followed closely at Iris' heels, keeping up with her brisk pace as they followed the flow of pedestrians.

"We have great crowds in Laran, but they move around a bit more chaotically than this. Everyone is so nice about staying on their side of the path here." Delly giggled as she walked in almost a comically correct way, stepping with knees raised to exaggerate her careful steps.

Iris turned and, noticing they had fallen behind, spoke over her shoulder, "Look, we are just heading to that building across the canal up there." Iris motioned for them to follow her to the footbridge over the canal to their left.

Lara followed Iris's hand motion, and her chest tightened. It was a building she was already familiar with. "Oh, do your parents work at the Parliamentary building?"

"Yes, they are both senators and spend most of their days in meetings. I was glad to move into the Stone House finally. I barely ever saw them anymore and was super bored at home."

"Well, I've already met a few senators. Maybe I met one of them?" Lara thought back and realized it was unlikely since none of them had Iris's dark skin.

"Oh, you'd know if you met my mom. Everyone says we look just like each other. But there are around a hundred senators, although most of them aren't very active."

Delly called from behind, "Why were you meeting with Senators Lara?"

As Iris looked back with the same question in her eyes, Lara suddenly felt the closeness of the crowded streets increase. She didn't really know how to explain what happened to these young girls. Would they understand her story? Would they judge her as harshly as some of the senators had? That seemed unlikely since they had been so open to her even though she was older and had shown up in her blacks, but her insecurities made her heart pulse, and she felt a bit lightheaded.

She decided this definitely wasn't the time to get into it and said, "It's a bit of a long story. Let's talk about it when there is less going on?" Both of the girls nodded without any worry. Lara was glad to find that as they stepped onto the bridge, the crowd lessened and both girls stood on either side of her. She felt comforted by the easy way of these young ladies and was reminded of walking with Sally and Anna back home. It was nice to not be alone in this.

Their path bridged over the canal and Lara took a moment to stop and peer down into the water. Fleck peeked out too and was entranced by the light flickering over the tiny crests of waves that lapped against the edges of the canal caused by the boats moving through the water. The sounds of water lapping against the edge of the canal were mesmerizing to Lara. Oh, how she had missed it. They stood there, cheek to cheek for a few moments until Delly called, "You coming?" And she realized they had dropped behind.

As they came up to the building, Lara noticed how different circumstances changed her whole feeling: the building did not look nearly as imposing and scary as it had on her first visit. The same man stood at the entrance but looked much less formal as he raised a hand in greeting to Iris, "Good morning, Iris, I heard you had moved into the Stone House. You look so official in your uniform."

"Thanks Jake," Iris said, giving a little silly half curtsy. "These are a few of my new friends, Lara and Delly. They are both new to Azural and I thought I would bring them along, since I had to check in with the parents." She said 'the parents' in a tone that was heavy but lighthearted and it gave Lara the impression that she loved them but felt a bit burdened by the expectation.

"Ah yes, Ms. Lara was here the other day. Many of us have been wondering if we would get a chance to see you again," he smiled, but Lara could feel the questions from his greeting. "Glad you brought her by. Well, head on in, your parents are on the top floor right now for a meeting. The view is great from there too. Your friends will appreciate it." Jake waved as they walked into the doorway.

Again, it was a thin, sheer doorway of water and Lara had another chance to practice putting her hand to her forehead. Only a trickle was left dripping down her face as she came out on the other side, shaking her hand dry. Delly, on the other hand, had walked straight through, face upwards, and her wild curls had flattened against her ears. Her smile was infectious, and Lara grinned back.

"I just can't get enough of this water. We don't have much in Laran. The traders bring plenty in for drinking and washing, but we certainly don't have enough to just be walking under it like this."

Lara took in the entrance hall in a new light this time around, noticing more without her mind being preoccupied. The room was even larger than the Great Hall, and people bustled around busily. Large arches were dispersed evenly along both sides of the room. Lara felt a pang in her stomach as they passed the one she had been brought through just yesterday. What a difference a day had made.

"What is this room for?" Delly said. Pulling Lara's attention from her memories. She saw Delly in front of a huge arch at the far side of the room. Hastening to catch up to the two young women, she understood Delly's interest.

The room was a large amphitheater with seating in rows of steps toward a large stage with a dais. Everything in this room was gorgeous. The chairs were soft, light blue leather. The aisles leading to the seating and stage were carpeted in a smooth navy. The walls were hand painted, with flowers of all shapes and sizes and shades of blue, from hues of lilacs to teals. But the far wall behind the stage was the highlight.

The whole wall was a clear glass pane, aside from a small circle of blue glass in the center of it about two feet in diameter. The glass reached from floor to ceiling and side wall to side wall, and the view was stunning. Unlike the small canals that they rode on to get around town, here she saw an actual river, the source coming from the waterwall and reaching toward the sea. The raging water of the wall filled the river, but by the time it reached directly outside the windows, the water danced along calmly, sparkling as it reflected the blue sky above. Lara could see families beside it, young ones splashing on the banks.

She tried to remember what the river looked like on the other side of the waterwall and realized it wasn't there. Somehow, this wall was keeping all the water stuck here in Azural.

"This is the Senator Hall. They only use it rarely, when they have meetings, everyone has to attend. I can't remember the exact number, but I think there are like 100 senators? Most of them don't get very involved in everyday decisions, but big things come up they meet in these chambers." Iris answered.

A hundred was more people than Calambria current population.

"All the weavers are senators, too." Iris said.

"Really?" Delly said. "In Laran, our weavers don't get very involved in politics."

"Here, anyone who has earned four bands becomes a senator. The Great Stone House is a big piece of how our leaders are trained."

Lara held back a bit from the conversation. She wasn't sure how she felt about the politics of Azural. So far, she was not very convinced they took people into account. It all felt too large to see the needs of an individual. Back home, when there was an issue, people knew each other. They could discuss things when there was a problem or get a friend as a mediator. The sheer size of this realm was starting to intimidate her. The room suddenly felt imposing, and she turned her back on it and walked out to the main hall.

Iris and Delly were not far behind, Delly ready to see whatever was next. Their lighthearted energy healed Lara's, and she followed along, a bit less tense.

Iris grabbed Delly and Lara by the hand and pulled them through an arch off the back left of the main hall. The room was small and led to the exterior of the building.

There was a large glass tube on either side of the room, each one wide enough to fit Lara lying down on her side. Water rushed through them, one upward and the other downward. As Lara craned her neck to see all the way up, trying to get a handle on what they were, Iris walked right up to one and walked in.

"No way!" Delly exclaimed. "I've wanted to ride one of these since I saw them when we entered Azural."

Lara looked more closely at the platform that sat in the water tube and the water gushing around it. "Wait, so we ride this up to the top?" She wasn't too sure about this.

Iris saw her discomfort and quickly jumped out. "Oh, I totally forgot. This is new to you." She gestured to the top of the building. "These are great. The stairs would take so much time to climb, and we would be exhausted. All you have to do is jump in here onto the platform. We can all go together. And then the water moves just like in the canals. It will take us up to the top."

"I don't know. Maybe I should just wait here."

"No, you've got to come. We need to see the view!" Delly chimed in, "And I have heard they are super fun."

Iris came up and placed a hand on Lara's shoulder, breaking her long stare at the heights above. Once she had Lara's attention, she said, "I understand. All of this must be so overwhelming, but I promise that I will stay with you the whole time. It is worth it. Plus, I've done this a thousand times." She met eyes with Lara. Once Lara gave a sigh of agreement, Iris gave a quick nod of her head, her dark tight braids swinging forward and backward and the beads making a quick satisfying snapping sound.

"Ok, let's go, but I need for you hold my hand I think." Lara laughed.

They stepped onto the platform and with Lara in the center, a hand in both Delly and Iris', and Fleck wrapped tightly around her neck, the platform shot up through the tube. At first, all Lara could do was squeeze tightly to their hands and hold her breath. After a few moments, the momentum of going up decreased a bit, and she caught her breath and looked around. The platform had open sides, but a frame with a solid glass top. She could look up and see the gushing water as they pushed past it, but that made her feel the motion more acutely, so she looked forward.

And caught her breath again.

"Oh my," she whispered.

"This is even better than I thought," Delly squealed.

They rose above the town and although Lara couldn't see details through the stream of water, she could see the buildings and houses and canals. Then she saw them shrinking and tightened her grip again. This was so high up.

The platform stopped and Lara felt as if her body kept moving without her for a moment. Then she came back to herself, feeling her feet settle, then finally feeling firm on the platform again. She happily followed Iris off of the platform.

They stood at the top of one of the tallest buildings in Azural. The room was completely open, with a large round table in the center. Iris' parents were already walking towards them. They both were wearing the Five bands of Head Statesmen on their shoulders. Lara was amazed at how similar Iris looked to her mother, not only their dark complexion and almond-shaped ebony eyes, but their bearing was the same. They both had a way of standing tall even though they were slight of frame.

"Oh Iris," her mother exclaimed, clasping both of Iris's hand tightly in her own. "How is the Stone House? Which room did they put you in? These must be some new friends?" Lara noticed that her kind eyes also had a hint of mirth, like Iris', as she spoke.

"Mom, this is Lara and Delly. They are both from outside Azural, so I wanted to give them a tour. And these are my parents, Simon and Hyacinth Mere."

Hyacinth engaged with them while Simon stood back and let her take the lead. A kind smile came from the tall man, but Lara got the impression he was used to his wife doing most of the talking. Hyacinth jumped right in speaking quickly, but with the diction of someone who obviously gave public speeches often; her words crisp and firm, while still sounding pleasant and engaging.

"Nice to meet you," Lara began, but was quickly struck silent when Hyacinth locked elbows with her and started leading her to the North windows.

"You've got to see the view of our beautiful town from up here."

Lara looked out at the town below them. She had never been this high up, but she was getting used to seeing amazing things she had never seen before. Directly in front of her, she saw the cliff wall to the north. She could just see over it to the distant tops of a thick green forest in the land of Grevendale, the Green Realm. To her left was the Water Wall. The top of it was impressive. She could see the smooth water on the Azural side inside the wall and a hint of frothy white at the far edge as the water began to fall off the back side.

She craned her head to look to her right. There she saw the top of The Great Stone House and the gardens. From here they looked organized and neat, pathways and walls built to control the space in circular patterns around the house in the center. The harbor was calm, with the cliffs on either side, but beyond, the sea looked dark and turbulent. The darkness reminded Lara of home, and she shook her head to clear it.

"It is impressive. I have seen so many amazing things since I left home."

Hyacinth looked to the left and right, confirming they were alone, before continuing. "I actually heard about you yesterday. There is quite a stir about the town of the 'Wasteland woman trying to take our stone.' There are a lot of people who don't like seeing outsiders from Azural try to stonegraft blue. I'm glad Iris brought you by, because we feel very different. Too many around here are so stuck in the ways of Blue that they forget, or are too young to remember at all, that the world has not always been this way. My mother told me stories my whole life about how we used to all be one land, before the stones were found. I'd love more people to cross borders and connect us all again. But don't let me go on," Hyacinth paused and turned to face Lara. She spoke the next words slowly, "I'd like to hear from you. Why are you here?"

Lara hadn't really expected this conversation when she had left The Great Stone House with the two young ladies. She realized she had a wall up, holding all of her stress and obligation close to her and hidden from everyone. The question brought that wall down suddenly and not just to mind, but to heart. She felt tears prickle the edges of her eyes and she put her hand to her chest as if trying to hold the emotions back.

"Sorry," Lara barked out a small ironic laugh as she said it. She took three quick deep breaths to get a handle on herself. She pictured Sally's hollow cheeks and Anna's eyes sunken in her face. The difference was much more pronounced now that she could compare it to the flushed cheeks of Delly and the bright eyes of Iris. She pictured the whole town sitting in that meeting house again, everyone's tired eyes on her with hope.

She breathed in and squared her shoulders in order to hold the burden more firmly. "I'm here for water." She whispered. Then she looked out the window again at the town, so blue with its canals and decorative ponds, water everywhere, most of it wasted and unnecessary.

Taking a deep breath, she turned to Hyacinth and said in a clear voice. "I am here to bring water back to my home. The Hope River has run almost completely dry because the water magic has been hidden here behind that wall. I am here to try to save my family and my town. I am here to become a colorweaver and return the water magic back to our corner of the world."

She felt like a fake standing here in front of someone who was so obviously successful in Blue, who had gone to study at the Stone House, who had earned five rings and still had not stonegrafted successfully. If Hyacinth couldn't become a colorweaver, how could Lara aspire to go further than this accomplished woman? Her insecurity hurt.

Iris' mother seemed to see into her soul. "I didn't realize things were quite so dire out beyond the waterwall. There is nothing like need to make us do and become great things." Hyacinth looked at Lara one last moment and said, in such a matter-of-fact way that it helped dispelled Lara's doubt, "I can't wait to see you waterweave."

Lara felt a strange balance of lighter but heavy as she stepped out of the tube at the bottom of the building. The conversation with Hyacinth had definitely focused her resolve. She was here for a reason and was capable of getting this done. She just needed to focus on the tasks needed to get to her goal. She was a bit lost in thought, and following along behind the two younger women, so was not paying much attention to the surroundings.

Fleck's emotional spike brought her out of her thoughts and as her head snapped up, she saw the cause of his reaction. Stella was walking up to Iris and Delly.

Her head was held high with her nose in the air. She had already been talking, so Lara only caught the end of her sentence, "Are you sure you should have brought them here?"

Iris had the ability to look like she was not tipping her head up, even though she stood almost six inches shorter than Stella. Iris held her shoulders back to lift her line of sight. She remained calm, but Lara noticed that she had stiffened a bit. She obviously did not like the tone Stella was taking, or the connotations.

"I stopped by to see my parents. I saw your dad up there, too." Lara wondered which of the people milling about in that room full of important people might have been Stella's dad. "My mom was very happy to get a chance to meet Lara. They have a lot in common, both being amazing mothers." Iris turned and smiled at Lara. "I'm very glad to have her with us at The Stone House."

"Me too!" Delly piped in with a smile.

Stella gave a quick look at Lara but avoided eye contact and went back to her conversation with Iris.

"Listen, I just don't think it is good etiquette to bring outsiders to the Round Room. That is for VIPs only."

"Oh Stella," Iris laughed, "what makes you and me anymore VIP than these two?"

Stella spluttered at that. "Iris, you can't be serious." Then she did look Lara in the eye. Her tone was biting as she stated, "You shouldn't be here. I don't even understand why you were allowed into our classes."

Lara looked Stella back directly in the eye and responded quickly in kind, "Because I passed the admittance test, just as you did. I am not here to take anything away from you, but to try to return something to my home that has been taken away. There is more to the world than your shining blue city, and it would do a lot of good if you and the rest of the people in Azural started to see that."

She didn't wait to see what Stella's response might have been. She was not in the mood to deal with moody teenagers. Indeed, she had raised four of them and knew better than to engage. As she walked away, she reminded herself it was best not to respond in kind, but it was so easy to be baited by them. She remembered what a great relationship she had with her daughters now and took a deep breath. Stella was not her daughter, but she was at that tempestuous age. She needed to remember that when dealing with her in the future.

As the three walked silently back toward the canal, they all seemed to be in their own worlds. Delly was looking around at the people and buildings. Lara was still preoccupied with her interaction with Stella. And Iris seemed to be focused inward.

When they were back on the boat heading toward The Great Stone House, Lara commented on it. "Everything alright Iris?" she asked.

"I feel awful," Iris said, mumbling her words. This was such a drastic change in character that Delly whipped her head around from watching the passers-by.

"What about? Did something happen I didn't see?"

"I never should have said that about Lara and my mom being amazing mothers." Iris said. She turned to Lara and grabbed both her hands. "Don't get me wrong, you totally are. But I shouldn't have said it like that in front of Stella. Her mother has been gone since she was little, and it was a low blow to say that to her."

"What happened?" Delly asked.

"She left. We don't know much, but my mom once said that Azural wasn't a good home for her, and she decided to leave. She chose to leave

Stella. I am sure it still hurts her. I really shouldn't have done that." Iris' head dropped.

Lara looked at the top of her head and the tight braids that sat there for a moment. "I am glad to hear this. I should have known better than to get so angry about little things she said. I was feeling bad about my interaction with her just now, too." She looked at Delly, who just pinched her mouth to the side with a painful, quizzical look. "It's a good reminder that others have their own story, and we are often not aware of the pain others are in. Thank you."

Delly grabbed Iris's hands from Lara. Iris looked up at her as she did. "We can do better. You and I are fast friends right away. Maybe we can work on getting to know Stella, just a bit more slowly? Who knows? Maybe we can all be friends."

Iris smiled at her. "I have known Stella my whole life. We have never been friends."

"Well, maybe it just wasn't the right time," Lara said, as if she was on a new mission. Lara felt an emotional pushback from Fleck and thought she and the girls might have a shot, but he was less likely to come around.

# Mentor Meeting

Lara had her first one-on-one mentor meeting with Detmer later that afternoon. She knew this was an important visit, so asked Fleck to stay in the rooms. He was tired from the outing, so had no issue. He jumped to the bed and curled up, wrapping his long, floofy tail all the way around him like a nest. Lara loved that floofy tail. He was asleep before she even reached the door.

She was reminded of her kids when they were young and marveled at the ability of youth to put all of your energy into everything from playing outside to falling asleep. Indeed, when you run with all you have in play, it can sure tucker you out. It made her wonder why, as an adult, she slowed her pace so much and then struggled to fall asleep sometimes. What was she reserving her energy for? Worry?

Detmer's office was on the first floor, down a corridor with all the other mentors. The doors at the beginning of the hall had three and four intertwined blue circles on them, and as she progressed down the hall, she saw that Detmer's was all the way at the end, marking his highest seniority. It was the only door with five rings. She knocked and entered at his call to come in.

The room was very sparse, with only a desk and chair and a small sitting area with four chairs in a circle. It felt clean, open, and inviting. Detmer stood from behind his desk and invited her to sit in the chairs with him. He walked over with a steady, solid pace. He reminded her of Jada's brother Stewart, a bear of a man who had the heart of a lamb. "Do you play any instruments, sir?" she asked him.

He looked up, taken aback by the question. "I used to play the flute but haven't in years. Why do you ask?"

"You remind me of a friend back home. He plays the fiddle like nobody else."

"I never did like a string instrument - having to tune it before you can even play, mostly. Now, why don't you tell me a bit about yourself?"

"What do you want to know? I come from the Wastes, raised in a small village that every year gets darker and more broken; the resources harder to come by. Still, my husband and I managed to have a family and fill our days with learning and love. I have been married for 30 years now. Nothing too exciting, just a life lived day by day."

"So, you were a mother?"

"I am a mother," Lara corrected. "I raised four amazing children. They are the pride of my life. They are unique, smart, and dedicated to their passions."

Detmer looked at her appraisingly. "Why are you here Lara?"

She knew she would have to address this sooner or later. After all, everyone looked at her like a fish out of water. "I need to bring the blue magic back to Calambria, my home. We are running out of water."

"Why did they not send a youth? We have many young people from the other color realms enter the waterwall to try to join the Stone House."

"Our town met and discussed options. Everyone believes that I have the best chance to earn the stone. We don't have many left in our village, most youth have left over the years. My son actually just headed to the Yellow realm a short time ago."

"What about you? Do you believe you have a chance? What makes you the best fit for the blue stone?"

"The town only knows bits and pieces about the color realms, but we know the tenets of each. Peace, Intelligence, Honesty, Responsibility, and Order. To be honest with you, being a mother seems to have taught me all the Blue Tenets."

"Your classes will follow those Blue Tenets, and you will get a chance to really dig deeper, beyond just your life experience." He looked at her without much telling on his face. "You might be right about being a mother, but the stone looks much deeper than our actions, it looks straight into your soul." He sounded a bit harder than he had the moment before and Lara wondered again why he had all five rings but was not a color weaver.

Lara decided she wasn't quite comfortable asking him, so she brought up another question she had been aching to ask. "I am excited to see magic. Do you know when I might see a waterweaver in action?"

"Probably in the morning during your first class tomorrow - Responsibility with Fallon. He has a very different personality than Shauna." His voice gave away a hint of humor in the statement. "Any other questions?"

"I was hoping to use the library. Are there any rules about it?"

"Everyone at the Stone House is welcome to use the library. You can ask Penny, she's the librarian, for any help you need with the rules."

Lara braced herself to ask her final question. "I brought a kind of pet along. It joined me on the journey here. I don't want to be sneaking around, but he is important to me. What are the rules about animals?"

Detmer looked a bit confused by the question. "I don't think anyone has ever brought a pet here. You are unique in quite a few ways, I see. I will have to speak to the weavers about it at their council meeting next week. Until then, it is fine as long as there is no trouble." Lara felt a tension leaving her that she hadn't even realized she was carrying. Fleck meant a lot more to her than she could have imagined. He really was like her fifth child.

"Oh, thank you," Lara said.

As Lara walked toward the library to find books on the Pelanor, she fretted over what she had learned. The timeline was too slow. She had people at home desperate for water and here they expected her to go to classes and meetings and slowly jump through the rings of Blue to reach the right to try for the stone. She felt the burden and insecurities hit her. Could she do it, and even if she did, would it be too late?

# Books & Friends

The door to the library looked like all the others leaving the main hall. Nothing too exciting or amazing. Just a wooden door with the same twisted silver handle. Her hand felt comfortable as it wrapped around the metal, as if the waves in the silver were crafted just to hold the shape of her hand. As she pulled the door open, though, her breath caught.

Never had she seen so many books. She had expected to see more than they had back home, but the difference was beyond staggering. Her town had happily shared books with each other, knowledge was important to the people of her home, and books were valuable beyond any monetary worth. Looking at this room floored her. She walked to the center and slowly turned. Each wall was covered in shelves of books from the floor to the two-story tall ceiling.

As she turned, she saw each cardinal direction aside from the main entrance had alcoves built into the shelving. Doorways to tiny rooms filled with books. The largest of these had small worktables with students studying, while the other two had comfortable chairs with lights behind to sit and read. Lara continued to turn slowly around wanting to take in every detail.

Her second time around she noticed that the second floor of books had a balcony that was accessed by narrow staircases on either side of the doorway entrance. Bookshelves built into both sides of the wall, so the stairs were practically hidden from view when looking directly at the doorway. Ladders were placed along the taller sections braced to the wall with metal brackets that looked like the same waves as the door handle.

There were small signs throughout the space, with category titles. The largest being based on the tenets of Blue "Organization," "Calm," but then she saw other, smaller signs that piqued her interest, "Cooking," and "History."

Finally, she noticed a woman standing at a tall desk with books piled high. This must be the Librarian Detmer had mentioned.

"Excuse me," Lara started quietly.

The woman smiled up at Lara from behind big, round glasses. Her bright blue eyes, made larger by the lenses, held a sparkle of laughter from whatever she had been reading. "Oh, hello." She closed the book, keeping a finger in, to hold her place. "What can I help you with?"

Lara was immediately aware that this woman was close to her own age. She had never been so aware of her age, but it felt like it was constantly on her mind here. "Detmer recommended I come and ask you for help to find a few books?"

"Of course!" She took the book she had been holding and looked at the page number. Lara noticed the woman taking a mental image of the page to remember later- a quick focused stare and a slight nod of her head. Then she set the book down on one of the many high piles at the desk. "What kind of information are you looking for?"

Lara laughed. "So much. I have never seen so many books!"

"We have such a great collection here at The Stone House, but if you ever get the chance, you should visit the library in town. They don't have as many intellectual books, but they have tons more fun books."

She came around the desk and Lara saw that she was about six inches shorter than Lara. She wore a comfortable blue dress with no rings on the shoulder and Lara categorized her with the kind man who served dinner last night. She was hopeful of making a few friends.

"I realize this might be a stretch, but do you have anything on Pelanor?"

The woman's eyes lit up as she looked up at Lara's face. Lara noticed light freckles along her round cheeks and thought they were endearing. She had been around so many hard personalities here in blue so far that the soft person in front of her felt comforting beyond the smiles.

"I love those stories! Do you read a lot of fairy tales? My favorite might be the tale about the rabbits and the sorrowful farmer, such an endearing tale."

Lara smiled at the memory of her own mother telling her that tale and then her telling her own children, wrapped up cozy in a blanket or two, in front of a fire back home on a dark night. "That was my daughter Brie's favorite as a kid. She made me tell them all the time. I think she hoped someday to come across a field of bunnies herself, although I occasionally wondered if she hoped to turn them into a fluffy army rather than leave them to the meadow as the farmer does."

"How many kids do you have?"

"Four, but I guess I can't call them kids anymore. They are all grown and live lives on their own. Do you have any kids?" Lara asked as she followed the woman through the stacks to the fiction area.

"Oh no, but I do love them. My name is Penny, by the way." she smiled over her shoulder at Lara.

"Lara."

"I am so glad to meet you, Lara. It's rare to get time with new adults here at The Stone House. Ah, here we are…" she stopped in front of a shelf full of fairy tales. Lara saw all the classics, and many she was unfamiliar with.

Penny pulled three books off of the shelf and handed them to Lara. "The best one is probably this children's storybook with great illustrations by Wilson. If you want to get into the lore of the story, this one by Siegel is the best. I have read it a few times, and each time I learn more. It is pretty amazing how in depth he goes. It is almost as if they were real rather than imaginary." Her gaze drifted off as if she was picturing the pages and re-reading them.

"I think that is definitely the one for me, then." Lara marveled at the cover alone. Unlike many of the books in this room, the cover wasn't blue. Instead, it was white leather, with streaks of every color of the rainbow across the binding. Lara wanted to go back to her room to read this book, but she had learned a long time ago not to be rude. So, she continued with the conversation and asked about the other books she was interested in.

She found conversation with Penny easy. She was friendly and Lara valued knowledgeable people; they always had something to talk about. As they walked down the history stacks, Penny slowed and looked over her shoulder. "I would love to hear about your home. I have never been outside of Azural."

Lara was a bit taken aback. It hadn't occurred to her that she had information to share with this obviously intelligent woman. She was reminded that everyone has their own experiences, and that one can likely learn something from any person we might come across if we are open to asking and listening. Lara suddenly felt a bit more comfortable in her own skin here, rather than feeling so out of place, and felt that much closer to this new friend.

"I'm from a small town called Calambria in the Wastelands to the West of here, on the far side of Morchast." Lara said it a bit tentatively. She wasn't sure after the inquisition she received on her initial entry to Azural how Penny would react to the mention of the Wastes.

Penny stopped and turned toward her. "I had heard. You will find a few of us in Azural feel differently than the consensus."

Penny's bright blue eyes penetrated Lara's, the look lasting a moment longer than natural, and Lara felt a bit uneasy, suddenly tired of all the new interactions. "A bit of friendly advice?" Feeling as though Penny was waiting for permission, Lara nodded her head encouraging Penny to continue. "Wait until you know where the people you speak with stand before sharing about your home. Blue has a lot of great qualities, but there is a general bullheadedness that can keep people from seeing a new version of a familiar story. Unfortunately, your experience downtown might be the most common response." Lara was suddenly aware that Penny knew a lot more about her than she had realized.

Penny led her to one of the cozy nooks with two wide leather chairs of dark blue. "Why don't we sit, and you can tell me about yourself?"

Lara and Penny spent the next hour or so chatting away. They started with a light talk about families. It felt so good to tell stories of her children and James. It was interesting for her to hear about Penny's parents and how it was growing up in Azural. Penny had gone to a regimented school downtown where all the kids were taught lessons with lots of tests. Penny had always excelled in the intelligence area and did very well in her courses. Lara explained how the schoolhouse had been closed down when she was twelve because the teacher had to leave town, and since there were only a handful of children left, the families and mayor had decided to have them learn at home. Lara shared her days of reading and working alongside other community members learning from them.

Penny was engrossed with the explanation of how things slowly began to crumble in Calambria. As Lara shared the story of Brie leaving, she began to cry, and Penny cried along with her. Lara choked on a laugh. "This story is so common for those in my home, but it is no simpler to say goodbye to loved ones. Each time it hurts. But I know Brie is happier wherever she ended up. She felt the emptiness of the Wastes more than anyone there. Her heart ached to escape it."

Penny responded with a knowing nod. "I felt that way a few times when I was younger looking at the waterwall, but I know we have it better here than you did in those wastelands. Also, I have found my place here as an adult. Once you find your place in Blue, you get fairly comfortable." Penny smiled at Lara with a hint of sadness in her eyes. "Do you think you might find your place here?"

"Oh no, I can't stay. I am here for one reason alone, to help my home. I need to find a way to bring water back to Calambria." The sadness in Penny's eyes deepened and Lara felt her pulling away a bit. Although it hurt, it reminded her again of her purpose.

A loud deep bell chimed, and Lara looked at Penny, who seemed barely to notice it. "What was that?"

"The dinner bell. You won't be in trouble since it is still your first day, but you should already be in the dining hall. Let's get your books officially checked out to you so you can get some dinner." Penny led her to the main desk and disappeared behind it.

"I really appreciate the chat. It was nice to just have a moment with a friend, rather than all of this chaos my new life has become. Everything is so different and everyone is so different." Lara thought she noticed another shift in Penny and wondered if she shouldn't have said 'friend' so quickly. Maybe she had misunderstood this librarian's kindness? No, it had been a lovely chat. No need to worry about things she has made up in her head. *There is enough on your plate that is very real Lara.*

# Guardian Dragon

Lara entered her room, barely managing the door with all the books she carried. She had never seen a library like the one here, and she couldn't help herself grabbing books until she couldn't carry anymore.

Fleck was sitting up, perched on the windowsill, and she felt his need immediately. She opened the window, and he scuttled off into the gardens, his relief and excitement at the new space to explore filled her. He was happy to be in a natural environment that actually had nature. The Wastes had been so dismal; she agreed with him that at least the nature was an improvement. She still wasn't so sure about the attitude of many of these Azurans, but she had met a few really good people today.

As Fleck explored outside, she started sorting her books. She created three piles on the writing desk. The first was the books she found on the Pelanor, also known as the White Dragon and Guardian Dragons, according to Penny, who had behaved as if they were make-believe. The second was a pile on Azural, including a book on the history of The Stone House and a few about Axel, the leader of Blue, and the blue power. The third pile was a motley mix of titles ranging from the flora of Azural to a book about cooking stews.

She started with the Pelanor books. The large white tome by Siegel was at the top of her list. The leather cover felt luxurious and strong, like it could last ages, and she wondered for a moment how old it was already. Placing it in the center of the desk she opened the first page of the heavy book, and she was thrilled to see it was filled with images. Her excitement brought Fleck speeding back to see what she was seeing.

"Look Fleck, it's you." The page showed a drawing that was the spitting image of Fleck, with the perky little ears with fur sticking up, to the long flowing tail, to the tiny claws. The section was labeled Infant Pelanor. Lara was amazed.

To Lara, this confirmed what Van had said. She looked in shock at Fleck and his eyes shone back at hers, "You are a Guardian Dragon."

They both looked back to the book, Fleck perched on the pile of history books. She turned the pages, not worrying about the words for now, and found images of the Pelanor in later stages. The youth Pelanor was larger, similar to a fox, but with a much longer tail and the eyes showed so much intelligence. The final images were of full-grown adults. These were majestic looking. The faces had a wisdom that came through, more fur on the face than the younger ones, a few had long whiskers and beards. One picture showed it floating in a blue sky. There were no wings and Lara wondered if this was even possible. She felt Fleck become engrossed with the image. His tail flicked back and forth, tickling her arm as it brushed in her direction.

He looked up at her and then back at the image of the grown dragon. He set his paw on the image, and she felt his confusion and apprehension. She took a moment, just staring into Fleck's eyes. He looked too adorable and tiny to become such a wondrously monumental creature.

"We have some mysteries to solve, Fleck, but time will teach us a lot, too. Growing up is an adventure, and yours will be extra exciting since you don't have mentors, but I will be here for you."

Lara felt exhaustion hit her. She sat on the bed and slumped a bit. She was still very worried about the process of earning a stone. This was going to take forever. With the rate that her home was disintegrating, would it even still be there after the months or even years she might take here jumping through Azural's hoops?

She pictured Anna and Sally walking to the river daily since the well was now dry. In her imagination, she envisioned them happy as usual, and then when they arrived, the river was dry. Their smiles disappeared, and the jugs remained dry. She immediately let the fears take over her emotions. She was so worried about her loved ones. She felt the pull into the deep darkness, but suddenly there was a tug at her thoughts. She felt

Fleck reach out with a soft push to her mind. He sent a vibe of concern, and she looked up to see him propped up with his head tilted to the side. Aww. She was instantly snapped out of her doldrums by his adorable expression.

"We have to speed things up. I need to find a weaver and get them to help us. Surely someone will understand how serious this is. Tomorrow, I will see if I can talk to Fallon or Shauna, or one of the other color weavers. Someone here must see the dire situation of the Wastes. Someone must want to come and help our home."

She sighed a bit of relief at the forming of a plan that made more sense to her than earning a blue stone herself.

Picking up one of the lighter dragon books, Lara sat on the bed. "Let's start with reading through this. It is written as fiction, but I bet we can get some morsels of truth about you and your history from it. Remember these are likely written by people who have never met anyone like you, but then again, I have to wonder how they got the picture of you so correct? There will still be some things we need to take with a grain of salt." Lara tried to send her meaning in emotion. Trust in himself, and he reflected it back to her, sharing that she should trust that she could achieve her goals, too.

# More Answers

Before classes the following morning, Lara joined Fleck for his romp in the gardens. The paths led in circular rings around the Stone House, and she found many small walled off areas, each with their own atmosphere, but all had elements of water.

The first she walked by had a high wall and as she peeked in the opening, she saw a single stone set next to a calm, ripple-less pond. Another she saw had enough benches to seat twenty surrounding a low glass aquarium where people could chat across the top and watch the small fish in a multitude of blue hues dart around.

She finally decided to sit for a while when she found a low wall with a large opening. The space was a long oval with a brook running down the center. On the far side of the garden was a short waterfall, the source of the brook, and she was reminded of her home and the bubbling, rushing sound she used to enjoy when the resources had been more abundant.

The bench she sat on faced the opening and the main path, so when she saw Van walk past, head down and lost in his own world, she called out a hello.

He stumbled a step and looked up, confused.

"Over here, Van." Lara called again

As he turned to see who called him, she saw his face brighten. His features transformed from the mousy look to an engaged smile. Lara thought for a moment about how handsome this young man was and remembered her own son. Yellow had better be treating Peter right.

"Good morning, Lara. Is Fleck with you?" He looked around hopefully.

"Of course," and Lara gestured to the waterfall where Fleck was darting back and forth through the falling water.

"Ahhh!" Van sat carefully on the bench next to her. They both sat watching him for a few minutes. Fleck spent some time deep under water, then perched up on a rock. In one moment, he was skinny with his fur plastered to his body, then with a fierce shake, his fur clustered in clumps around him, and he looked twice as big. Lara laughed and looked at Van.

But Van wasn't laughing. He looked in awe. "I just can't believe I know an actual dragon."

"He is amazing. I am excited to learn more about him, but my home and family are my priority right now. Maybe once I return with water, we could travel to meet another Pelanor."

"They are also called Wish Dragons, you know," Van said.

This sparked a memory, and Lara immediately pictured her little town square with the fountain. The stone dragon statue curled above her. "Wait, what? The Pelanor and Wish Dragons are the same?"

Van smiled at her. "One of my favorite fairy tales is about this. Want me to tell it?"

Lara nodded enthusiastically, and Fleck came running over to sit on her lap. She was expecting him to be sopping wet from his frolic in the water, which Lara wouldn't have minded, but somehow, he was completely dry when he settled in to listen along. "Of course," she said.

Van almost transformed as he stood up and began the tale. It seemed to Lara that he had experience with this. It was practically a performance.

# Kira's Three Questions

Once upon a time, there was a princess who lived in the tall towers of Morchast. She was lonely living in such a remote location and longed for friends. Her three brothers were all older than her and never included her in their play.

She would approach the oldest as he studied the stars. "Can I look through the looking glass, too?" She would ask.

"Go away, Kira. I'm busy."

She would join her middle brother in the dining hall. "Can I help you cut vegetables?" She would ask.

"Go away, Kira. You'll just be in my way."

She would follow her youngest brother as he entered the library. "Can you read to me?" She would ask.

"Go away, Kira. I need to concentrate."

And so, she would wander the halls alone.

One evening, after being turned away by all of them again, she wandered all the way to the tallest parapet and climbed up to the patio garden there. Laying on the cool stones, she stared up at the night sky.

She knew she was young, but she could do amazing things too, and how would she ever be able to show them if they never let her join in? She began to cry, feeling lonelier than a girl in a large family should.

Suddenly she noticed the stars above her blinking out, startled she looked closer and saw that something was flying above her. It was definitely a creature of some kind. She saw the sleek long shape with a long tail. She squinted her eyes to try to see into the dark night sky. She didn't have to look hard because the creature was coming closer. It was large, but Kira wasn't scared. She had heard about The Wish Dragons before. She had never believed they were real, but this proved they were.

It alighted right beside her on the parapet, and she saw it clearly in the light from the torch she had brought with her. She was still small for twelve, but she didn't even come up to the chest of the magnificent creature. It had the largest round eyes that reflected everything around, like the mirrors in the great hall. Its ears were poised on top of its head and folded over. It had sleeked white fur that got fluffy at its paws, bringing attention to the giant sharp claws there. It was studying Kira the same way she was studying it, and after a moment it smiled a large grin. Kira saw teeth that could tear a tree down, but the smile was friendly.

"Hello friend," the creature said. His voice was strong and reverberated through her mind. She had not so much heard the voice, as felt it.

"Hi," she said timidly. She said it out loud, because she had no clue how to communicate any other way.

"I heard you crying and wanted to see if you were okay. Would you like to tell me about it?"

Kira had never been given an opening like that. She went right into sharing all her emotional turmoil. How she was so lonely, even though she wasn't quite alone.

Her new friend listened intently. He understood her emotions and was patient with her telling the story. When she had talked all she could, she took a deep breath and found that she felt much better.

The Pelanor came to visit Kira regularly on the parapet in the lonely towers of Morchast. She began to live her days in a happier way. She kept busy, so she had things to share with her friend Salzan. Each time they met, Kira talked for hours. Salzan was not very chatty himself and Kira began trying to find out more about him.

He always turned the conversation back to her, and she realized after a few months that she only knew a handful of facts about him.

Years passed and Kira decided that it was time to get the answers she had been wondering about.

When he arrived, she gave him an appraising look. "What are you up to?" He asked, "You have a glint in your eye."

She laughed and said, "It is your turn to talk. You have listened to me enough. I want to get to know you."

He laughed. "I love listening to you. It's why I travel the distance to see you. You may ask three questions. One for each visit. I will tell you a complete answer, but nothing more."

On the first night, Kira asked her first question. "Salzan, where do you live?"

"On a mountain top to the North of here, it takes me a few hours to fly there, but it would take you weeks to walk, even with the help of those horses you humans have. It is a beautiful place, a paradise. We have rolling fields full of colorful flowers. We have caves to protect us from the elements. We have waterfalls and freshwater springs to drink and cool off in. I can look down on the land in each direction and see the whole of our beautiful continent."

On the second night, Kira asked her second question. "My friend Salzan, do you have a family?"

"All Pelanor is my family. We are all born of eggs and when we hatch, the whole of our kind work together to raise the young ones. We bind to each other and learn though emotion at first, and then as we grow, we learn to communicate in more detail. We also have ancestral memories that bring us knowledge from the past. Words, as you know them, are often just the skimming off the top of the information we convey to each other.

My family consists of twenty-three of us. A new hatchling arrives about once every five years, so we should be adding a new one next year. Our Oldest sits on the rainbow throne to guard our treasure. Soon, that will be my job, for I have only two older than myself."

On the third night, Kira asked her third question. "Salzan, will you take me with you?"

Salzan considered this a long while before responding. He had spent many evenings over the years getting to know this young woman. She was fiery, energetic, creative, down-to-earth, honest, wise, and kind. He knew her brothers shared nothing with her, and she was still lonely in her towers, even after all these years. He thought of the world he knew and her place in it here, and he thought of the world he knew and what she could be if she was with him.

"Yes." He replied.

As Van finished, he slowly bowed, and Lara stood and clapped for him. "That was wonderful Van. You are a true performer. I never would have guessed."

"I used to tell stories to my grandmother back home. Her vision went bad, so she couldn't read anymore. My grandfather taught me stories, and we worked together to share them with her. It had been one of my favorite pastimes." His eyes teared up and Lara immediately knew that Van had lost her.

"Oh Van, I am so sorry. Some of the most painful memories are of loved ones we have lost. I just know that she must have appreciated all of those stories. I have never experienced such a telling."

Van sat quietly next to her. Fleck moved over and set a clawed paw on his knee. "Losing her was what pushed me to decide to come here to Azural. Granny Tanny was always telling me that I would find my place. She used to tell me 'Vanny, my boy, the world wasn't always like this. Not everyone fits in this green box so well as your mama.' I would never have had the courage to leave if she hadn't supported me in it."

"Sounds like your granny was a wise woman. I'd like to see more people break these color boxes the world has fallen into."

"I've never seen the Wastes. My trip from Grevendale to here was so direct. There is barely any wasteland between our two realms. That high cliff wall to our north is a barrier enough."

"When we were in town yesterday, I saw the treetops of Grevendale. I can't put into words how lovely seeing color is. The Wastes have lost everything. We have no water, no sunlight, no blue skies. Our trees are just skeletons of what they used to be. We have learned to make do with less, but having no water will be the death knell to our community. I have got to bring water back."

"Do you have a plan?"

"I am thinking I should approach one of the weavers about coming with me?" She raised her voice at the end in question since she was very insecure in this plan.

"I don't know. I have never heard of a Weaver leaving their own realm. At least that's the way it is in Green and Blue."

"I have to try. Everyone back home is counting on me." Lara lapsed into silence, watching Fleck play until she felt Van sit up a bit straighter next to her. She looked up and saw Iris and Delly walking down the path towards them.

# Kids in the Garden

"Hi there!" She called out.

The girls waved and headed into the walled area. The bench they sat on was the only one and Delly just plunked herself down between them a hand patting stoutly on each of their knees, Van jumped up awkwardly "Um, you can sit here, or, I mean, um there, if you'd like." He didn't make eye contact, but Iris smiled and thanked him but continued to stand next to him.

"Oh, I'm fine standing. Oh, look at Fleck! He is so adorable." Fleck had been pouncing on the tiny minnows in the pond but stood back on his hind legs to look at Iris when she spoke.

"I can't wait to learn more about him. This Pelanor thing is an exciting mystery." Lara said.

"Oh, it's a common topic around Laran." Delly said.

"Van was just sharing a fairy tale about them with us. I had no idea the Wish Dragons were real." Lara shook her head, trying to make sense of her adorable little friend being one and the same as the legends of the Wish Dragons she had shared her dreams with as a child.

Van stumbled over his first few words, "We...we actually know a lot now. In Grevendale we have been st—, um, studying them a lot recently." His gaze darted under his bangs at Delly and Iris.

"Really? What happened recently to get the studies going?" Lara asked, and as he looked up at her, she noticed him relax a bit.

"Well, we only know of three in existence. Well, four now, I guess. The Grevendale scholars started studying them extensively when the first one was seen in the South Forest about ten years ago."

"So, they only have ten years of research? How can they know so much about them already?" Iris asked.

Van didn't look directly at her, but rather at Fleck splashing in the pond. "Most of the information is from the copies we had of Siegel's journals. Siegel was a scholar from before the stones had been found, you know, the time long before the world broke."

"That's who wrote the book I got from the library yesterday! I haven't had a chance to look at it much yet. Have you heard anything about this connection we have?" Lara asked.

"Oh, Lara! I would love to see that book. Siegel said the psychic link you two have was used originally with their dragon families. Siegel postulated that they had to connect with humans since they no longer have family. The first we know of them connecting with humans happened in Orange with a person named..." He looked to Delly for help.

"Soren. No one has seen him in years, but his Pelanor Exu still flies over the capital sometimes. They can fly. Did you know that?"

Lara shook her head, as she was reminded of the picture in the book. It felt preposterous. Fleck couldn't fly.

"Right," Van continued animatedly, he was becoming more engaged by the moment. "They start flying once they reach puberty. We have two younger Pelanors in Green. Not so young as this guy, but they looked similar to him. My first glimpse of a Pelanor when I was eight. She was beautiful, and came up to about my knees, like maybe a baby goat?" Lara let out a little snort, picturing her husband's goat Sheila next to a grown-up Fleck hanging out in the yard. "A full sized Pelanor is supposed to be larger than a horse, and even prettier."

Fleck seemed to appreciate the positive things being said and she could feel his happiness in her own chest. He had jumped back on the bench to stand facing Van and Iris, looking at Van expectantly. "Go on," Lara said. "What do you know about this link we have?"

Van looked up toward the sky and set his mouth to the side, eyebrows furrowed. "I just don't remember much, the connection has something to do with emotions. I know the two we have at Green; they're named Harmony and Clarity after tenets of Green. Anyway, they are connected to two of our color weavers and I had heard that the link helped the connected person be more in tune with their emotions."

Iris popped in. "Wait, I think you're talking about what we call the Guardian Dragons! We only have stories about them, but we have heard of the emotional connection. It is said that as babies, they connected with their mothers and then slowly their connection grew, and all the dragons were connected. There are children's story books about them. But I thought they were made up by parents trying to get their kids to sleep."

Lara looked with wonder at Fleck and was suddenly worried about her tiny friend. How much had his ancestors lost, and if any of what her new friends here were telling her was true, Fleck could not just be her little pet? He had come from the stuff of stories. This was big. "Guardian Dragon, Wish Dragon, Pelanor. My goodness, little friend, you have some big shoes to fill."

Delly's face lit up. "Hey, Lara, you were going to tell us why you had already been to the Parliamentary Building."

"I guess I can fill you in." Fleck looked from Lara to the three youth and realizing that the topic had changed from him jumped down and dashed into the low bushes along the edge of the garden.

"Where's he going?" Delly asked.

"He's just tired of the conversation now that it isn't about him." Lara said lightheartedly. Suddenly, they all heard a tiny, satisfied growl from the low bushes, and they all went over to see what Fleck was up to. Through the upper branches they saw him, four paws in the air, he was scratching his back happily in the dirt and fallen leaves. With a swish to one side a tiny bark came out and all four let out peals of laughter.

"Awe, he's so happy." Iris cooed. "What a sweet baby."

Fleck's upside-down face, smiled at them and then he suddenly scrabbled to standing, dirt all over his back. He flashed past them to dive into the water and was back to his games from earlier. The four of them settled down again, and Lara shared her experience from when she entered the waterwall until she was escorted to the gatekeeping trial.

"Wow." Van said. "I have already noticed a lot of people here are unaware of anything outside of Blue. I get sideways glances a lot."

"It seems ridiculous to me," Delly said. "In Laran, we have visitors all the time. We hear stories of other realms, of the traders, of the Wastes. Not only ridiculous but super closed-minded believing that it just isn't real."

"I don't think they realize how much has changed since that waterwall went up," Lara said. "I am not sure I can convince them how serious it is when so many people refuse to believe anything I say about it. I worry I won't be able to convince people when they aren't even willing to listen."

Iris sighed. "My parents have been talking about the rumors for a few years. I think there are people here who are starting to believe it?"

"I had really just hoped to find a weaver who would be willing to come help me fix our water problem back home. Now, I am not sure that is an option. I am excited to meet more of the weavers today and tomorrow in classes, maybe one of them thinks more like your mom."

Iris suddenly raised both her hands to her cheeks. "Oh no! We were actually on our way to meet Stella in the Great Hall. We are totally going to be late. We better be on our way."

Delly rolled her eyes, then speaking in an obviously loud whisper. "Ugh, I can't believe I got roped into this with her. That Stella is a pain."

Iris and Lara, both gave her a disapproving look. "Don't forget what we talked about in the boat yesterday. We need to try to give her a chance, I think." Lara said.

"Yes, and I promised my mother I would be nice to her. She doesn't have a lot of friends, and we have known each other our whole lives," Iris explained.

"Well, I think her attitude explains why she doesn't have many friends. I mean, look how quickly we all became friends." Delly put her arm around Lara's shoulder and squeezed.

"Oh Delly, you, Van and I have a lot in common being outsiders. The question really is, why is Iris so nice to us?" Lara smiled at Iris.

"That is a ridiculous question. I love learning from other people, and the more different we are, the more likely we can learn things! But we really do need to get going."

"Fine," Delly sighed, "but she won't be happy to see me with you."

"That's fine. I am thrilled to spend my day with you." Iris responded in a cool tone that covered just a bit of the mischievous smile she had on her face. She seemed to enjoy the idea of doing the right thing while also still annoying Stella a bit. "See you two in class in a bit."

As the girls left, Lara noticed Van staring extra long at their backs. He looked sad.

"Whatever is wrong, Van?"

"Nothing," he replied, kicking a loose stone into the brook.

"Van?" Lara's tone was soft and careful. She was beginning to see Van as a ground squirrel, super anxious when out in the open and quick to retreat to his hiding place behind his curtain of hair.

He looked up at her and she saw a pained look on his face. "I just don't know how to interact with them. I am so awkward." He sat back down on the bench, but this time there was nothing careful about it and he shook the whole thing.

"Both of the girls like you, and they are super nice. You don't need to be nervous around them. Just talk to them like you do with me."

"It's not the same..." he paused, "I just..." he paused again. Lara gave him the time he needed. "It's just that Iris is soooo pretty and smart. And she obviously belongs here in Azural. I don't think that I could ever fit in anywhere the way she does here. And she is so confident in the way she speaks and..., and don't she and Brandon just look so perfect for each other? He knows how to speak to her, and he's at home in Azural, too."

As he spoke, he opened up so quickly that Lara was almost surprised by it. She was careful not to startle him and chose her next words carefully. "I agree with you that Iris is amazing. She is confident, smart and lovely, but I think you are missing the mark on yourself. I am very impressed with you. You are passionate about your knowledge of Pelanors, and I believe that carries on to other knowledge too. You are kind and careful, and those characteristics are difficult to find. Indeed, I think they might be some of the most important."

He looked up at her, and even though his shoulders were slouched, he held his head a little higher. "But I don't even know how to talk to her. Or what to talk about. Every time I try, I stumble and bumble my words.

You saw me just now. It's terrible." His head fell back down, and he studied his fingernails.

"I think you just need a plan. You need something to bridge the gap. Can you think of something you have in common? When you share your knowledge about Pelanor's with me, you really open up. Maybe you can find a topic that you feel confident about? She seems really interested in learning about different realms. Maybe you could have a conversation about Grevendale?"

"Maybe…" His voice trailed off, but he looked more comfortable than before, and behind his eyes Lara could see he was already thinking. Young people really had as much to learn about themselves as they did about the world around them.

# Responsibility Class

The classroom on Responsibility was the largest Lara had seen at The Stone House. The room was set with rows of long backless benches facing a tiny stage at the bottom center. Lara had wanted to sit up close so that she could hear better. She also had hoped to get a chance to speak with Fallon after class. But when she entered, the room was already mostly full.

She estimated about two hundred students lined the benches. So, she was left to find a seat wherever she could. It was strange how the hubbub of chitchat from the youth filled the room, making it quickly feel like she was in a tighter, smaller space. Lara was more aware than ever of how many people were around her. The gardens and small classes hid many of these people away. It wasn't just downtown Azural that had crowds. She chose a seat on the outer left edge to avoid the feelings of claustrophobia from kicking in further.

Once seated, she looked around the room for the familiar faces of the students she knew. Delly, Iris and Stella sat near the front on the far-right side of the room. Delly squirming in her seat as Stella and Iris spoke. She saw Brandon sitting with a group of young men he obviously knew from before the Stone House. Finally, she found Van seated in the back of the room, his nose in a book he had brought along.

Fallon entered through a small door at the bottom of the room, close to the stage. He wore bright sky-blue robes and had loose blue hair falling over his face. He was older than the students in this room, but not nearly as old as Lara. As he moved across the stage, he practically danced. He was filled with calm but graceful energy that reminded her of the little blue butterflies she used to try to catch as a child.

As he reached the center of the stage, she noticed his magic, even from this distance. A blue swirl of magical light was beginning to pool around his right arm. He reached up and a sudden wall of water cut the room in half.

Lara was floored. Water that had been nowhere in sight was suddenly shimmering across the length of the whole auditorium. Magic. It hit her suddenly that this really was the answer. This water magic was going to save her home.

Fallon stepped through the water to the side, away from her, and she couldn't hear what he was saying. There was a rumble of laughter from the students on the other side of the room and all the students with her on the outside of the water began whispering to each other.

"Can you hear what he said?" Someone said loudly from the far back.

"No, he's cut us completely off," a young girl sitting in the front row next to the water called back.

They didn't have to wait long before Fallon swept through the water and stood on her side.

"Apologies," he said. "I have a theory I want to test out, and since you are a captive audience, you all are joining as participants." He reached his hand up again and the water wall sucked back toward him. She hadn't realized that they could control the water to make it disappear also, these weavers had an awesome power that could be very dangerous. "Now," he continued, "Responsibility is more than just about yourself. It represents your view of the outside world, the people around you and the surrounding environment."

Lara scoffed internally. If Blue was so responsible and cared about the environment, why did the Wastes even exist? Their view of the 'outside world' was a bit limited.

"The goal of this class is to prepare you for the Responsibility Trial. Once you have proven yourself in class, you will be invited by me to attempt the trial, and that is where you will attempt to earn your Responsibility Ring."

Fallon held out his hand, and a shimmering ball of water appeared. "I have just created this water bubble. I am now responsible for what I do with it." He turned his hand over and it dropped to the floor in a splash, tiny droplets flying in all directions. He created another one with a flourish of his hands, which Lara devised was stage presence, a bit of acting, since the hand motions hadn't been needed before. "Again, here is another. I can guard it carefully," he hunched over it with his hand around it, shoulders bent. He added a comical, shifty look to his eyes and got a few laughs from the room. "But I am limited now. I am stuck. What about teaching the class? How can I fulfill my responsibility to you and my responsibility to my water baby?"

He looked at the water droplet with loving eyes and then back at the crowd, suddenly blue wisps split the water into three smaller balls, and he began to juggle them, his hands not quite touching the water balls, but the motion moving along with them.

"I carry many burdens, and I must be able, at all times, to weigh my obligations, keep in mind people and things that depend on me, and balance my time and self to meet all of them. And the better you get, the more ends up on your plate." The three balls split into six, and he continued to juggle them. "This is the ultimate truth of responsibility."

He let a flow of blue mist out and it encompassed the water droplets as they spun in the air. The mist took over for him and he stepped away from the show. He stood at the side for a moment watching the movement, then turned to the crowd.

"There they spin. I have left them to take care of themselves. The magic will keep it running. I can now focus on other things." He reached into his pocket and took out a piece of candy and popped it into his mouth. His eyes shifted to the water. "See, there it continues with no effort from me. However," his voice had turned suddenly serious, and the students all listened a bit more intently. "I am still responsible for those water droplets. What about the next class taught here? What if Headmaster Shauna came in while reading a book and walked straight into it?" He walked over to the circling water and stepped right into it, the balls smashing into his face. He mimicked an outraged, spluttering face.

"The blue stone magic is great and powerful, so it must be held by those who understand the responsibility of carrying that power."

He pushed a hand through his damp hair and slicked it back across the top of his head. He looked powerful suddenly, the bangs not covering his eyes as they looked around the room. Unlike Shauna, he didn't look at each student. Instead, he only made eye contact with a few. As his gaze moved around the room, the students got very quiet and fidgety. Lara watched in awe as this huge room of youth who had been all giggling and whispers was suddenly so engrossed in waiting to see if he would meet their eyes. She almost forgot to wonder about it and prepare for herself, and when his gaze locked with hers, she was not ready for it. Just as Shauna's had burrowed right into her, Fallon's did too. This connection felt more friendly though, like a "nice to meet you, can we be friends" type of greeting. But with much more intensity than a greeting at a community picnic.

It was over quickly, and he finished his perusal of the room, locking eyes with a few more students.

"As I said before, the final test in this class is the Trial of Responsibility. When I feel you are ready, you will be invited to attempt it. But we must start with the basics, for many of you have never held the burden of responsibility, and it is not always simple to learn. Experience is often the best teacher." Lara felt sure she saw a flick of his eyes towards her.

"So, we will start with experiences. Your homework is to take one of the water balloons from the back of class. You will be responsible for it until our next meeting."

"Oh, but before you all leave, I want to tell you a joke." Reaching his hand up, he pretended to knock on a doorway, "Knock, knock."

"Who's there?" everyone chimed in from the audience.

"Water,"

"Water who?" This sounded a bit like a groan from the right side of the room.

"What are you waiting for? Open the door!"

The students around Lara laughed along with her, but the kids on the other side seemed less amused.

"Just as I thought! That joke only hits the first time told. Ah well, someday I will find the joke that is funny even when you know the punch line. We all must have our goals in life. Go, get your water balloon baby, I will see you next class."

Lara rushed back to her room, excited to share her experience with Fleck. When she opened the door, Fleck was already perched up on the bed expectantly. She realized her excitement must have been strong enough to wake him up.

"It's amazing Fleck! They actually control the water. When Fallon's tattoo started glowing and the blue light flowed from under his robe, I was floored. He plucked water from thin air and juggled it!" She giggled with glee. As she continued speaking and sharing all she saw, she took her new water balloon baby and wrapped it up in a shawl. She figured she could hold the doll the same way she had held her own children when they were young.

After surrounding it in the shawl, she took the small throw blanket from the back of her reading chair and set the wrapped 'baby' into the center, next she placed it against her chest, finally pulling the sides of the blanket over her shoulder and waist, tying the ends at her hip.

"This balloon doesn't squirm nearly as much as my own kids used to, or even you, for that matter. I am not sure if a water balloon is the best comparison to a real child. I realize we need to be responsible for it, but real kids are a lot more complex."

With the balloon securely tightened to her back, she turned to Fleck again. "I think our best bet is to try to find one of these waterweavers to come with us." Fleck immediately sent doubt her way, and Lara raised her hands. "I know, I know. But not everyone feels the way those senators at our first meeting feel. Hyacinth was very supportive. Maybe we can find a waterweaver who actually sees there are larger problems than just what is here behind their waterwall. Fallon was so fun. I think I could speak to him about it at least. Not like that Shauna, she was super intimidating."

Fleck sent her a reassuring feeling, and she realized she was letting Shauna get to her even now. How is it that someone who wasn't even in the room, or directly being aggressive to her, made her feel this way?

"I know. I have enough to worry about without adding Shauna to my list. What is it about her that rubs me the wrong way so much? I think I was upset about her little speech about the rules. I feel like the rules are my nemesis here. They are keeping us from getting the help out of Azural. But it will be a lot faster to convince one of them to come help than to actually go through all their trials myself." Lara sat softly on the chair, being careful not to lean back on the water balloon.

"Plan time. I think the next steps are to actually meet individually with a few of the waterweavers and ask them for help. They wouldn't need to stay in Calambria. We just need a quick fix at first. I would love to bring a stone back to our homeland, but if that is not an option, at least someone who can come and refill our well and riverbed…" It wasn't the best solution, but it felt like the most realistic one now that she had been in Azural for a few days.

Lara took a look at the schedule she had written for herself sitting at the desk. "Next comes lunch and my first Intelligence class. Wanna join me for some outside time and food?"

Fleck's joy hit her before he did. Jumping to her shoulder and scrabbling under the blanket knot she had there. "You better watch those sharp claws around my water balloon baby!" Lara laughed.

# Intelligence Class

When Lara walked into the Intelligence class, she expected a large room again, but this was much smaller. With only six desks, it looked like it was just her cohort in this one. She was reminded of her schoolhouse back home with a cozy space, small desks for each student, and a large one up front. It even had a chalkboard.

Iris and Delly were chatting animatedly in the front row, with Stella sitting on the far side of Iris, looking aloof and uninterested in joining in their conversation. Lara suddenly felt sorry for her.

With only six desks in the room, there wasn't much of a choice for seating. Lara went to sit directly behind Delly, who spun in her seat when Iris waved to Lara. As Delly turned, she hit her water balloon baby, knocking it off the side of her desk. The whole class held their breath for a moment as the blue balloon fell. The splash of the water exploding from the rubber as it hit the floor broke the silence. Looking around Lara noticed that all the students had placed their baby balloons on the desk in front of them. Hers was still strapped to her chest.

"Oh no!" Iris gasped, reaching her hand out to comfort Delly.

Stella gave a short laugh, while Brandon and Van each quickly grabbed their own balloons up from their desks.

Delly just shrugged, "I knew I wasn't going to last with that one. I am so clumsy." She laid her head down on her folded arms on the desk, mumbling, "What am I even doing here?"

Lara sat down at her desk and reached to touch Delly's back reassuringly, "Delly, it could have happened to anyone in here. The whole point of the exercise is that it isn't easy to take care of something."

Delly looked up appreciatively, "We just started, and I am such a fish out of water here, or maybe that is the other way around, I am not a fish in water? Ugh, hopefully Fallon isn't upset. Hey, we didn't see you at lunch," Delly said.

"No, I ate outside with Fleck." Lara said.

"What did you think about Fallon? I thought he was super fun! I hope all of his classes are like that." Lara started to answer, but Delly was too excited, all but forgetting her balloons demise, and continued. "I hope all of our other classes are like that too, although I can't see Headmaster Shauna being any fun. Anyway, I heard that the Intelligence class is a bit more serious." She smiled at Van, who was seating himself next to Lara. "I bet you'll like this one. Excel in it even."

Van smiled. "I, um, yes. I am excited about this. I heard from Brandon that the teacher is kind, but tough."

Brandon, at hearing his name on the far side of Van, leaned forward, the water baby still in his hands, and said, "Yup. She is super smart, too."

Lara was just wondering about how different Fallon and Shauna were and thought she had no clue what this new leader might be like, when in walked Penny. It took her one beat, then she realized she had gotten it all wrong. Penny was not a general worker here at the Stone House. She was a Weaver?

Van saw her too and immediately said to Lara, "Wait, the librarian is a weaver? She seemed so normal when I went in there yesterday. I mean, smart, but normal."

Lara just nodded slowly in response. She was wildly sorting out in her head this new information. She had opened up to Penny about everything. About how dire things were back home and how much she needed help, and Penny hadn't said anything about being a weaver.

Had this been some tactic to glean information from her? Had it been fake? Lara thought back through the conversation and how comfortable and natural it had been. She really trusted that the friendship had been genuine, but why had Penny kept something so large a secret? She could save Lara's home and family. Why keep that to herself?

Penny stood at the front of the room. She wore an adorable dress in light blue with tiny dark blue flowers all over. It swished around her calves as she spun to write her name on the board.

"Welcome class. I have had the chance to meet a few of you when you came to the library and encourage the rest to stop by there anytime. I love getting to know you all outside of the classroom setting.

"Now, down to business. Intelligence is a key tenet of Blue. Our stone values intelligence. An informed mind makes better decisions. Anyone hoping to become a weaver needs to prepare their mind."

Penny turned and pulled her glasses off her face to wipe them. Her eyes seemed to shrink in size. "We will begin our studies with a history of Azural. Then we will move on to the science of water: makeup; physics; states, that sort of thing. Finally, we will learn about the stone and weaving. If you are still in the class at that point, we will set up individual studies for you that follow your interests."

She popped her glasses back on and looked around the room. Lara knew what was happening. She was starting to get used to it, but this time it was different. She already knew Penny and wondered how that might change things. It didn't. The look was exhausting. Lara didn't get any read from it, but the color of Penny's eyes, while she felt laid bare before Penny. It didn't really seem fair to her.

As quickly as it had begun, it was over, and Penny started passing out books to the class. The book was heavy and covered with a dark blue textured cover. The only word on the front was AZURAL in bold letters with a shiny silver text.

Penny finished passing them to the six students quickly and moved back up front. "We will have a clear schedule for this course. For each lesson, I expect you to have completed the assigned reading. Then in class we will hold a discussion to answer any questions you have and at the end of class you will be tested on the reading. This will be the routine through all of our studies until you reach your independent research."

She turned again to the board. "You will all need to write out the assigned reading schedule, so you have it. I do not plan on writing this out again." The class shuffled to pull out a pencil and paper. Lara grabbed her journal and began copying.

It took most of the class time to write out the syllabus. At first Lara was excited about learning, but as she slowly added items to the list, it was obvious this was a yearlong class. The schedule of a single chapter a class might fine for these students who all were here to learn and grow, but she had pressing issues. She needed to be brave and talk with Penny after class and just ask outright for help.

When the bell rang, everyone was packing up their book and papers and picking up their balloon babies, Lara smiled to herself as she saw Delly place her empty popped balloon into her pack. Lara wanted to speak with Penny, so she spent a few extra moments fiddling with the books in her bag. She already had quite a few from her classes and she always carried the Siegel book with her in case she had free time to read more of it. The soft leather of her pack stretched comfortably to hold the books. Pulling the flap over the top opening, Lara touched Sally's heart representing home for a bit of courage for the upcoming conversation.

Iris looked back from the door. "You coming Lara? Calm class starts in ten minutes. I can show you the way."

Lara debated, but decided it was too important for her to get an answer out of Penny. "I think I can find my way. I am just gonna ask a quick question. I'll see you there."

Iris waved and was off.

Penny looked like she knew what was coming. She stood a bit tense at the front, loading up her own papers, but watching the interaction between Lara and Iris.

Lara had spent a bit of time while writing deciding how best to broach this discussion with Penny. "I had no idea you were a weaver. I'm a bit surprised you didn't tell me." She stopped there even though there was more she wanted to say because when she had played the possible conversation over in her head, she felt it was less rude to give Penny an open chance to explain.

She didn't want to come out and accuse Penny of not caring about her family. She knew that was a bit extreme, even though she felt that pain in her heart right now. Did no one care, but her?

Penny looked up at Lara over her glasses rims. "I'm sorry Lara. To be honest, I was just enjoying our conversation so much. I haven't had someone talk to me so comfortably for years. Ever since I became a weaver, everyone has treated me differently. They all want something from me or think I am something sacred or foreign. It was so nice to just have a chat and hear about you as a normal person."

Lara stopped up short. Her whole plan to ask Penny for help fizzled. This was exactly what Penny had worried about - being used. But she needed help. She would have to think this through a bit. And they didn't have time to discuss it right now. She couldn't risk getting kicked out of The Stone House for not getting to class. "Well, it's nice to know now. Maybe we can sit down and talk again soon?" Lara said. "I have to get to the Gardens for my next class."

"I'd love to visit again. Come by the library any evening." Penny said, and Lara walked out the door feeling conflicted about responsibility, friendship and family. How could she keep all of these intact?

# *Calm Class*

Lara had already explored quite a bit of the grounds with Fleck, so she found her way easily to where the Calm class gardens. She was just in time, though, and all the other students were already seated on cushions throughout the space. She saw her cohort of students seated to the back of the garden under a lovely, flowered tree. Van and Brandon were chatting amiably, laughing at their twin popped balloons sitting on the grass in front of them.

It was obvious that there was no rhyme or reason to the spacing, just far enough away from others, so she grabbed a pillow from the stack by the entrance and found an open area. She placed hers on the ground between a few students with two bands on their shoulders. Taking a moment to gear up for the pain she would feel in her joints as she sat. Once seated she appreciated the size of the soft pillow, her knees resting gently on the puff of the edges

It was already pretty quiet in the garden. Anyone talking was doing so in a hushed tone. But when the weaver entered, it went completely silent aside from the sound of the water in a narrow stream, tripping over the smooth rocks that had been strategically placed in its path.

Lara recognized him from her first evening on the island. He was the same man sitting in the back of the gatekeeping trial. His curls bounced against his head in a rhythmic way as he conscientiously walked toward a pillow already set up at the head of the stream on the far side of the garden from the entrance. Each step he took seemed to be thought out and purposeful. He arrived at his cushion and in a fluid motion folded his knees and sank into a cross-legged seat at the same time as the bells went off for the start of class.

Lara was impressed.

She sat waiting for him to begin. But many of the other students, who had been here for longer than her cohort, nodded to the weaver and then closed their eyes.

Lara and her classmates were left looking at each other, a bit quizzically, over everyone else's heads. Finally, she shrugged her shoulders and closed her eyes, too.

She found that her thoughts immediately started sorting through all she had to figure out, and it was a jumble. She had to get the water home. She had to convince a weaver to help her. But she realized she couldn't just bash one over the head with it. She had to convince them to help her and that seemed impossible with the Azurans' closed off worldview.

She thought of the friends she had made already. Good people live here in Azural. Hyacinth, Iris, Delly and Van, all had told her they support her and wanted to help her figure out how to accomplish her task.

Penny seemed like a friend. Lara thought that she had been a friend. The short conversation they had just held seemed to confirm it. Penny just had her own life. Lara had to remember that as she dealt with people. Sometimes it was so hard to look at things from the other person's point of view, especially when your home was at risk.

Lara could hear the twittering of a few birds, and there was buzzing from some flying bug close by. Focusing on the sounds calmed her a bit, and she realized that she had been getting stressed with her thoughts so intense.

She breathed in and reminded herself of her plan. She needed to ask Penny if she would help her. If she could help her. That was the clear next step. She was very nervous about it now that there was the added stress of hurting one of the few friends she had here. She didn't want Penny to think that she was using her, but she needed her help.

Maybe she was using her. That thought made Lara feel unsettled. She hated the idea of being inconsiderate, but this was bigger than one person's feelings. The world outside Azural and the other Color Realms were crumbling away. She pictured Nessa and her girls; she pictured her neighbors in the town hall. Heck, she even pictured Stella sitting at home without her mother.

This made her open her eyes and look over the group for Stella. She was sitting next to Brandon. Eyes closed, but a tight look on her face. She looked so young. Lara wondered how long ago her mother had left. Life was hard in so many ways. There was a struggle for everyone.

She looked up at the dais where the weaver sat on his cushion. He looked so calm and comfortable, what struggles did he have that she couldn't see? She wondered how he could sit cross legged without his ankles feeling like they were digging into the calf of the other leg like she was struggling with.

He must have noticed her attention, for he opened his eyes as she looked at him and she was caught in another of the weavers' stares. She felt more prepared for this one than any other, wondering if perhaps it was the quiet state her mind was in? She still felt an emotional tug and exhaustion, but again, it was over quickly.

He nodded to her and closed his eyes again. Strange.

Lara closed her eyes herself, and listened to the songs of the birds. She felt the warmth of the sun on her shoulders and neck as her head bowed forward. On the light cool breeze, she could smell the sweet flowers from a few gardens over. She thought if she opened her mouth, she might be able to taste the sweetness of it. She couldn't, and she laughed to herself for having tried.

As she settled into the quiet, she found that she could sense Fleck back in their room. He sent her an image of the closed window and a feeling of wishing he was out with her in the garden. She was a bit surprised to realize how easily she understood what he was conveying. The connection with him was getting stronger by the day.

As she started to sort through what she had learned about Pelanor, the bell rang, bringing her eyes open with a start. The time had flown by. Class had been nothing more than sitting and thinking.

She followed the other student's lead and left the garden quietly, placing her cushion on the pile by the door. Once outside the garden, she found the youth much calmer than they had been that morning in Fallon's class. She looked back over her shoulder at the weaver as he continued to sit on his cushion. Well, color her impressed. He had accomplished teaching them all about calm, simply by example.

# Honesty Class

"Honesty begins in your heart. There is a need to know the truth fully before we can acknowledge it, then speak it and finally live it. To live an honest life is to know, understand, and validate your emotions. This class will be delving into these facets so that we may all know ourselves better and therefore learn the value and complexities of the Honesty tenet."

Lara had noticed right away that this class was different from any she had seen so far. It was in a larger room, but there were only seven chairs, and they were in a tight circle.

When Lara had first entered the color weaver sat with her back to Lara, her cloak giving her status away. The grey streaks in her black hair were also a clear marker that she wasn't a student.

Layla turned to look over her shoulder and Lara was pierced by her bright blue eyes. The gaze only took a moment, but Lara felt staggered by it. She had never been standing when she had met the eyes of a color weaver before. She was surprised at the energy it had pulled from her. Layla smiled and asked the others to make room.

After a few moments of arranging to let Lara into the circle, she had been seated in the last empty chair next to Iris, to the right of Layla. Lara was again struck by how much older she was than these youths.

"I keep my honesty session sizes limited so that we can all get comfortable with each other. It is important to build trust as we really get into sharing our inner truths out in the open. Let's go around and introduce ourselves now. I want you to share your name and why you are here. Not in this class specifically, but why you are at The Great Stone

House trying for the blue stone." Layla turned to her left and prompted Stella to begin.

Speaking in a clear, concise tone, she started them off, "My name is Stella Molina, and I am here to earn the blue stone." She turned curtly to Brandon.

"Oh, I'm Brandon and I am here to follow in my mom's footsteps. She came to the Great Stone House before she had me and earned three rings." He turned to Van on his left.

Van kept his head lowered, "I'm Van. I'm here to learn as much as I can about Azural." He nodded his head slightly to show he was done.

Delly jumped in speaking quickly, "I'm Delly from Laran. I came here to learn about Azural, too." She turned to Iris, beaming.

"I'm Iris. I came here because it is what was always expected of me, to be honest." She turned a warm smile on Lara.

"I'm Lara." She gave a nod to Stella, "I am also here to earn a blue stone." Lara turned to Layla.

Layla looked up at the ceiling for a moment, taking a deep breath. Lara knew that look. She had used it many times when her children were young, and she had been trying to sort out her thoughts on what to do next. It was disappointment.

"We have a lot of work to do students. I asked for your honesty and all you gave were pleasantries. Here, I will return the favor. I'm Layla and I am here to teach you." She slowly looked around the room. After a moment, she continued. "Disappointing and hollow, right? There is honesty there, but it doesn't reach down to the core, it isn't genuine. It doesn't bring the truth out into the light. Honesty is about the truth being set free, speaking with candor. This group is for us to really open up, talk with sincerity to find our honest selves."

"Let's try it again, but this time I will go first as an example. My name is Layla. I have been teaching the classes on the Honesty Tenet for ten years. I continue to enjoy teaching this class because I learn more about myself each time I lead lessons. I have found that when I feel lacking and empty, all I have to do is lead a discussion with a small group and the interactions open my heart just a bit more to the truth inside myself. I love getting to know myself better, and although sometimes the truths are hard to admit, being honest with myself makes me stronger.

And it helps me be a better color weaver because I connect with my stone more strongly."

She turned back to Stella. "Your turn."

Stella sat quietly for a moment. To Lara, it looked like she was practicing lines in her head. When she spoke, it was clear, and she sounded almost like she was giving a speech. "My name is Stella Molina. I am here because I want to make my father and all of Azural proud by earning the five bands and becoming a waterweaver. I want to take my understanding of the tenets that I learned since birth," she stressed that word a bit harshly, "and increase it until I am ready to stonegraft and become a leader in our realm." She nodded her head succinctly, clearly pleased with how she had phrased her answer.

"Like I said, I am Brandon." He spoke with his head down, looking at his fingers as they fidgeted in his lap. Lara was a bit taken aback, because Brandon had always looked so confident before this moment. "I'm here because my mom has always wanted me to come to the Great Stone House. It was one of her favorite times as a young person and she wants me to get those experiences too. Honestly, I'm not really sure if I belong in Blue. It is just all I have ever known." He looked up at Layla but also darted quick looks at the rest of the youth in the group, taking stock of their reactions.

"That was well done, Brandon. That is precisely what these classes are for. You will find out more about yourself as we progress. Thank you for opening up to the group. Van?"

"My name is Van. I came here from Green to attempt the blue stone. My family is all in green, but I never felt comfortable there. I wanted to find a place that prioritized the same things as I do. Blue's tenets really rang true for me, and I hope to be successful and earn a stone or at least earn enough bands to prove that I am in the right place." Layla smiled at him and then looked at Delly.

"Well, here goes nothing," Delly began a bit more slowly this time, "Delly, from Orange, and honestly, I came here because I was tired of the chaos. I had heard about the peace and order of Blue and I really was just hoping the change would help me relax finally." She looked at Iris, and Lara noted a slight tinge of fear in her eyes. As Lara listened to the youths in the class attempt to open up, she found it adorable. They so wanted to know themselves and set themselves apart from the rest. But they also wanted so much to fit in. The battle inside them was apparent to her in her older age.

Iris smiled warmly at Delly, then sighed, turning toward the whole group. "I'm Iris Mere, and I am here at the Stone House because I want to see what I am capable of. My parents thrived here and now hold leadership roles in the Senate, and I hope I can live up to their example. I was most excited to come here to meet new people." She turned her head to look back at Delly to her right, then turned to look at Lara and smiled such a genuine smile.

Lara smiled back. Then it struck her. It was her turn. She realized she should have been thinking about what to say.

She began slowly to try to sort out her thoughts. "I'm Lara. I came here from Calambria. It's a small village in the Wastes." She quickly realized she would just have to wing it. "Our village is running out of water, and we needed to find a way to bring the power of the blue stone back to our home. So here I am. I am trying to accomplish something I have never even considered before." Her words began to tumble out quicker. "I know I am out of place, and I feel scared that I won't succeed and my whole village, my family, the people I love will have to leave the only home we have ever known." She realized tears fell down her cheeks. She had been keeping the burden so close to her chest that opening up felt painful.

Painful, but also there was relief.

She looked at Weaver Layla and saw a glimmer in her bright blue eyes, and Lara thought maybe she saw a tear there too. Lara began to realize she might learn a lot from this woman.

# Order Class

Lara had been looking forward to her next afternoon meeting with Detmer. She had been to all of her classes now, and thought she understood the timeline much clearer. She needed to know what kind of options she might have to get this on a faster track.

After the class on Honesty, she felt like sharing her story would be the best tactic. The more people who started thinking about outside of Azural, the better. After talking with Iris and Delly, she believed she could trust him with her real concerns and story. He had been a mentor here for a long time, and according to Iris, he had surprised everyone by turning down the option of trying for a stone. He certainly followed the codes of Blue, but he also went to the beat of his own drum.

Lara had laid it all out, telling him about her family, the town meeting, her trip here and how her first days had gone. He had listened patiently. He really was a great mentor. Finally, she finished up, "So, although my classes are interesting and I wish I had all the time to enjoy them, I really just don't. I need to know what options I have." She paused. "Do you think I might be able to convince one of these weavers to break their codes and come with me? Or is there a chance I could speed up the trials and attempt stonegrafting more quickly? The fact is, that at this point the only thing I can do without some help is fill a bucket from the waterwall and carry it home. That is no help at all. I feel useless. I feel powerless. I feel like I have wasted so much precious time already."

Detmer's answer was short and sweet to her ears, even though it came out in a gruff, detached manner. "Lara, there are people in Azural who might help you. You aren't alone in seeing the damage the wall has done to our people here, but also to Chroma at large. I have a few friends I will talk to, but it will be up to them if they want to reach out. They have been looking for solutions too, so have hope."

"Oh, thank you," Lara professed her appreciation, feeling a huge weight off her shoulders.

"Don't get ahead of yourself. I can't make any promises; you need to keep on your path. The classes are your only option right now."

The next morning Lara sat in Shauna's Order class and tried her best to hide her frustration. James had always told her that her emotions were clear on her face. She hoped it was just because he knew her so well, but was fairly sure most people could read her like an open book.

Shauna was so focused on the rules that she seemed to not care about anything else. She sat at the front of the classroom ticking off all of Blue's expectations large and small to the point that Lara wondered if the only way Shauna would be happy was if everyone was a complete copy of herself.

The class had started with a very large binder already set at the desks in front of them. Lara had opened it to find that it was full of all the codes of conduct. They were numbered and organized by section. The binder looked to be heavier than the history book she had brought back to her room yesterday.

It seemed that Shauna expected to just read aloud the binder from start to finish during class time, and the past hour had been a monotonous reading of each tiny rule. This first section covered conduct in the Great Stone House.

# I. Uniform

## 1. Levels

    i. Initiate

    ii. First banded

    iii. Second banded

    iv. Third banded

v. fourth banded
vi. Fifth banded
vii. Employee
viii. Weavers
**2. Cleanliness**
i. Where to clean
ii. How to clean
**3. Damage**

It went on and on. Subsections dealing with each small infraction to the code. Shauna read each line. When Lara had tried to look ahead in the book to see what else it covered, Shauna had called her back to attention.

Lara hoped they would get to take the binder with them. It might have some real answers about the stone.

"Code I.4.i.a. Uniform Replacement location for initiates. If an initiate must replace their uniform from irreparable damage (see code I.3.iv.a) initiate will contact their mentor immediately."

If rules were so important here, maybe there was a way to work with the rules to save her home. She needed to look through this book in detail, but Shauna was keeping them stuck on the first section, reading page by page.

The others in class seemed about as interested as Lara was. She even caught Stella staring out the window a few times.

When the bell finally rang, she was happy to find that she was told to pack up the binder and remember to bring it back next class.

# *One Week In*

Brandon and Iris walked out of their Order and Rules Class side by side in front of Lara, and she couldn't help but notice that Van was totally right. They did look beautiful next to each other. Two of the most peaceful and kind Azural natives she had met so far. She didn't see any spark of romance between them, though, just a comfortable friendship.

Shauna was the most difficult teacher they had in all five classes. The tenets were clear to Lara. She understood the basis behind each emotion and felt confident she could define them in her way, but Azural had a different way of looking at them, especially order. To Lara, an orderly home was one that ran smoothly, but also happily: dishes washed so that you had them for the next meal, tools put away in the proper place so they could be found the next time they were needed. To Shauna, though, order seemed to consume every decision: what time to arrive and leave a place, how many times to turn up the cuff of a uniform sleeve. Lara inwardly groaned, not to mention when someone was allowed to leave Azural to help a small community in need.

Her past week of classes had her on an emotional path of highs and lows, and she always was at her lowest after interacting with Shauna.

She had enjoyed Responsibility class again this morning. Fallon had a way of entertaining, while also teaching these young people that life had a lot to keep track of.

Her favorite classes by far were the Calm and Honesty ones. She was learning a lot about herself in these classes that forced her to sit and think and then share. Life had always been such a rush from one thing to the next while raising the kids. The short time she had before leaving Calambria for Azural after Pete had left had been just enough time for her to mourn the loss of her busy daily life with children. Not much time to think about her feelings and process emotions.

She was also getting much closer to Fleck. They had gotten better at communicating. Although he did enjoy coming with her to classes sometimes, he was tired quickly, so they spent a lot of time communicating from a distance. She always knew when he woke up.

Other strange things were starting to happen around him, too. While studying with Van for loopholes in the Code in the gardens the other evening, twilight and shadows creeping in, Fleck had just started glowing. Van and she stopped short, but as soon as Fleck saw them looking at him, the light disappeared. "What was that, Fleck?" She had asked, but he seemed as confused by it as she had.

She really wanted to read Siegel's journal but needed to focus on the codes. She was hoping to find something to take to Penny or Layla, that showed it was allowed for them to leave to help her. Unfortunately, so far, she and Van have found a lot of rules that said just the opposite. Azural first. Blue stays in Blue, was the story the rules told.

# Ulterior Motives

Shauna's clipped steps along the path sounded a bit angry to her ears, so she controlled them and stepped a more softly. She didn't want anyone to notice her agitation. When she reached the end of the path, she gave a sharp turn, the pebbles grinding underneath her heels, and walked in the opposite direction. She knew that Fallon would be by in a few minutes. He always came this way after his Responsibility class.

She noticed the gravel crunching beneath her boots and she decided it would look better to passersby if she just stopped pacing. So, she stood next to the bench. She was too tense to sit.

Finally, she saw Fallon's light blue robes turn onto the path, so she started toward him to meet him part way.

"Was she in the class?" Shauna asked in a clipped tone.

Fallon laughed. "Of course she was Shauna. It's not like the woman is just going to disappear."

"I realize that." She spat out, then caught herself and spoke a bit more calmly. "I just hoped that she came to her senses. She obviously doesn't belong here. We haven't ever had someone over the age of twenty-five and she is likely double that."

Fallon looked at her with kind eyes, and she hated him a bit for it. He was always so at peace, while she had to work for her calm. The tenets were her life, and she put effort into every moment to fill the expectations of Azural and her Head Waterweaver status. He had no need to try when it came to calm, because it was just part of him. She felt the depression she fought constantly leaning in on her, almost like she was struggling to breathe.

"I need a better understanding of what her plans are if I am to deal with her. When I gazed with her, I felt her practically push back on my own mind. There is something unsettling about her beyond these age and Wastes issues. I can't put my finger on it, but she scares me a bit." Shauna looked up from studying her wringing her own hands, to see Fallon bouncing water from one hand to the other. "Fallon! Our magic is not to be used for idle purposes." And she raised her hand and pulled the water he was playing with to the ground, watering the lilac bush to their left.

Fallon was used to her behaving this way, so she knew he would forgive her for her outburst. He knew the stress she was under to keep the Stone House running now that Axel had finally stepped down from his role in leadership.

And thank the East Star that Axel had decided to step down. Lately he was speaking gibberish half the time about how wrong he and his friends had been. How the waterwall was the biggest mistake of his lifetime. Imagine that the crowning glory of Azural, the thing that kept them all safe, and he regretted it. Well, Lara was her problem to deal with, not Axel's.

Fallon broke a bloom off of the lilac bush and brought it to his nose. "Lilacs are my favorite. They smell divine. Now, Shauna. I agree that there is something special about Lara. You are right that she is much older than the other students, but that doesn't mean that she can't complete the trials. Indeed, in my gaze I found she might already be ready for the responsibility trial. Her feelings of responsibility for her home are striking and real. I didn't feel unsettled at all, but your feelings are valid. Once you figure out how to put a finger on it and explain what specifically bothers you, I am ready to hear it. Until then, I think we need to keep treating her as we do the other students. The senators voted to allow her to come. She passed the entrance test, and she has been following our expectations of her. So, my recommendation," Fallon paused and looked Shauna directly in the eye, "if that is what you are here asking for?"

She begrudgingly gave a short nod. "Yes. I guess that is what I came to you for."

"My recommendation is to let her continue on. Let's see where this leads. She might just surprise you and teach us a few things. And if things go terribly wrong, I know a dozen or so super powerful mages who can deal with her." His eyes danced as he conjured up a blade made of water and slashed the lilac bush with it. The water broke apart on the flowers and the sun on the droplets made the bush sparkle. Shauna enjoyed the bright glints of light for a moment and then shook her head.

"More than ready for the responsibility trial, you say..." Shauna contemplated out loud. "That's it! Let's assign her the trial in the morning."

Fallon spun around. "Shauna, we have never done a trial that quickly. What are you thinking? She has barely had time to settle in, let alone plan and prepare for a trial. In fact, she didn't even know about them until a few days ago."

"Exactly. If this isn't the place for her, it is best for her to see quickly. Maybe she will get discouraged enough and just leave." Shauna felt her eyes dance at the thought, and she reined it in a bit. "Besides, you just said you thought she might be ready for it."

Fallon groaned. "Is this a recommendation, or are you telling me to as Headmaster?"

"Fallon, I appreciate your willingness for input, but every choice I make is as Headmaster. I think it is the best course of action. Now, I have to get to my afternoon meeting with the junior mentors. Maybe we can encourage this woman so much that she gets overwhelmed and turns around to head right back to wherever she came from."

She turned and walked down the path toward the Great Stone House and couldn't help but think that she might be the only one who saw the problems that Lara represented to the status quo. Shauna had a responsibility to the Stone House as it's headmaster to do right by Blue's tenets.

Fallon looked out at the sea of faces in his class. He loved teaching. Becoming a weaver had been one of the best moments of his life, but teaching was his passion, and mixing the two together had made each day a pleasure. This was one of the first times he was not excited about announcing a trial.

Generally, a trial was considered a rite of passage for one of the youths. It was a celebration of the effort the student had put into their class work. This felt rushed to him.

"A show of hands, my friends," he called out in his stage voice, loud but not shouting, from the diaphragm. "Show of hands, how many of you still have water in your balloon babies?"

There was a tittering of uncomfortable laughter as only about thirty of the two hundred in the room had hands go up. Many of them were older students with a few bands, he even remembered clearly a few of them having done this balloon experiment in the past. There among the hands raised was Lara. Even in her school uniform she stood out from the crowd. It wasn't just her aged face and graying hair that pinpointed her as different. It was her calm. She sat with these youth comfortably and smiling. Enjoying their amusement at their own failure as much as Fallon did.

He knew that Shauna had told him to do this trial in hopes that she would go packing, but Fallon saw in Lara a kindred spirit; someone who appreciated responsibility and the encouraging of these young ones like he did.

"I am proud of those of you who have been successful. For those of you who did not, I hope you learned from the lesson. When we have responsibilities, it isn't always about big choices and big actions, it is often about the constant vigilance to keep invested in the responsibility."

He paced, gearing up for the news that he knew would shock many in this room. "Now, before we end class for the day, I have an announcement. Every now and again, there is a momentous occasion here at the Great Stone House. When a student is invited to stand Trial in one of Blue's Tenets."

As expected, there was a quick rumble of excitement through the crowd and then a quick hush. This was the usual reaction, everyone wanting to know who was next. Who had earned the respect of the Weaver enough to try for the band on their arm?

He took a slow breath. There would be no going back after this. There would be some who might question his decision, but none of the students would. He was respected and loved. The other weavers would likely wonder if Shauna had pushed it, but they would understand, they all had to deal with her also.

His biggest question was how he felt about it himself. He felt the honesty of his feelings thrum in the stone at his shoulder and he let the magic push out of him. He was confident not only that it was what Shauna wanted, but that it was what he thought was right. Lara was ready for this; he had seen it in his gaze that first day.

Fallon loved a good show, so he took the sparkle at his shoulder and spun letting it curve around him, he sent it into the air with a splash of water, creating a line that he began writing in a lovely script he had been practicing, "I would like to invite the next student to attempt the Responsibility Trial tomorrow morning."

There, for the class to see, was a sparkling blue water sign with the name, Lara Soleil. There was no going back now.

# Responsibility Trial

Lara stepped up to the entrance. It was a lovely arch of large light gray stones; she thought of how strange it was that the gray could be bright and clean - she had a momentary flashback to her home with the grime and dirt - the constant weight on her shoulders increased and her chest tightened.

*Concentrate*, she reminded herself, *focus, and breathe.*

She walked under the arch and was presented with a round area sealed off from the rest of the gardens by a high stone wall: too tall to see over, with smooth stones. In the center of the circular space, there were three short column stands. Each one had an item on it, and she took her time studying them.

On the first was a bowl. It was an oval shape, large enough that she would have to hold it with two hands and made with an unsealed blue clay. The insides and outsides had been hand engraved with detailed patterns of a map of Azural. It reminded her of Sally's painstaking work when adding embellishments to her leathers.

The second held a glass bird statue, a perfect size to sit nestled in the palm of her hand. It was a cute, fluffy, round bird. When Lara bent to look closely, she could see the stone wall behind change to a bright blue through the thin glass of the statue. She recognized the round rings that showed it was hand blown. A beautiful piece of fragile art.

The third stand held a silken shawl in deep, rich shades of blue. It lay folded across the top of the pillar, and she could see the light catch and flash on the soft threads of silk. She marveled at the intricate patterns and how this piece had at least ten different shades of blue.

A responsibility trial. She knew nothing of what they expected of her. The room had no doors other than where she had entered. As she turned to look back at it, she heard a loud slam as the arch was closed off with a heavy door. Her only entrance, and exit, had been sealed off. Looking around at the walls, she saw nothing of interest. The only interesting items were sitting on these pedestals.

The garden was peaceful, and she could hear the birds chirping on the other side of the walls. She could smell the fragrant hyacinth. She could hear the waters from the garden next to her bubble along its path. The waters of that garden were not quiet. They made a musical melody as they hit stones, it was meticulously planned for a calming song. Lara closed her eyes to listen for a moment, steadying her mind as she tried to think what the point of this exercise was.

Was she supposed to choose one? Maybe she needed to pick one up? Would something happen? She went over to the blue bird. She carefully lifted it, and it felt lighter than air. Suddenly, a gush of water started flowing over the back of the wall. It was a heavy flow, and the water was up to her ankles almost immediately. Her mind raced.

The water surged in roughly and she realized that if she set the bird back down, the waves would for sure crash it against the hard walls destroying it. Her eyes flew to the bowl. It wasn't sealed with anything. Even if it was heavy enough to withstand being bashed against the wall, the design would wear off in the water. She sloshed through the water, now above her knees, to the bowl. She lifted it. It wasn't light, and she had to balance it against her chest so she could continue holding the bird.

The water was up to her mid-thigh, and she looked at the final piece. The blue of the shawl stood bright against the churning white of the waters. She jumped to move through the waters toward the fabric. She knew the water would destroy the dyes in the silk fabric, as well. She set the glass bird onto the silk shawl and gently, but awkwardly, wrapped the fabric around it with her right arm. Then she set the bunched-up fabric into the bowl that she held in her left.

Holding the bowl in both hands, she thought about her options. The walls were about seven feet tall. The columns were about three feet. If she climbed up onto one, she would be tall enough to hold the bowl above the water line, and hopefully still breathe. She quickly clambered up awkwardly onto the nearest column, holding the bowl against her body again. She was quickly reminded of all of her years slinging a child against her hip as she did a multitude of chores. She slowly stood up on the column, the water was sloshing around at the level of her toes even up on the column. She spaced her feet to get a sturdy set base and rested the bowl to her tummy, arms reached out in front of it with her fingers wrapped around the lip of the bowl.

She looked out and saw that she could see over the top of the wall. That felt like a good sign. The water should flow over the edges and keep her head above water. As the water rose and hit her knees again, she bent them to keep the rush from pushing her over. The water hit her hips, and she pulled her arms around and under the bowl, pushing it upwards and rested it against her chest. She pulled her elbows in and left the weight of the bowl in the palms of her hands. She hated the feeling of the cool water creeping up her body. She had always been one to jump straight in as a child. She knew the worst part was when it hit the belly button, so she bent her knees and got the pain over with bringing the water just under her breasts. When she stood, she felt the cool air and as the water rose, it warmed her rather than feeling cold.

The water continued to rise, and her body felt lighter. She tried to make herself as heavy as possible, bending her knees to keep her footing on the pedestal. As the water rose to her chest, she pushed her arms up and rested the bowl on top of her head, placing a hand on either side of the bowl and grabbing the rim with her fingertips. She had been right. As the water reached her shoulders, it also reached the tops of the walls, and it began to flow over the edges. The water became quiet, and the flow sounded like a light waterfall rather than gushing rapids. Lara breathed a sigh. The waters around her knees quit pushing and shaking her, and she felt only a slight undertow of the flow from the water coming in. The top of the water smoothed out as the churning ended. Then she felt even the flow of water stop and all was silent again. She heard the birds and the bubbling of the musical waters in the garden beyond.

The waters receded quickly, and Lara started to shiver. She slowly maneuvered her way to sit without dropping the bowl. Once she was seated and had a good grasp of the bowl, she hopped down and splashed into the puddles left behind. She thought about setting the bowl on the pedestal, but realized it was still wet from the flood. The door clicked and swung open, and Fallon stepped in.

He walked up to her and with a flick of his wrist, she felt him pull the water off her. She stood dry before him. With another flourish he dried the closest pedestal, then gently reached forward and took the bowl from her. Lara had to slowly flex and unflex her fingers as they felt so stiff from holding the bowl so long.

Placing the bowl on the nearest pedestal, Fallon smiled. "Amazing Lara, you have saved all three." He shook his head slowly from side to side.

"Did I pass the trial?" Lara asked, feeling foolish as the words left her mouth, because she was certain she had.

"Lara, most people who pass only protect one of the items. By saving all three, you have done what only one other has accomplished." Lara noticed his eyes shift quickly to Shauna watching from the doorway and realized that it had been Shauna. "I would say you passed this test with flying colors." He looked past her at the door, where Lara could see a few people looking in. She saw her friends Iris and Delly with grins across their faces, and she saw Shauna, her face in a settled mask that Lara couldn't read. She wasn't sure what to make of that woman, but she certainly didn't look happy about Lara's success. She returned her full attention to Fallon. "Your new uniform will be brought to your room soon. Congratulations."

〉〉〉

As Lara walked out of the circular garden walls, Delly came running up and gave her a huge hug. Delly's exuberance broke Lara's strain over the trial, and she began to laugh along with her. Delly grabbed her hands and spun her in circles. Lara felt a wave of nostalgia. Youth had just a vibrant outlook. So much energy.

"We couldn't see anything that was going on in there. When I heard the water pouring in, I had all sorts of crazy worries. I just started worrying that you might never have learned to swim!"

Lara patted her shoulder. "No swimming necessary. I learned to swim as a kid, but you're right, I am out of practice. Wait, maybe we could go swimming?"

Delly turned to Iris, and said with uncommon quiet for her, "Do you know a place we could go without many people?" She looked conspiratorially from Lara to Iris, then gave a wide sweep of her eyes to see who was still hanging around. "I never learned."

"Oh!" Iris showed a moment of shock but quickly got her bright mind thinking. "I know of a few places. We could try all of my favorite quiet spots. It's a great way to see some of the best views in Azural too."

Lara gave a contented sigh. She was so lucky to have found these young friends. Iris obviously understood Delly's need for a discrete place to learn to swim, and rather than making a big deal of it, she was respectful of her needs. Meanwhile, Delly was a great balance to that, with an attitude that was quick to uplift the spirits of those around her.

Lara wondered if Blue was the right place for Delly. She must have come here for a reason, but she didn't seem to fit here the way Iris and even Van did. Speaking of Van, he had been playing with Fleck in the music garden before she went into her trial. She looked around to see if they were close and found Fleck bounding happily toward her, with Van rushing to keep up.

"We heard everyone talking about your success as they were walking down the trail toward the Great Stone House. Congratulations!" Van beamed at her, and she felt so grounded in the friendship they had. All of these youth. They had welcomed her more than the adults here.

"Thanks." Lara's smile was as wide as his. Lara opened her arms and Fleck jumped up into the crook of her left elbow. He nuzzled his nose into her armpit and let out a gruff purr. Oh, he was just so cute.

They walked up to the Great Stone House, listening to Iris discuss a list of quiet spots to swim. She had already listed six, and Lara was again reminded of the differences between Azural and Calambria; when it came to water: overabundance vs. lack of resources. Lost in her thoughts, she didn't notice Shauna's calculating gaze as she watched Lara and Fleck walk away with the others.

# Forced Choices

Shauna repositioned the third chair by two inches. As headmaster, it was her job to lead the weekly meeting with the Weavers. The four weavers who lived and ran things in the city came each week and joined the rest of them here. The last time they had met together was to decide about letting Lara join the House. That had not gone well at all. She needed to be sure to keep Axel in line. He was quick to mess everything up.

Today she had the whole agenda written out. She had rehearsed what she was going to say. She had a plan, and she needed things to go smoothly.

Once everyone was seated in their high-backed chairs facing the center, she called the meeting to order.

"I, Weaver Shauna, call this weekly Water Weaver meeting of the first week of summer to order."

With a quick hum she pulled a tight, soundproof wall of water around them.

Her plan was to keep the goal of her meeting a small decision rather than making it obvious she wanted a certain outcome. If she made a big deal about it, then there are those here who would stand up and counter her. And so, she bided her time.

"We had two successful bandings this week. Lara Soleil passed her first trial in Responsibility and Greg Meglan passed his third trial in Honesty." She shared her practiced smile and nodded to both Fallon and Layla as she spoke of these two.

"I turn the floor over to Weaver Sheldon to update us on happenings in the city proper."

While Sheldon shared items that she would normally find important, she instead focused on what was coming up. She looked around the circle and indeed, many of the weavers were starting to look like they were wrapping up. These meetings often were a rote checklist covering the same things.

When it was turned back over to her, she looked down at her paper, as if she needed to check what it said. She didn't. "There have been a few code infractions that will need to be voted on and dealt with.

"First, Code 2.i.c. We have had a two-banded student fail to pass room inspections for the third time. They will be put on probation for two weeks to see if there is an improvement. All in favor?"

"Aye."

Next, Code 4.ii.b. One of the one-banded students has been found to have a pet they brought along. This is against code, so we will need to remove the pet, or the student will be asked to leave. All in favor?"

"Aye." It was unanimous. No one questioned her motives. And indeed, how could they? She was being responsible, calm, following the order of the law, indeed all the tenets were being followed here. They didn't need to know who it was. She wasn't dishonest here.

"Finally, Code 5.iv.c. Two of the students were found in a boat heading to town after dark. Both students will be grounded from visits to the city for two months. All in favor?"

"Aye."

"That is all for code violations." And Shauna happily closed the meeting with a feeling of immense relief. Maybe this problem was going to walk under the waterwall of her own volition.

$$\gtrless\gtrless\gtrless$$

Lara felt amazing. This morning, she had dressed in her new uniform. The band around her arm made her feel like she was closer than ever to her goals. Fleck had stood upright on hind legs and then after watching her spin for him had mirrored it and spun for her.

Her morning classes had been her favorites. In Calm, Weaver Onya had waved for her to sit with him. He had spent half of the class slowly wrapping the garden in a magical mist. Bringing it up and then letting it dissipate. The mist was filled with blue sparkles from the magic, and Lara had been entranced by it. It had taken some of the stress off her mind as she was distracted. And when class was over, she found her shoulders were less tense.

In Honesty class, she had a huge breakthrough with Stella. Lara had been thinking hard about how to connect with Stella after the debacle at the Capital. She had been thinking about the advice she had given Van about finding something they had in common, and today during Honesty class Stella had brought up sewing. Lara loved to sew and had a lot of experience, especially with mending. She thought she might have just found a common interest, if she could find a way to spin it that didn't sound fake or pushy.

The afternoon had been pleasantly spent studying for intelligence class with Van in their favorite garden, Fleck playing alongside them. These were the best afternoons because it meant that in the evening Fleck was ready to sleep rather than keep her up all night with his constant push of communication.

As they walked back to her room, she noticed immediately something was wrong. Two of the young guards, wearing uniforms similar to those who met her at the waterwall, were stationed outside her door. Fleck jumped up into her arms, watching them warily.

"Lara. You need to come with us." The older of the two stated as she walked up.

"Can I just drop my pack inside?" Lara asked.

"Best just come along now." She said and started down the hall.

So, with a bit of trepidation, Lara turned to follow. They led her to the Great Hall, where they were joined by Shauna.

It was late in the evening and most students were in their rooms for the night. The few that were around knew better than to hang out this close to the Bedtime Bell, especially with the headmaster right here. And so, although a very public space, they were mostly alone.

"Lara," Shauna began in a formal tone. "It has come to our attention that you are breaking Code 4.ii.b. I had hoped you knew better than to flout our rules. Especially considering the way you arrived here."

"I'm sorry. What is Code 4.ii.b. supposed to be? I didn't realize I was breaking any rules. I have been doing my best in class to learn the rules around here. Aren't we just on section 3 of the Code in class this week?" Lara tried to keep the annoyance out of her voice, but she was tired, and these rules were ridiculous if you asked her. Which, of course, no one had.

Shauna lifted a finger and punctuated each word, pointing directly at Fleck, still perched in Lara's arms. "No pets allowed."

Lara froze. Her arms instinctively squeezing Fleck tighter in her grasp. She felt his confusion and realized she was confused herself.

She thought her best first step was to explain. "Fleck isn't just a pet. He is a Pelanor." Hoping that alone would clarify things for Shauna.

"There is no way that creature is a Pelanor. They are make-believe and at your age you should know better. The Code is clear. You have the choice of removing yourself from The Great Stone House, or we will have to remove your pet." To Lara's ears, Shauna sounded just a bit pleased with herself.

"Wait, so you are asking me to choose between Fleck and the possibility of staying here and earning a stone?"

"Well, Lara." Shauna stated with a bit of derision, "You can't have everything go your way all the time."

"But I have a responsibility to him. He is still so young."

"Then that can be your choice."

Lara suddenly got the clear understanding that Shauna did not want her here. She had gotten the impression before, but this was different. This was coercion in Lara's eyes. She bit the inside of her cheeks to keep from saying what she wanted to and instead started thinking rapidly through the situation.

Fleck was just a baby. They had a psychic connection. Tearing them apart would be beyond difficult. In fact, Lara wasn't sure she or Fleck would be able to get through a day without each other. But that was silly. Of course they could. There had been days this week when she was gone all day, and he was fine. And she had been able to communicate with him from a pretty great distance in the woods before they arrived.

But she didn't want to leave him. There were just so many hurdles blocking her way. She needed a friend here. Suddenly, an image of Van,

Iris, and Delly laughing in the garden flashed in her mind. Fleck was communicating with her.

She had a responsibility for him. She was there to help feed him. An image of the dark riverbed where they met flashed in her mind. At first, she thought it was her memory of feeding him, but it hung there. Fleck was pushing it on her, and she realized he was trying to make a point. The dry riverbed, the dying trees, the dark clouds overhead. Their feelings of responsibility for their home were more important than anything else. She realized he was right. She was amazed at how much he understood what was going on, and how much she just knew what he was communicating without words. She felt it as much as she felt her own feelings.

*I can't let them take you and put you in some cage, Fleck.* He showed her the field of flowers on the far side of the waterwall, next to the Brown travelers' outpost.

"Lara, we need your decision. You have your pack. You can head out now if you want," Shauna said in a sugar sweet tone.

"No. I need to stay. I'll drop Fleck off on the far side of the waterwall." Lara paused, realizing she needed permission from Shauna. "If it's alright for me to be late to bed tonight."

Shauna's eyes got a bit larger. "Lara, I thought this animal was important to you?"

"Yes, but I have to stay," Lara said with the determination she was mustering up. "I have to stay." She said again quietly to Fleck, who sent her the agreement she needed from him.

Shauna turned to the two guards and nodded curtly. "Show Lara to the waterwall. Don't bring her back unless the animal stays." She looked at Lara one more time and with a tone Lara felt was just a bit too smug, said, "Rules are rules, Lara. They are the cornerstone of blue, and necessary for society to run. What would this world be without our order?"

Lara knew it was a rhetorical question and also knew that Shauna would not want to hear her thoughts on this topic. Indeed, Lara was beginning to think she was not a good fit for the blue stone at all.

The two young guards joined her and Fleck for the walk to the waterwall, but as they reached the guards on the city side of the bridge, they stayed, joining them. Lara, on the other hand, walked under the water slowly, clutching Fleck in her arms. She had not wanted to let go for a moment since leaving Shauna. Each step felt surreal.

When they reached the far side of the waterwall, it was dark out. She sat on the grass near the side of the path, placing Fleck in her lap. Looking up at moon in the sky, she marveled at the ability to even see the moon. The shape was an odd semi-rounded shape more than half full, but not completely round.

Slowly she stroked from the tip of Fleck's nose all the way down his narrow back, then cupped his fluffy tail and pulled all the way to the tip. He purred lovingly, and she continued to pet him for a few minutes. She hadn't heard him purr often, and at that moment, she was pretty sure it was the cutest thing she had ever experienced. Then she remembered her own children running down a path with peals of laughter and sleeping with their curls soft on the pillow. Fleck really was that precious to her. She loved him. How could she do this to him?

Would she even be able to earn the right to a stone, and would she even get a stone? Hyacinth and others had been supportive in her quest, but she had trouble believing it was worth losing Fleck over. This could take months, years, even.

Fleck didn't seem to think so. He showed her an image of the full moon. *Come on, there is no way I can stonegraft that quickly.* She laughed. But he just jumped out of her arms and ran around her joyfully, like it had already been accomplished.

"I really don't think I can do this without you. I don't think I can leave you. Look, I have my pack right here already. We could head back to Calambria. You can meet James and the goat. You can meet my daughters!"

He stopped short in front of her. He looked at her with his deep gray eyes, which seemed to hold so much wisdom. Then he scampered over to her adorably, in stark contrast to the wisdom she had felt a moment ago. He placed his tiny paws on her cheeks, and she lowered her forehead to his. It was soft and warm. Then he inundated her with images. The dark sky. The drought ridden fields. The dry riverbed. The naked trees, trunks tipping toward the ground from lack of dirt to hold on to, their roots pulled up. And again, the dark sky, a moving image of the clouds gray and hostile, rolling across in stormy waves.

She felt ill. Slowly, he dropped his paws and stepped back. "It's up to us, isn't it? There is no one else." Fleck seemed to understand what was needed. He was willing to stay on this side of the wall and wait for her to accomplish this. But was she willing to leave him?

She stood pulling him up in her arms and gave him one final huge hug. She worried that she might hurt him, she squeezed so hard, but he just purred and confirmed his affection. When she loosened her grip, he leapt to the ground and scampered toward the field.

She turned from him, stiffened her shoulders, and walked back through the waterwall. She didn't have to watch him as he bounced into the field, because he sent her images as he did so. He wasn't worried at all.

She, on the other hand, worried that she was making the biggest mistake yet. But she had no choice. This had to happen, and it had to happen quickly. It had been too easy to lull into feelings of accomplishment from successfully completing her first trial, but four more to go and then stonegrafting too? And Fleck thought she could do it before the full moon?

She laughed at his faith in her, and that started a flood of emotion. The tears started coming fast and furious. He was going to be OK. She was not so sure about herself.

# Possibilities

Lara had avoided the lunchroom so far, opting to enjoy lunch with Fleck and Van in the gardens. With Fleck gone she and Van had decided it would be less sad for them to just join the other students in the rush and chaos of the cafeteria.

She found Delly easily in the crowd of tables, her bright orange curls shining. Sitting down on the uncomfortably narrow bench at the crowded table Lara thought she might continue her lunches outside even without Fleck.

"Where's Brandon?" Lara asked as she realized he was the only one in their cohort of students not already seated at the table.

Iris smiled a sly smile, and Delly just laughed. Lara looked more closely at the students waiting for an answer, and noticed even Stella had a bit of a smile that might be touching her eyes at least.

Van looked at the girls with confusion, "What's so funny? Where is he?"

Stella nodded to a table on the far side of the large room. There was Brandon at a table with a bunch of two-banded students. "I don't get it, why is it funny that he is over there?" Van asked.

Delly added an exaggerated dreamy look to her eyes and clasped her hands to her chest. "Brandon is in loooove." Then she and Iris broke into peals of laughter. Stella looked at them both reproachfully, their behavior obviously unacceptable.

Stella said in a stiff, but kind voice, "He always sits with Daniel."

Lara watched Brandon across the room. He was sitting with a young man a little bit shorter than him. Well, everyone was a little shorter than him. Daniel wore round bright blue glasses and wore his hair in a sweeping loose curve across the top of his head. Lara thought it must take a lot of time to keep it styled that way. Brandon said something and the whole table laughed, and Daniel rested his head on Brandon's shoulder, and Brandon kissed his swoopy hair. "Aww, it's nice to see him so happy."

Lara took a sidelong glance at Van and noticed he suddenly looked pretty happy too. She also noticed his furtive look at Iris. Ahh, young love.

"Brandon has been in a relationship with Daniel for two years." Stella said. "It was hard last year when Daniel was already over here, but they figured out the best way to make it work. Now, whenever we have time with the whole school, he is generally choosing Daniel's group over ours." Stella sounded a bit put out. "He even spends his nights with him. It has made studying a bit difficult. I had hoped to be his study partner." She gave Iris a searing look. "And now my back up study partner would rather study with an outsider."

"Oh Stella, grow up. Delly is great, and you know it. I've seen you smile a few times at her jokes."

Stella froze; her eyes narrowed. "Iris, I just don't understand how you can possibly think that these are your friends, they have nothing in common with us. Azural is best when we are true to blue."

Lara had never seen Iris angry, but her temper was flared now. "Stella," she gritted out through clenched teeth. "I would rather be true to the blue tenets than be true to stuck in the mud blue-before-anyone-else followers like you!" She slammed her hands on the table and grabbed her tray, storming off.

Stella sputtered and then looked around the table realizing it was just the outsiders she had just complained about left sitting with her. Lara recognized the pain in her eyes and felt sorry for her. Stella didn't know any better. It seemed that her father had not been as honest with her about the rest of Chroma as Iris' had. She had a lot to learn.

"Stella," Lara said quietly, trying not to push after the heated conversation, "if the blue tenets are important to you, I think you might benefit from thinking about what they really mean to you, not just what Azural and the rule books say."

Stella looked at Lara with a harsh demeaning look, "You don't know anything about Blue. Our tenets, our rules and laws. Who are you to tell me about Blue?"

Lara took a deep breath. "The blue tenets are human attributes Stella. We all have them. They are important to everyone. You don't have to be born here to understand how important it is to be honest or responsible. Azural isn't the only place those characteristics exist."

Lara thought she saw Stella's eyes show a bit of a quizzical look before she huffed and pushed away from the table herself.

Lara picked up her grilled cheese sandwich and was wondering at the fact that everything here looked blue. How could food that looked blue be so delicious. She remembered the blue sparkles of Fallon's magic seeping into the ground and thought that the magic had seeped into everything here.

"I wonder what Detmer is doing here." Delly commented across from her. Lara and the others looked up and turned to see what Delly was looking at.

Detmer was walking along the tables. It was obvious that this didn't happen often because most of the students in the room who had noticed him had heads together and were watching as he walked through the room.

He walked up to their table and after a nod to the table at large said, "Lara, can I have a word please?"

"Of course," Lara placed her sandwich down on her tray and stood, following Detmer to a more remote corner.

He handed her a piece of paper, "I have an addition to your schedule."

"I'm not sure I can take more on Detmer. Losing Fleck was-" she couldn't quite find the words. "Last night was horrible," she whispered.

"You want to go Lara." He added an unsaid weight to the words. Lara suddenly realized this might be the meeting she was waiting for. Looking down at the note it simply said, *One o'clock - East Water Garden*. When she looked back up to ask Detmer for more details, he was already walking away. Well, she would get her answers soon enough.

ǏǏǏ

Lara's mind was reeling with possibilities, could Detmer's mysterious friend finally be reaching out to her? She hadn't been to the East side of The Stone House and really wanted to see the ocean. She had felt the pull of it ever since she arrived but had not found the time with all the rules and schedules.

The archway to the East Water Garden was closed off with a thin wall of water. She was getting better at traversing them without the water getting in her eyes, the lifting of the left arm almost second nature now. When she passed through, she got her first full open view of the ocean. It was stunning and powerful and pulled her toward it. She felt suddenly small and insignificant at the same time as she felt fulfilled and empowered. It was a strange balance. The stone paths from the house changed to sand beneath her feet and the wild grasses that grew out of the peaks of sand dunes quickly hid the Stone House, and the tall buildings of downtown beyond the House from sight.

She saw a tall figure standing in a deep blue cloak near the water's edge. Assuming this was who she needed to meet with, she headed over. Not wanting to startle them, Lara called out "hello" when she was nearing, since they hadn't responded to her so far.

"Hello, Lara." It was a deep voice, but it crackled with age. There was patience with it, the words spoken slowly and carefully. He didn't turn to her, so she went to stand beside him. As she came to stand beside him, she could feel a hum of power. It even distracted her from the raging sea and waves before them.

At his side, she finally got a look at his face. He looked to be decades older than her, but healthy and stronger than those similar to his age back home. She felt something stronger from him, though. The power that radiated from him was that of dependability. She felt an immediate sense that she trusted him, not that she could trust him, but that she already did. She felt calm and at peace, as though he was taking on her burdens.

The power than emanated from this waterweaver left no question that he was a founder. She stood beside the vast energy of the ocean and it was diminished by Axel's vibrance.

"Tell me why you have come to Azural." He didn't sound judgmental to Lara, as most of the others in powerful positions had. His question was that of an intelligent person wanting to understand.

She thought for a moment about how much to tell. "I'm here to save my home. Our village has run out of water, and we need the power to restore water, or everyone will have to leave."

"So, it's true," he said quietly, "the Wastes are real."

Lara turned to face him, the blue of the ocean reaching out to her right, the blue of the sky above her, the dark blue of the shale cliff behind him. He even stood before her in a blue cloak. She was surrounded by the thing she most desperately needed back home: water, but also color. They had lost so much to these color realms. She couldn't even put it into words. Her sadness at what her home had lost sat on her chest as she tried to communicate all their needs. "Yes, the Wastes are real, and we are losing more resources every day. Can you come? What we need is a color weaver to bring blue back to the Shadowlands. To bring our river back to life."

He smiled at her and reached out his right hand to her right shoulder. An awkward motion that brought him very close to her. She could suddenly see the age on his face, the lines of years lived, and the dullness of eyes that couldn't see clearly. She realized he was older than she had thought. He was frail, but his hand on her shoulder sent a shock of pure peace through her. "I am afraid I cannot. I am not the one who will fix it. You are."

# Absolutes

Lara was struggling to concentrate on what Axel was saying to her. She had been so hopeful that he might just come along with her and fix the river, and instead he was saying it was her. All of her fears and insecurities hit her, and her mind reeled again, wondering if someone else, anyone else might have been a better choice to be standing here with one of the most powerful stonegrafted in the Realm.

She knew she needed to be more present, and focused her mind on the words, making herself listen to Axel rather than the stream of consciousness fear mongering of her mind. "There are two sides to all emotion, as there are to all things in life. For balance to exist, nothing is all positive, and so we shall discuss all the emotions of the blue stone.

"As you have already learned in your classes so far, we strive for peace, honesty, intelligence, and dependability. Being a giver rather than taker, having a serene spirit in all things, being a reliable and trustworthy companion, for we truly take pleasure in helping others. We love to live in organized environments and feel at peace when we are surrounded by less. We strive to be good listeners and create order and harmony in our actions and environments. Blue loves to communicate, be supportive, and a dependable friend. We feel emotions and are sensitive and aware of the feelings surrounding us. We are nostalgic, appreciating our past and what it has taught us."

As Axel droned on Lara was reminded of Granny Sanders speaking. Was it something that came with age that made people give soliloquies?

She realized that at another time she might have thought this interesting, but right now she just wanted answers, solutions.

"But as I shared, there are dark sides to the blue stones' power also. Emotions that risk our hearts and souls. They still power the stone, but they come from a place that will drain you, and possibly even hurt yourself and those around you. Loneliness and coldness could push you further from people, feeling that others have betrayed you and hurt you deep to your core will certainly connect with the blue stone, but these emotions come at a cost to you." Here Axel paused, and Lara knew there was a real memory connected to his lesson. He shook his head slightly and continued. "If we are not surrounded by order, we can become overwhelmed by disorganization and chaos, cutting us off from our connection to the stone. Nostalgia could go too far, with us lingering in the past rather than the present."

Lara heard the emotion push through when he spoke of nostalgia. She considered her own busy life and thought of how much more this man had been through. She wondered about what he might be nostalgic about.

"Blue's love of order can go too far and become rigid and authoritative." Lara's mind immediately went to Shauna. "The balance is tenuous, and it takes a strong person to know when they have crossed the line. Often though, even if there is a better way, the status quo will be followed, for change is difficult for Blue. Predictability is revered for order helps calm Blue's nerves.

"Too many of our weavers have become cemented in their beliefs that they know what is best. We have a very passionate group of leaders here at the Great Hall and in the city. But often, passion can blind one to the truths they don't want to see."

He led her over the dunes, back toward the stone arch, and sat slowly on a bench beside a pond. "I am about to tell you something I have told no one but Detmer." He held a hand for her to be seated beside him. As she sat, she saw blue filter from his arm and a rush of water surrounded them in slow swirls, cutting them off from any watching eyes and muffling the outside world, and their conversation, from unwelcome ears.

"When my friends and I first found the stones, we were so very young. Youth looks at the world with such absolutes, looks at the moment, and reacts to it. Do you know the history of the waterwall?"

Lara nodded. "I have heard the basics. You put it up not long after the stone collecting had been completed to protect Azural."

"Not my proudest moment looking back. I reacted in pain and all of Azural has followed suit. We have remained closed off from the world living behind our wall, focused on the Blue tenets, order most of all.

"Every year I watch these youths enter The Stone House, and with each year I see our lessons focus more and more on Order. I am not sure that is the most important tenet anymore. The more I see of these young people, the more I think our choices are too controlling. We are making decisions based on what we have always done, even if we know there is a better way.

"I realized watching you these past few weeks that you bring something none of our weavers or initiates have brought before earning a stone. Wisdom. We all became weavers in our youth. Hotheaded and so sure that we knew what we were doing. It has taken me a long time to admit where I was wrong, and it has been very difficult to open the eyes and change the minds of our current leadership.

"When my fears have been brought up with the other Blue Weavers they react with indignation. The order here, the internal peace and responsibility to our community, have clouded the judgment of the other weavers and they see only Blue. I now feel the responsibility to the whole of our world. I remember fondly the days before the stones. My childhood years where we were surrounded by the rainbow the world used to be. I love Azural and Blue, and believe in everything it stands for, but I feel the loss of my friends, of the benefits they brought to my life. I would like to see all of us here in Azural reach past our borders and see the world start to right itself."

Lara felt his sincerity. His words brought her own struggle with the breaking world over her lifetime into a succession of images. As a girl the bright blue sky, yellows of the wheat fields, green of the pastures, red of the roses. Then as a teen the slow sapping of the color until it was just a dull gray, even the water they had reflected the dust and overcast skies rather than the radiant blue she saw around her here.

"I don't have time. Water is running out now." The pressure of her responsibility to her home pushed on her and she sunk her shoulders, feeling the impossibility of the situation. "You say I am the one to bring water back, well by the time I jump through your rings, my home will be a ghost town, all of my neighbors having moved on."

"Aha, but Detmer and I have come up with a plan." He sounded like a child with a sneaky secret. The thrill of it seemed to take years off of his face, the wrinkles switching from lines of concern and burden to laughter, raising his face she saw the adding twinkle in his eyes. "We shall just skip the rings." He said with triumph.

"Detmer and I can sneak you into the Stone Chamber and you can attempt to stonegraft. Do it as many times as you need to. By day, go to your classes, and each evening we will try. I feel your energy. I have seen a lot of youth over the years, and I have never been wrong about who has the potential. I remember the day each of the waterweavers first walked into that Great Stone Hall. You can do this."

Lara was taken aback. She had thought that everyone here was on board with the hoops that you had to jump through. And here she was with the original Blue colorweaver, one of The Finders, and he was encouraging her to skip ahead.

"But what about Order? If I skip the rings, won't I be flouting the emotion that the blue stone needs?"

"Don't be fooled by the definition of our tenets. We have defined them to distraction and now the meaning we adhere to at the Stone House is too absolute. The stone does not work in absolutes. It works with the individual, one on one with emotions. You are working to bring order to the whole world. That will resonate with the stone." He said. "Also, you will need to have a clear connection with the stone on multiple levels. Order is just one of the pieces of the puzzle in the connection."

# Memories

As Lara walked away from him, Axel turned back to the beach. Slowly, he lowered his creaking bones into the warm sand. He relished the feel of the gritty sand in his hands and smoothed away the top layer to reveal the cool, damp layer underneath. Memories flooded in as he sat quietly with his face turned up toward the sun in the bright blue sky.

At the time, they had felt so grown up and sure of themselves. Carlie had just turned sixteen, so they all were celebrating by exploring the paths up the mountains. It had been wild and difficult terrain, but the day had been sunny and cool. Perfect for a long hike.

The group of seven friends had been traipsing along the overgrown path near the river for hours. They often went exploring together on free days, but this day was the beginning of everything. The beginning of a change in the world that there was no coming back from- a change in themselves that there was no coming back from.

They came across a small cavern cut into the hillside and stopped short. The cave opened up into a secret hideaway. Never in their lives had they seen such beauty. It was a space that held the bluest of waters next to the fire-red of the lava flow, with rich shades of green and flowers in all colors. There in the orange rock of the cavern on the bank of the river bend, they felt the pull of some power they had never felt before. As they neared, they each had different emotions, and slowly they found they were not pulled to the exact same spot.

Carlie felt so excited, she couldn't take her eyes off of the bright orange stone, and as she neared it, she felt the power of it start to reverberate through her.

Artie was always happy, but never had he felt more clearheaded and like there was nothing that could go wrong as he stepped toward the yellow stone.

Mary felt so grounded in the moment, like everything was right and balanced in the world as she moved closer to the green stone.

Becca practically floated and danced over to the pink stone, her heart full of love.

Blade walked with purpose and power up to the red stone.

Stevie slowly reached his hand toward the purple stone. It pulsed with energy as he reveled in the mystery of it.

Axel had been in the rear, so was the last to enter. and saw his friends look more like themselves than they ever had before. He felt more at peace, and he felt the pull of the blue stone set in the banks of the shallow waters. The closer he got, the less he noticed his friends and the more he only felt the stone. It sang to him, called him. In answer, he reached out to pick the stone up, but before he could, it jumped into the air and wisps of color flowed out of it.

Slowly Axel stood as the blue color spun around him and poured into his skin through his outreached right fingers. He was at peace and content. There was nothing scary about this power flowing into him. It was right. As the stone grafted itself into his upper right shoulder, he felt the power surge into him. Blue streaked down his arm and across his shoulder blade, leaving what looked like an inked tattoo in patterns that reminded him of the spray on the crest of a wave. He was pulled into the experience fully and it took him a while to settle once the flow of power subsided. He still felt it there, but it was no longer pulling him toward the stone, for now he and the stone were one. He felt the pulse in his shoulder and knew the power was his. With full trust that the flow would create something beautiful, but without knowing how to put it into words, he reached out with his right arm and focused the power outside himself. The blue reached from his hand and a fountain of water pushed up from the lake. He marveled at his ability. He looked to see if his friends had seen what happened and realized for the first time that he was surrounded by many colors, magic like he had never seen swirling around them all. Purples, reds, pinks, greens, oranges, and yellows reached through the small cove. They all stood and looked at each other, amazed.

The memory faded and Axel looked out again at the sea. He felt a strange feeling of still being that young man, while also being a stranger. Time had taught him so much that he wished he could go back and tell those youths. If only they had known at the time, understood what would happen, how the world would change around them, and how they would change towards each other.

It hadn't been until recently that he had come to terms with their mistakes and admitted that he had been part of the problem. It had been a difficult few years coping with the knowledge that he had to fix something that he was no longer strong enough to undertake. His magic was still powerful, but his body was weak. Lara had shown up just in time. He slowly made his way to standing and turned his back to the waves. He looked over the stone house to the top of the waterwall in the distance.

Lara could help.

# Attempt

Lara headed out to the gardens later that evening. She arrived in the music garden and sat down on a wooden bench, where she was scheduled to meet Detmer just before midnight. She looked up at the night sky. She saw the moon peeking over the treetops. She had still not gotten used to the sight of it. Back home, they hadn't seen the moon from behind cloud cover in ages. Here it was like a clock sitting there in the sky, so reliable. Time had gotten away from her. She had been disconnected in this new setting. The moon was waxing gibbous tonight. It would be full within a week. She felt the weight of time, worried about those back home. The moon had been a waning crescent when she had first seen it on the road to Azural. It had already been weeks. How much time did her loved ones have left?

Time was slipping away from her. She needed to figure out how to control these emotions. She needed to be successful tonight, but was she even capable of stonegrafting?

When Detmer arrived, he didn't say anything to her, just motioned for her to follow him. She nodded and stood. The path he led her down was covered completely by closed off trees. He pulled back a branch and revealed a narrow path leading down a hill. The surrounding trunks were thin and close together. It twisted and turned and had no outlets, just where they had come from or forward. This was not meant to be found by accident. It took about half an hour of walking, and they finally exited the closed space and were in front of a building. It had a domed roof and round walls.

Detmer stopped in front of the door and turned to her. His voice sounded loud and a bit jarring after such a long silence between them. "I have never completed this task, so cannot give you advice, but I know that Axel has faith in you. Focus on your emotions, your feelings, and you can do this. I will be waiting for you here."

"Thank you Detmer," Lara whispered. She already knew her emotions were all over the place. This was never going to work. She stepped through the door. It had to work.

The interior was just one huge room. It had an outer ring of stone about five feet wide, then a channel of water about five feet wide, and then an interior circle. There was an oculus in the center of the ceiling and below it on a pedestal similar to the ones in her trial was sitting a small pile of blue stones. There wasn't much light in here. She imagined that most people came to attempt the stonegrafting during the day and no one had planned for nighttime lighting needs. There was a bridge leading across the water, so Lara walked across and went up to the pillar. The stones were beautiful, and each one unique. Lara reached out and touched one. It was smooth, and she felt a pulse emanating from it. But there was no magical connection. She wasn't quite sure what to expect. She should have asked Axel more questions. She was so ignorant about this, she wasn't ready.

She closed her eyes and focused on her emotions, as Detmer had said. She was feeling stressed. What if she couldn't accomplish this task and she failed? What if her town never got the help it needed?

She was feeling inferior. She thought of Detmer outside, who had all five bands and still had not stonegrafted. She didn't know his story, but if he wasn't good enough to do it, what made her capable?

Lara realized her thoughts were focusing on the wrong emotions. Repeating the tenets: Responsibility, Honesty, Calm, Intelligence, and Order, she would start by calming herself. She took deep breaths and relaxed, trying to keep her mind from the rampant worries.

Once she felt a bit more in control and the tension in her chest had lightened, she focused next on responsibility. She was here because of her need to help her home. What could be more responsible than that? She looked at the stones and thought of her home. She needed the water that these stones could bring. THEY needed the water that these stones could bring. Why was the world so messed up? Why was it her problem? She felt her heartbeat racing and tried to tune into her emotions. She was feeling angry and resentful. These were not blue emotions. She calmed herself.

She began to focus on why she was angry and resentful, so she could work through it. The world was broken and messed up. The stones were all conglomerated into separate spaces and the resources were being practically hoarded, purposefully or not, in these color realms. She couldn't magically snap her fingers and change the big problems, but she could focus and actually maybe change one issue at a time.

The water magic would give Calambria a fighting chance. At least they could continue to survive, and she had an opportunity here. Again, she stood and looked at the stones.

Responsibility - check. Serenity - mostly check. Order - no idea. She hadn't really learned much about this yet, aside from the Codes which she didn't like one bit. But she did like her lists. Honesty - she was always honest with people. Hadn't she told the Senators, Detmer, Shauna and even Axel her true reasons for being here? And what about Fleck? She had been honest there, even though it had hurt.

She wasn't sure where she was lacking, but the stones just sat there, glinting in the pale light of the large room. She had failed.

She knew the main reason was likely how raw her anger felt at this moment. She could practically feel it crawling under her skin. The stones were right there. Everywhere she looked in this realm, water just sat. They used it as decoration, as a plaything. And her family and friends were thirsty, dehydrated.

They had been depending on her and they had made a mistake. She was failing left and right. The headmistress hated her. The people who said they would help were cryptic and only gave her the smallest hints of support. Penny, Hyacinth, Axel, Detmer. A short word of support, but when it came to actual action? They all sat on the sidelines.

Did any of them actually want her to even succeed? Maybe they were just placating her. Maybe they were just sending her on a wild goose chase to keep her busy until she finally just got out of their hair and decided to leave on her own?

The anger she felt turned in on herself. Wasn't she the one her community had sent to fix it? Why did she expect others to do it? This was on her.

She looked up through the oculus window in the center of the room. It showed the black night sky and for a moment she felt a connection with home. The dark emptiness of her homeland. She crumbled to the ground, her hands hitting the stones hard to catch herself. Pain shot through her arms, and she felt agony keenly in her joints. Wrists, elbows and shoulders all held the discomfort, and she relished the suffering for a moment. Those at home were still suffering, and so should she.

Tears of anger and self-pity wracked her, and she heard her sobs echo around this large, cavernous room. They only made her feel her torment more fully. Her own pain feeding itself becomes swelling waves of emotion.

She worked to catch her breath. It wracked through her body and brought her awareness back to the moment. Although her torment was in her head, her whole body felt it. The struggle and strain of her tears were raw in her throat and all of her muscles were tense from the effort.

How did anyone expect her to do this alone? She missed Fleck. He had been her support. She looked up through the oculus again. From her vantage point here on the floor, the cylinder pedestal sat in her view also, and she could see a slight hint of one of the blue stones as it sat on the top of the pile.

She wondered if she might be able to connect with him from this far away. Slowly, she reached out with her thoughts. She tried to picture the field he was in. The image she created felt superficial. Maybe… She tried imagining walking down the path to the waterwall and under the waterwall and then the field on the other side was there. It was a much more powerful image, but it was just a memory of her time there when she dropped him off.

She didn't feel any connection. She wondered how he sent her images so clearly. She wondered if he saw images she sent toward him. Maybe she needed to turn this around.

She centered her thoughts and stood. She focused on the sight in front of her.

The image became super clear in her mind. She scored her brain with it. The stones glinted with the edge of the moonlight peeking into the oculus. The blue color overwhelmed her, and she felt the tears that she thought had been used up continue down her cheeks. She closed her eyes and felt a twinge of pain searing her face from her puffy, red eyelids. Once closed, she realized she had a complete image in her mind. The magical stones sat in her mind as clearly as they did in front of her eyes. She focused on the little details, the variegated lines, the different hues, the range in sizes. Once she felt completely settled in the image, she sent it out. She wasn't sure what she was doing or where it was going. She just sent it out in every direction, she sent it with clear thought. *So close, but I failed.*

It was a strange feeling. There wasn't any power to sending out the thought. It was just a clear image in her mind. But then. She felt a ping. She couldn't explain the how, but she knew exactly the where. She felt where Fleck was. It was powerful. One moment they were disconnected and suddenly she felt his thoughts. She was scared to open her eyes and break the connection. His excitement was powerful.

The image of the stones in her mind was suddenly drowned out by a blinding puff of orange. She opened her eyes to save them from the bright color that permeated her mind but was startled to see that the orange sparkles sat in the air surrounding her as well. When it cleared, she saw Fleck sitting on the edge of the pedestal, staring at the stones with reverence.

"What!?" Lara sputtered.

Fleck looked up at her with innocent eyes. His excitement at being with the stones and back with her was all he could convey.

She looked down at the stones again. His excitement rubbing off on her. She felt it seep into the cracks in her psyche. She might not have succeeded tonight, but she was closer than ever. Fleck agreed.

Lara watched as Fleck looked down at the stones. His eyes, though light grey, looked almost blue to her, and she felt a subtle shift in him. He looked possessive. He looked back up at her and his eyes held the blue color even though they were no longer reflecting the stones.

The mystery of Fleck came front and center, hitting her hard. "Fleck, what are you?"

But he didn't know either. His mind was run over by confusion, and he jumped into her arms for comfort. *I guess we will just have to figure these things out as we go,* Lara thought.

Fleck was in her arms, relishing their connection. They both resonated with concern and care for the other, and she felt how much her own broken-ness felt mended as she felt a similar pain in him. She soaked it in. It helped her immensely. She was not alone.

She had been so focused on her failure to connect with the stone that she had forgotten to separate herself from the specific task. She was not a failure just because of this single moment.

Fleck sent a wave of cheerful emotion toward her and made a small chittering sound that sounded like laughter. He again sent her an image of the full moon, and Lara recognized it to be set in the center of the oculus above them.

She slowly smoothed her hand along his head, it felt so good to have him back with her. "We are going to have to keep you hidden, I don't think that Shauna will give us a second chance if she finds you." Lara heard her words echo through the cavernous room. *I wonder if we should practice thinking to each other instead, it's probably good practice anyway.*

She felt his agreement. *Well, best hide away, probably best no one but maybe Van even knows you are back.* Fleck slid under the cowl of her cloak and when he settled, she walked to the door and smiled sadly at Detmer. "No luck, I am afraid."

He stepped inside, smiling encouragement. He quietly walked across the bridge and stood at the stone's altar, looking at the stones reverently. Lara could sense his contemplation.

"Detmer, do you want to talk about it? About why you haven't stonegrafted? If you don't, I understand."

"My mother was one of the first blue color weavers after Axel. Her name was Sansa, and she was the most beautiful person I ever saw, black hair in tight curls, deep blue eyes, tall and strong. She and Axel were young and always so sure of themselves. They just knew that what they thought was the best way. They never considered consequences and just pushed forward. She was integral in the process of collecting the blue stones. She was a shining example of how great these stones are. People looked up at her and were awed by her power. When I was a kid, I ran around the halls of this grand building when it was brand new. My whole life I have watched the youth come and attempt to earn stones. I have watched the process, and I have seen successes and failures. When it was my turn and I was of age, I did what was expected of me. I took the classes; I passed the tests. But when it was time for me to come into this room and finish the process..." He paused and looked almost startled that he had spoken so much.

He shook off his cobwebs of thoughts and continued, "I came in here all alone, just me and these magic blue stones and I thought for the first time about what I wanted - about what I thought about the process - about where I wanted to be when I grew up. I stayed on the far side of that water. I never even made it over that bridge and this close to them." He raised his eyes and looked at the far side of the room and Lara pictured a younger Detmer with sad eyes standing there. "I was sure that I did not want to be a color weaver. I didn't like what they did with their days, stuck here in The Great Stone House with an attitude of assurance that they were always right. I also really didn't like the fact that the choice had never been mine. And so, I took my control, and I walked out. My mother never really understood it. I never had the strength of character to be honest with her about what happened in this room. And when I finally was mature enough to tell her, she was gone. She passed away about twenty years ago. Her stone was returned to the pile, that one there was hers."

He reached out and almost touched one of the lighter colored blue stones near the back of the altar. "The real irony is that I am still stuck here, a cog in the system; one that I have known my whole life is wrong." He gave an ironic laugh and then looked up at her with a sparkle in his eye. "But I think things are about to change. Between you showing up and Axel's new attitude, I think we might just fix things. Maybe there is a future for me in a world where things are balanced and considered, rather than assumed and taken."

He looked happier than he had when he had first started sharing with Lara. She was always glad to hear what was in people's hearts. It often helped her see her own heart just a bit more clearly. She liked to understand people and that helped her understand herself. She gave him an encouraging smile, and they headed toward the door. Feeling Flecks heartbeat against her back she was reminded of how good it felt to know she really wasn't in this alone.

# Mending

Lara picked a garden she thought would be quieter on the far side of the island to take Fleck to play the next morning. It had been a bit chilly, so as she was taking her cloak out of the armoire to attach to her uniform, she had seen her original black cloak, the tear in the lower side gawked at her. She never would have left something like that for so long at home. She had bundled it up and added it to her pack along with the sewing kit that she had found in the storage of her room.

As she sat listening to the waves crash on the far side of the wall, she pulled out her cloak and the sewing kit. Opening the kit, she saw it was full of brand new tools, a shining thimble, an assortment of needles in many sizes, and of course, the thread was all blue. As she began to thread her needle Fleck, who had been playing in the sandy area near the wall sent her a warning and darted into the fronds of plants along the edge of the garden.

She looked up to see Stella walking along dejectedly. Lara had never seen her in a natural state, it seemed that Stella was usually wearing a mask of control, because this Stella looked much more human and real to Lara. Her heart ached a bit for the poor lost daughter of a mother who made the choice to leave her. Lara took a moment to hate the mother for the choice, and then realized she had no idea what her story was. But she sure did hate what it had done to Stella.

Taking a calming breath and then sending Fleck a warning about staying out of sight, Lara called out. "Good morning, Stella."

Stella looked up startled and Lara saw the mask of indifference cover her open emotions. "Good morning."

"I'm just sewing up this hole in my original traveling cape. You are welcome to join me. This is a nice garden; I hadn't seen it before this morning." Lara motioned to the bench seat next to her and was surprised when Stella came over to look at what she was up to.

"I've always wanted to learn to sew." Stella said quietly, as if it was a secret.

"Oh, well, have a seat. I have taught tons of people how to sew, including my own four kids. There are plenty of needles in this kit."

Lara spread her old black cloak across both of their knees and walked Stella through the threading of the needle and some basic straight stitches using her cloak to practice on. Once Stella felt confident, Lara moved on to mending the large tear from her fall down the cliff at the beginning of her trip. She was stuck in contemplation, thinking of how far she had come with little real success yet, when Stella called out to two more walking down the path. "Good morning, Weaver Fallon, Weaver Penny."

Well, this was not what Lara had been expecting in what she thought was a quiet corner of the island. She shook her head as she realized that there were too many people on this little island, someone was always close by. "Come join us if you'd like." Lara called out. "We are just working on some sewing."

Penny and Fallon walked up and joined them on the bench facing them. "Is that your cloak Lara?" Fallon asked.

Stella looked at him incredulously. "Of course it is. No one else here is from the Wastes are they?"

All three of the adults took a moment staring at Stella. The young woman had been very vocal about how although Lara was an outsider, it was unlikely she had come from the Wastes. Lara raised her eyebrows and said cautiously, "Stella, I thought you said you didn't believe in the Wastelands?"

Stella sighed. "Well. I've been paying attention, and Weaver Penny can vouch for me, I am pretty smart. This cloak alone tells us the truth. You must have owned this for decades. It's threadbare and has been mended so many times that my practice stitches have passed over multiple others."

Penny smiled. "Yes, Stella, you are very bright. I agree Fallon, of course it is Lara's cloak, what a silly question."

"Of course." Fallon smiled at himself.

Stella looked up, and Lara was happy to see that her face was not the usual mask of indifference. "Weaver Fallon? Lara and I were talking yesterday, and she said something that has had me thinking." Lara was surprised again. What was this about? "She said that Blue tenets are human characteristics and that they aren't just true for Azurans."

"I would say that I agree with that Stella. We are all human. Any of us, whether from Orange like your friend Delly, Blue like the three of us, or even from the Wastes like Lara here. We are all capable of the virtues that our Blue stones embody. We are all capable of holding those tenets clear in our minds and if dedicated enough becoming waterweavers."

Stella wasn't done, Lara could see her truly processing the information, thinking it over and more questions appearing. Lara loved watching young minds open to new possibilities.

"But I don't understand. If we are taught to be responsible, how can we close the water off and keep it from communities like Lara's?"

Lara was floored. Here, she thought that Stella was the last person in Azural to come around and she had been listening on the sidelines to all of the conversations Lara had been having. She had been thinking and processing and she was now speaking the very thing Lara had been trying to get across to the people she most needed to hear it.

Lara looked with tear-filled eyes to Fallon, wondering what his answer might be.

He looked as confused as Stella, like it was a new concept for him. "I just don't know. The rules are here for us to take care of our home, our loved ones. I am not sure I have ever questioned it before." He looked desperately at Penny for help and support.

Penny looked at Stella, then locked eyes with Lara. "Sometimes we need to hear the truth from the right source for it to sink in."

# Responsibility to Whom?

Lara was preoccupied with her thoughts as she headed toward the hidden entrance to the stonegrafting hall path. The morning conversation with Stella had shown her that there was a real chance to convince people in Azural of the need for help. The conversations just had to be held. People needed to talk about the hard things they didn't want to. Being herself and kind to Stella had opened Stella's eyes to the truth about outside the waterwall.

Fleck was curled around her neck, sending vibes in support or discouragement as she sorted through her plan to approach the stone this time. She took a moment to be amazed at how well they communicated now. Fleck didn't use a single word, but she knew that he understood her emotions and thoughts. He was still such a baby, and they had only been connected for a few weeks now; she knew this connection was just going to become stronger as he grew up.

Her plan was simple and similar to the last time she was with the stone. But this time, she was not going to allow her fears to take over. She would meditate to start, settling herself into a Calm state. Fleck sent a wave of approval that almost felt like a pat on her back. So strange. Then she would—

Lara was abruptly pulled from her thoughts, hearing, "Ahem! Did you not see me, Lara?"

Lara turned in place and saw that she must have walked right past Shauna on the path. "Oh, I am so sorry, Headmistress. I was completely lost in my thoughts." Lara focused on impressing upon Fleck to stay out of sight. He seemed completely fine with that plan.

"I could see that. I am actually quite pleased to have bumped into you. I think we need to have a little chat."

Lara could tell immediately that this was not meant to be so much a friendly chat as a headmistress 'putting a student in their place' chat. "Of course, Headmistress. What would you like to discuss?"

"I am sure by now you are aware of how things work here at The Great Stone House. We have a process and clear steps. The Tenets, Trials and Rings help every citizen of Azural find the proper place for themselves. It helps our whole realm function with success. I have been a waterweaver for twenty years and seen us grow this land into the amazing, self-sufficient realm it is today." Lara felt uneasy. She had already figured Shauna for a lover of the rules, but being confronted with it directly was jarring.

"Yes. Azural is amazing."

The weaver seemed to square her shoulders. "Lara, you are not meant to be here. Our agenda is to strengthen the Realm by teaching our youth and preparing them. To be frank, you are not a youth, which is problem enough, but even more so, you do not even want to stay here in Azural. I think it is time to end this farce and for you to just head home."

Lara was floored that Shauna felt so strong that she would say this to her face.

"Yes, Lara," Shauna practically spat out the words, "I supported sending you away when you first arrived. You shouldn't be here. I know that, and I think deep down you know it, too."

Lara visibly saw Shauna control her temper. She pulled all of the anger in and her face became a cool reserved mask, the tendons in her neck tightening. "It must be left up to you now. You need to leave."

Lara paused before she responded. Shauna needed to understand. She was sure once she heard about the plight of her home and the truth of the Wastes, this intelligent waterweaver would come around. "I can't leave. I am the only chance for my home to survive."

"YOUR home to survive? You think that to save your home you must take from us here in Azural? The way of things is clear. If your home has turned into nothing but a wasteland, it is obvious to me that it is time to find the place you are all meant to be. The tenets of each realm are meant to help us all find our place in this world. You should go home and tell them that. It is time to see the world for what it is. Why would you all try to stay behind, when it is obvious the world is made anew?"

Lara's mind reeled. She shouted responses in her head but tried to keep them contained and keep her face calm. Take from Azural indeed. Where did Shauna think those stones came from in the first place? She remembered the stories her grandmother told her of the harvesters pouring into Calambria, they searched every corner of the world for the stones. If they had never been taken in the first place, Calambria would be doing just fine. Thank you. But she knew better than to say any of that, instead she said, "You are right, of course. The world is a new place."

Lara settled into a new understanding. The knowledge that between the Senators and Shauna there were many who benefited from the way the world was now. She would not find support just because she explained the truth to them. They might be open to believing the truth, as Stella had just taught her, but with them in power they were less likely to want change. "You've given me a lot to think about, headmistress. I had best be on my way."

"It's a bit chilly tonight. Where are you off to?"

There was a short spike in Lara's heart rate as she realized honesty was the only option here. But she couldn't tell Shauna about the stone chamber. Shauna would absolutely not approve of Axel's plan. "I was just heading to a meeting with Detmer."

Shauna gave her a short appraising look and then shook her head firmly back and forth. "I do hope you will reconsider your plans to stay at the Stone House, Lara."

"Oh, I am definitely thinking about that myself." Lara stated flatly and continued down the path. *I need to get out of here as quickly as I can, but I need to do it WITH a stone.* Fleck agreed wholeheartedly.

# *Stone*

When Lara entered the round room and closed the door behind her, Fleck jumped down onto the outer ring of the floor. The domed ceiling loomed high overhead, and the moonlight coming in the oculus shone down directly on the stones. She caught glints of turquoise and navy, all shades of blue. Slowly she crossed the narrow stone bridge over the water surrounding the center leaving Fleck behind to watch. The inner floor was a circle of solid stone about twelve feet wide.

Rather than walking straight to the center podium with the stones, she began by slowly walking around the floor along the water's edge. The tension in her neck from her interaction with Shauna and knowing she must succeed highlighted to her how stressed she was. She needed to let that go. Slowing her breathing and relaxing her muscles, she followed the ring of water, bringing her awareness to her steps. When she had gone full circle and reached the entrance, she was already much calmer, so she turned and took a step toward the stone, then turned again and walked around in the other direction.

This time, her focus was on organizing her thoughts. She needed to connect with the stone, which meant she needed to feel the emotions fully. Her failure last time had been from feeling too many emotions that clashed with the blue power. She knew she needed to focus on the Blue tenets: Serenity, Order, Intelligence, Reliability, and Honesty, but she thought she needed to go beyond. She was tired of looking at all of this through the rules of this Realm. She needed to start looking at the stones in a more personal way.

What about trust?

Her family, friends, and home trusted her with this. They had sent her because they knew that she could do it. She had their trust, which meant that she had already met the trustworthy criteria.

Reliability? She had always been reliable. When people needed her, she was there for them. She felt a weight on her shoulders when others needed help, as if the yoke was just assumed. If they needed help, she was the one to take it on.

Honesty? This was where she still struggled inside herself. She tried to be honest in her words and deeds, but was she honest in her heart? The stone's power connected with the truth there. She tried her best to think honestly about what she was attempting.

The blue stone's power would save her home. She felt confident that she could control the power the same way that the other waterweavers did. She was aware of the expectation from others, asking it of her. Did she want it for herself, or just for others?

She stepped a step closer. The stone lay just out of her arms reach to her right, and she continued with her slow circles around it. She closed her eyes and pictured the gardens around The Stone House: sparkling fountains of water, fish in the gurgling ponds, the ocean waves on the shore. Then she pictured the city: canals bustling with city folk, the shops and buildings, people going about their busy days. Then she pictured her home: the color immediately stripped from her imagination, the grime and dirt, the empty well in the town square, her favorite seat by the river now just a trickling stream.

She wanted to fix it. She wanted to be able to bring home the help that was needed. To show them that she could do what they believed she could. And, if she was honest, she wanted to show herself she could do it.

She was fully capable of being more than she allowed herself to be. She was tired of trying to define herself outside of her family. Had she not had the most success with Stella, when she connected with her the way she had taught her own children? Being a mother was part of her. She could accept that, rather than hide it. She didn't need to move past it now that the kids had grown. She would always be a mother; it was ingrained in her now.

A floodgate of emotion welled up as she admitted this to herself. She realized tears were running down her cheeks. She opened her eyes and saw that one of the stones had light blue wisps of magic reaching out slowly into the air.

She was going to help her community, but she would also be able to do so much more.

Maybe she could start to fix this whole broken world. So few held the power of the stones, and she could be one to bring new thinking to the power structures. Help them see that Order and Serenity were important, but that they had to reach out past the borders of Blue. They had to see what was going on beyond the waterwall.

She could be the honest voice that was needed for the Wastelands, now that she was being honest with herself. She wanted to be something great. She wanted to be more than the person others came to when they needed advice. She needed to be more. But that trust they held in her made her stronger. It gave her the support she needed to do the strong, impossible things.

She slowly reached her right hand up to touch a wisp of blue and felt a tingle of power as her fingers met it. As her hand passed through the wisp, it didn't dissipate as she thought it might. Instead, the cerulean magic followed her hand as it moved past. Slowly, the blue color shifted to darker shades and curled around her arm.

She held her palm up and moved her arm slowly from side to side a few inches and was engrossed in the way the misty blue tendrils of light mirrored her actions. They were winding around her arm and slowly reaching up. She turned her palm over and reached toward the stone, ready now for all that it meant to be a blue colorweaver. She knew it was time. She was ready. She reached out, but the stone met her halfway. It jumped up, lifted and surrounded by the blue misty light it flew toward her. In a flash of brilliant, bright blue light, that she saw as much in her mind as before her eyes, she felt a burning in her upper arm.

Power rushed through her, radiating from her shoulder to the tips of her right hand. She felt it all the way to her toes to a lesser extent. She concentrated on the feeling. There was a slight push on her thoughts, as if something new was in her brain. An idea that needed to be worked over, pushing just a bit for attention. She gave her arm a slight shake as it felt heavy with the power. The blue light flowed from her fingers and a shot of water pushed up from the outer rim of the room.

This startled her into awareness. She looked down in shock at her arm. She had done it! There on her shoulder the stone, in variegated shades of blue, an imperfect little smooth circle sat embedded deep into her bone. The blue tattoos looked just as she had seen on the other stone grafters, waves of blue reaching down to her elbow and across her right collarbone.

She looked to find Fleck, his body glowing blue from the sparkles of magic in the air and felt a bubble of laughter escape her. It echoed quietly in the empty room. She looked up at the full moon shining above her. Fleck had been right, his faith and belief in her astounded her, and her laughter turned into a choked cry. Emotions flooded her as she let go of her focus on needing to complete her mission. She had done it.

No longer was she scared for her home. No longer was she worried about whether her daughters would survive. No longer was she failing them. Letting these fears go was momentous.

Her long day caught up with her and she crumbled to the floor. Exhaustion mingled with all the emotions she had focused on trying to connect with this stone, her stone. They added to the toll the stonegrafting had taken on her body. She lay with her forehead on the cool stone and cried, laughed, and fell asleep.

# Training

When she awoke, Detmer was standing nearby, looking at the pile of stones remaining on the pedestal. Fleck stood there too, as if they were best friends. The morning sun was bouncing sparkling peach hues over the room and the blues looked a different shade than they had in the deep of night. Both of her friends contemplated the stones with such a serious faces that Lara wasn't sure she wanted to interrupt.

She slowly stood up, paying attention to how she felt differently. She had expected pain in her shoulder where the stone had grafted, but there was none. She felt a keen tingling of all her sensations. The water in the room rang in her ears. She heard the trickling of it as if it called to her, whispering a hello. She could smell the freshness of the water near her, she could feel the flow of the water in the ring around the room and also feel the moisture in the air. She could feel that moisture on her fingertips and knew she could probably pull the tiny droplets together.

Rather than feeling exhaustion and pain, she felt rejuvenated and powerful. She wasn't sure she had ever really felt powerful before. She had always been capable, but always working with her minimal resources and abilities. This was different. She knew this would change things.

Taking a moment to look into the cool waters, she saw that the bottom was covered in stones so deep blue that they almost looked black. She was instantly inspired to leave. It was time to get moving. Fleck perked his ears at this, and she turned quickly to catch him, as he had already jumped from the pedestal to her arms. Detmer turned to look at her.

"Congratulations, Lara. We need to go meet up with Axel. I updated him about your success, and he is waiting in a training chamber. Are you ready to go?"

They both stopped on the far side of the bridge. Lara soaked in the room. She didn't think she would ever be back here, but it was a memory she would never forget. She saw Detmer also taking in the space. Some places create and hold memories, that is what makes them sacred. This was a sacred spot.

Lara realized that because she was doing all of this on fast forward, she didn't know a lot about the way of things here at the Stone House. She hadn't even heard of the training halls, but when Detmer led her to the far west side of the main house, there was a huge square structure.

"There are four rooms surrounding a center courtyard. Each room has different purposes. I am sure Axel will take you into all of them."

Axel was sitting on a bench nearby when they entered. Lara was surprised to see that the entrance was just a simple, small door. It looked wrong on this huge building. Axel was grinning, and he let out a gruff laugh as they walked up. "I heard about your success. Congratulations, but we don't have time to celebrate beyond that. We need to train you so you can save your home."

"Yes, please!"

Detmer spoke, sounding happier than Lara had ever heard him, his voice light with a touch of humor there. "Well, this is where I leave you. Can't wait to hear about your progress." He paused for a moment and looked into her eyes. "And thank you. For listening the other day. I haven't opened up about that before. I believe it has been good for me."

Lara smiled in return and found she felt a strange pulling sensation. This was similar to the looks from the color weavers, but she was in control. It disconcerted her so she quickly broke eye contact. "I was happy to hear more about you. Thanks for opening up to me."

He waved a goodbye and she and Axel entered the small door.

The first room they entered had a hard dirt floor and high ceilings. There was nothing in the room aside from deep grooves in the ground and a pond in the center. A simple single chair set next to the pond.

"The chair is for me. I can't keep up like I used to." Axel said as he slowly progressed to the center of the large room. He lowered himself into the chair and then looked at her. "Let us begin."

The first task Axel started her on was pulling water from the pond through the channels in the ground. The small pond of water sat lower than the rest of the room. The deep grooved channels reached out of it like the spokes in the Wheel Road. They went slightly uphill, angled to drain everything back into the pond, so when left alone, the water pooled into the pond again.

Lara found what he asked surprisingly simple. She easily focused on the water and thought about home and why she was here and the blue started flowing from her and the water did as she asked, sloppy waves pushed through the channels. The dirt along the channels became a bit muddy and the water always sloshed back to the center when she stopped paying attention, but she was feeling ecstatic. This is what she needed to know how to do. She could pull the water from the river up here by Azural and, as she walked home, draw it along the riverbed back to Calambria.

Smiling, she turned to Axel. "I think I can actually save my town." Her last words faltered a bit when she saw Axel's face. He didn't look impressed, or even happy, let alone ecstatic like her.

He sighed. "Lara, you are a baby learning to crawl. You haven't even taken your first toddling steps."

As her mind tried to sort through what his meaning was, he stood and with a flick of his arms, the blue was instantly shooting from him. The water in the pond flowed lightning fast without a drop bouncing loose down the channels. He stopped the water instantly and turned to her. The water held. He was no longer doing anything. There was no blue sparkle, no look of effort (indeed he had barely put any effort in to do any of this) but the water held there, rather than falling back to the pond.

Lara looked at the pond. The whole of it was dry as a desert, dry as the well back home.

She looked at him in awe. "You're right. I have a lot to learn."

He nodded, "Let's try this another way. Undo, what I have done."

She slowly pulled the water back toward the base, still splashing water out the sides, but much more aware of it this time.

She spent the rest of the afternoon focusing on two main skills. Control and longevity.

Keeping the water in the channels, this was about control. Axel explained that the stronger the emotion tapped into, the stronger the stone's response. So, she needed to learn to tap into smaller bits of the emotions for these smaller tasks.

"What are your responsibilities back home?" Axel posed.

"Do you mean like my chores? I do the dishes every day and feed the goat?"

"No, deeper responsibilities, like emotional responsibilities."

"Well, my kids, of course. They are all grown, but they still weigh on me. I still worry about them and feel responsible for them. My husband and friends? They all mean the world to me."

"Those are some strong emotions, too. But not nearly as strong as saving your whole town. What about honesty? Little truths can spark the stone. We are working to create a spectrum of emotions for you to draw on. The large and powerful ones, like saving your hometown, will give you the magic, but not the control. The small ones, like your responsibility to do the dishes, or rather your responsibility to your family to do the dishes so they have clean ones, is a smaller one. But don't forget that all emotions lead to others. Maybe you think 'I will draw on the dishes emotion' and then realize you are pulling in some honesty about your frustration and depression from not getting appreciated for the task, and suddenly you have a well of overflowing power."

Lara was surprised at how quickly the power might consume her. But she didn't want to interrupt as Axel continued. "As we work through these rooms, you will find more memories and connections with emotions that you can use as touch points for the magic. But, speaking from experience, time will change these memories and what they mean to you. A memory of your childhood friend might bring you joy today, and in twenty years, bring you sadness. As a stone weaver, we must always stay honest with ourselves about these things."

Axel was still sitting in his chair and with a simple motion pulled water from the pool into an arch along the room. "Now, undo what I have done."

The afternoon went on like that. Axel pulling water in a specific way, and Lara practicing the opposite. After hours, Lara felt a strange mix of exhilaration and exhaustion. The magic danced in her veins, and she felt the power re-fill every time she touched on the correct feeling. But her mental acuity started to slip.

Across the large room Axel pulled water into a tightly spinning cone. He sent it toward her with the same, "Ok, Lara. Now, undo what I have done."

Her tiredness and irritation battled her respect for him, and she finally broke. *If I have to hear him say that one more time...* she threatened in her head to Fleck. Sagging her shoulders she let out an enormous sigh and whined, "But I'm tired." As soon as the words were out of her mouth, she realized she sounded just like her kids after a hard day. She instantly started laughing out loud at herself. Giggling, she bent in half and couldn't stop for a breath.

She finally got composure and stood up straight, but it was too late. The water tornado swept her up. She had no time to think, just react. As she spun within the torrent, she let the magic of the stone connect with the water's motion; she felt for the rhythm of it. This wasn't a moment for a tiny bit of magic, this needed some serious power.

She closed her eyes and imagined herself sitting in the zen garden with Weaver Han. A breeze drifting by, she grounded her mind in the peace of that moment where it was just her and her own thoughts. She let the consistent spin of the water, lend itself to the meditative state. Focusing on that calming energy, she imagined pulling it around herself. When she opened her eyes the energy she had envisioned surrounded her. There in a light blue sparkle of light, glowing about an inch from her body the magic pulsed. She pushed the energy from herself in the opposite direction of the spinning water and it slowed, lowering Lara to the ground.

When the last of the water had splashed into the earthen floor, Axel came over to Lara. "I know you are tired, but often we need to react when we are at our least prepared. You have made great progress. But you have a lot to learn."

Remembering the soft blue glow that had been around her body moments ago, Lara agreed. "What's next?" she asked.

# *Friendships*

"Where are you taking us?" Delly laughed as the four of them stumbled up the hill to the training building. "I can't believe how big this little island is! All the gardens hide away so many secret spaces."

"I know, right?" Iris giggled. She was always more relaxed around Delly. It brought out a less reserved Iris that Lara loved even more. "My parents met when they were in school here, and they told me about a garden they spent hours in each day with just the two of them. It supposedly has magical waterworks where if you put anything in, say a tiny leaf or a bracelet, at the entrance, you can watch it flow throughout the whole gardens, doing flips and flowing up and down. I have been trying to find it since I got here but haven't had any luck." She finished with resolve, "Yet."

Van smiled but was still so quiet around the girls. Lara hoped he might learn to open up and give them a chance to get to know the Van she knew. It has been two busy weeks since Lara had stonegrafted and begun her training with Axel. During class time, Lara joined in and behaved as if nothing had changed to keep Shauna and the others from realizing what had occurred.

Early mornings, and evenings, and any other moments they could, Lara had been walking this path to meet Axel and work on her waterweaving. Her young friends still had no idea.

Well, they were all in for a surprise.

As they came up to the large square building, the three youths quieted, looking at Lara expectantly.

"Come on in." Lara opened the small door, and the three shuffled a bit nervously into the large open room.

"What is this place?" Van asked in a hushed tone, his whisper echoing in the huge room.

"It is the training hall for waterweavers."

"I don't think we should be here..." Iris said, worry creasing her brow.

"Well, I have something to share, and I wanted you to be the first to know. Well, aside from Detmer and ..." She motioned toward the small door leading into the tank room and the three of them gasped as Axel stepped gingerly through.

Lara hated to see him have to move around more than he needed to, so she rushed over to him. The others followed; a bit more reserved. When she got to Axel, he took her arm and smiled at the three of them.

Van stood as straight as Lara had ever seen him. He looked Axel in the eyes as if he were meeting a hero.

Iris was curtsying, of all things. She smiled and looked like she was following all the rules her parents had taught her about polite society.

Delly was bouncing up and down, barely refraining from stepping forward to grab Axel's other arm in hers. Her smile hidden behind her hands, clasped together, fingers intertwined as if she were holding her own words inside her mouth.

Lara knew they were excited, but this was not even what they had come to learn. "Follow us." And she turned with Axel, and they took them to the open aired training hall.

This hall was the most natural setting of the four, and it was Lara's favorite. There was a shallow pond fed by a waterfall that fell over many slices of slate sticking directly out of the wall. Next to the pond, there was a large body of water deep enough for swimming, although the main purpose was to practice submerging yourself underwater and keeping yourself encased in air so you could breathe. There was no ceiling in this room either, because this is where waterweavers practiced making it rain. Building clouds by pulling the particles together in the air and pressuring them to the point of bursting and bringing the rain down.

Lara gave the kids a moment to take it all in, but finally realized she was just scared to tell them. They had come to mean a lot to her, these three. They had welcomed her when she had felt so out of place. She wasn't sure how they were going to take this. Best to do it quickly. "I want to share something with you before it becomes more common knowledge. You are dear friends to me, and I have had such a wonderful time coming to know each of you." She turned to Axel.

He saw the worry in her eyes. "I have long thought it was time for change here in Azural," he started, "and I think there is no going back now." He smiled and Lara realized it was just time to do it.

She pulled her cape back from her arm and showed them the tattoo and the stone. "What!?" Delly squealed and rushed forward, taking Lara's right hand in hers. Studying the tattoo intently, then a beat later reaching out and tracing it with her fingers. "Did it hurt? Do you feel the magic right now? When did it happen? Are you going to save your family now? Can you show us some waterweaving? Is Axel teaching you?"

As the questions stacked up, Lara looked over Delly's shoulder to see Iris shrink a little and step back, her fingertips gently touching her lips and her eyes wide.

Van stepped forward and was looking in wonder at the intricate detail of the tattoo.

Lara put a hand on Delly's shoulder and her questions were stilled. She took her hand from Delly's grip and stepped aside to address Iris. "Are you okay?"

"I just don't understand. You've only got one of the bands. How did this happen?"

"Let's sit on the bank and I will tell you everything."

⟩⟩⟩

"So, all this time, Detmer and Axel, our Founding Father Axel, have been working to sneak you in to get the stone, and then sneaking around training you? That is amazing!" Delly was on board from the get-go, and Lara appreciated her open heart and accepting nature so much at this moment.

Their shoes lined up behind them, all four friends sat along the bank with their feet in the pool. "I guess I just never really thought about how dire things were for your family, Lara. I can't even imagine what it is to not have water," Iris said softly, the tips of her fingers sweeping along the water before her.

"When I arrived, I was dehydrated, dirty and exhausted. Cracked lips, dry skin, tired from lack of nutrition." Lara thought back to it herself.

"And look at you now! It's not just the magic; you looked like a new person. Well, I think we all understand why Lara came here. I remember what you all looked like when you first walked into that dining room, and it's helping me see. It was so exciting for me at that moment to see Black, Green, and Orange walk into my life. But why are you here, Delly? I just don't get it. Why did you think you would fit in here?" Iris had said the harsh question with the concern of a friend and although Delly looked a bit hurt by the directness, she didn't look angry.

"At first, I thought I needed to come to Blue for the order. You all know the stories of my mom carting us around everywhere as kids. I just wanted to find the place that was the opposite, I think. I wanted stability, and I thought, of course, Blue, the realm of law and order, would give it to me. I have already realized after my classes that I was actually looking for something else. I still don't know what it is, but the rules here are so far beyond my wildest imagination that I know I will never find a forever home here. I love you all so much, but this cannot be where I grow old." Delly's eyes filled with tears and Iris rushed over to her, tackling her in a hug, Delly's feet splashing out of the water as she was knocked to the ground.

"Oh, Delly, I love you so. I don't know what I will do when you leave, but I understand."

Van quietly said, "I know exactly what you mean, Delly. When I first arrived at Blue, I expected to find some calm here. I have never been a very confident person, so I had hoped to just find a place of peace here, instead I have struggled as much as back home." He smiled at Lara and Fleck, sitting on her shoulder. "But I have made some friends." His eyes then darted toward the two girls.

"Of course you've made friends!" Delly practically yelled.

Iris chimed in, "I have been the luckiest first year! I have learned so much about the Blue tenets, but I also have learned about the world outside Azural. I am so glad I found such a diverse group of friends." She paused and placed her feet back into the water. "Now Lara, I think we better finally get a chance to see what you can do. Let's see some magic already."

Lara stood up and pulled her cape back from her shoulder so they could all see the magic in action. She loved to watch the blue light twinkle as it sparked into motion and knew what they wanted to see. She pooled the feeling of trust they all had with each other and focused it on the center of the swimming pool at their feet. She sent the emotion into the tendrils of water reaching toward the center and pushed the water into a tall jet straight into the air, spouting the water out in every direction at the top to make almost a mushroom shape of water.

The kids loved it. Delly jumped up from her place on the bank and ran to where the water fell down and danced in it. Iris took hold of Van's hands and began to spin around with him as the droplets fell. Van looked startled for a beat but was drawn into their excitement and circled along with her, Delly joining them, and they laughed.

Lara let the jet of water end and the last of the water dissipated and fell in slow drops to the ground. Next, she took a moment to practice her drying off skills. She reached out to Delly first, feeling for the surrounding moisture, letting the stone's magic do the work and focusing on her responsibility to clean up after herself, she sucked the water droplets from Delly's orange curls, condensing them into a small ball about the size of her fist. She slowly reached with her hand to move the magical ball, still ensconced in the glowing blue light, into the pond. Next, she moved to Iris and did the same thing. Pulling the water this time into a stream that flowed along like a ribbon slowly pouring into the pond as if it were running down a plank of wood.

Finally, she turned to Van, his bangs stuck to his face, and as she began to pull the water again into a ball, Delly giggled and distracted Lara. For a moment she looked to see what Delly had thought was funny and there she saw Fleck standing on a stone sopping wet. The water stuck his fur to him, so that he looked bedraggled and very skinny. He looked at her expectantly and sent her a feeling of impatience. "Oh, for heaven's sake, he is waiting for me to dry him off. Fleck, just shake it off like you always do. You'll catch cold." Just then, she realized she had completely forgotten to pay attention to her magic. She turned with sudden concern to look at Van and in that moment turned her magic the wrong way around and sent the water straight into Van's face in a flash of water and blue magic. His face momentarily turning bright blue, he spluttered and laughed as it hit him, "Oh, Lara, it's gone up my nose!" He continued to laugh, and the girls and Lara joined in.

"Oh, I am so sorry. I still have a lot to learn."

"It's fine. This has been so fun!" Van said, looking up through his once again wet bangs.

Iris stood behind him and Lara was pleasantly surprised to see a look she was familiar with on Iris's face. She hid it quickly, but Iris liked Van. Lara thought for a moment about what a wonderful future the two might have together. But they were young, no rush, life took care of itself.

"Lara," Delly said, her voice uncharacteristically cautious, "if you have the magic to save your home, what's keeping you here?"

Lara paused. "I had to learn how to control it. Axel says I've come pretty far, but now I think it is time for me to figure out how to get past that wall."

# Found Out

Shauna could hear the giggles before she saw who was coming down the path. Sometimes these youths just were much too chaotic. She preferred the older students who had learned to control their tempers and kept calm while walking in the gardens. These were definitely first years coming her way.

She turned to walk away so she could avoid them, but then she heard something that stopped her in her tracks, a young girl's voice echoing in her ears, "When Lara's magic blasted you right in the face, I couldn't stop myself from laughing. Those blue magic sparkles along with the water droplets turned your whole face blue for a moment."

"Me neither and I was the one with water up my nose," laughed a young man.

Shauna turned right back around and rushed down the path to where the children were walking. She was not surprised to see that it was Iris, Delly, and Van.

"What did you just say?" She demanded of them.

All three froze, their laughs dying instantly. Iris visibly squared her shoulders. "Good afternoon, Headmistress Shauna."

"Don't 'good afternoon' me. I asked what you were just saying."

"Nothing much. We were just playing around. We just came back from the stream, and um…"

Delly jumped in here, "Yes, we were laughing because um, Lara splashed Van right in the face with some water from the stream."

Van and Iris nodded along, much too aggressively.

Shauna gave the youth a penetrating look and realized she was not going to get anything useful out of them. She huffed and continued down the path they had been walking from. She would solve this right away.

A bit farther down the path, she saw Detmer and Lara walking at a leisurely pace. It almost looked like Lara had been studying with her pack on her shoulder heavy with books, but Shauna had doubts now. The moment they saw her; they paused the conversation.

"Hello Shauna." Detmer stated. Obviously not happy to see her, but he never was. Nothing out of the ordinary there.

Shauna did not deign to respond. She wasn't going to ask for answers when she knew she could get them herself quite easily. Thank you.

She walked straight up to Lara grabbed hold of her sleeve, pulling it up quickly. There before her eyes was the blatantly obvious answer that Lara had stolen a stone. She turned to look at Detmer and found no surprise in his eyes.

He already knew.

Without a word to him, Shauna looked at Lara and gritted out, "You will come with me right now." And she pulled Lara down the path toward the Great Stone House. Lara didn't fight her on it. Indeed, she just followed along at the break-neck pace Shauna had set. Shauna was almost sorry. She had hoped to at least enjoy the satisfaction of pulling Lara forcefully.

This was everything she had feared from the moment she saw Lara. How could they ever come back from this? Once someone had stonegrafted, the only way to retrieve the stone was death. Shauna wasn't one to condone murder, but she was also not interested in seeing this woman take what she had no legal rights to!

Shauna continued to pull Lara until they reached the center of the Great Hall.

They now stood with all the Blue weavers standing in a group around Shauna. Many of the students, after seeing Shauna and Lara enter, followed by Detmer, Iris, Delly and Van, had stopped to see what the fuss was about.

"The facts are that no one who has earned a blue stone has left Azural." Shauna stated matter-of-factly to everyone who had gathered in the main hall. "And this woman broke the rules to get the stone. Why are we even discussing this?"

There was a hubbub around the room as people spoke over each other and to those next to them. Lara felt her chest tighten in panic. She was not comfortable upsetting people, and here the most powerful people in Azural, some of the most powerful in all the lands put together, were all arguing about her.

Lara remained standing where Shauna had dropped her hand in the center of the hall. Fleck was curled in his usual spot, hidden by her pack strap. He had grown a bit this past few weeks, but with Lara's hood and thick braid, no one seemed to notice him there. Lara had to remind him frequently to stay out of sight, he was always so ready to be her champion. But she was in enough trouble with Shauna.

Shauna turned to Fallon, obviously looking for backup. Fallon, always aware of stage presence, spoke in a voice for the whole room to hear. "We have rules in place to be responsible. We have rules in place to keep us honest. We have rules in place to keep order. We have rules in place to keep the peace." Shauna nodded at each line. "These are our rules because these are the truths of Blue. We, more than anyone, have studied, practiced and learned these truths. But we forget that there are truths, responsibilities and order needed outside of Azural. We have been in our Great Stone House for decades, ignoring how small it is compared to the world at large. I feel that we have failed our magic, we have failed our true responsibilities. Lara has opened my eyes to that, and I support her in her quest."

Shauna's face visibly fell. Lara saw disappoint that quickly turned to anger.

There was a hubbub around her, and Lara noticed many heads bobbing along. Many of the waterweavers looked inclined to agree with Fallon. The students around the outskirts of the hall were more exuberant in their agreement, or disagreement, the assurance of youth. When they believed something, they believed it with all their energy.

Lara looked to see her friends just beyond the ring of weavers. All three supported her loudly. She was surprised to see Stella there with them, nodding her head in agreement as well. Lara took a moment to wonder at how, although youth were so confident and energetic in their beliefs, they were also much more open to listening to and considering new ideas. Lara laughed a bit to herself, thinking, that's probably because all ideas are still new to their young minds. That girl was really growing.

"Well, I guess it's fortunate that this isn't just for you to decide, Fallon." Shauna stated with vitriol. "I've already called the city guards. This discussion is pointless. You can vote your conscience at her tribunal."

There was a large intake of breath from the crowded hall.

Penny burst out, "Shauna, there was no need to take it that far. This should have been a matter resolved among us waterweavers."

Shauna gave a contemptuous look at Penny, then pointed it toward Fallon and a few others in the room, finally landing on Lara. "It was obvious to me that we needed to take this to the city government. Too many here seem to have forgotten our rules."

Lara filled her lungs with air slowly, searching the room and finding many friendly faces. She had made some close friends here, but she missed James and their little cottage. She missed her kids. She missed Jada, and the comfort of lifelong friendship. As her chest was filled, she held the breath there for a beat. When she let it out, she put her hand up and the room almost instantly fell silent. Everyone wanted to hear what she had to say.

"I have no problem taking my claim to the Senators. It seems I was going to have to confront this eventually." She looked at her young friends who had just encouraged her in this less than an hour ago. "Let's get it done, so I can go home."

# Tribunal

Lara let her pack slide off her shoulder heavily onto the floor next to the single chair they had placed on the dais in front of the large window. Her pack had all of her belongings in it, as she had been asked to empty her room before they left. One way or another, Shauna was not welcoming her back to The Stone House. Deciding what to take had been fairly simple. She packed up her personal belongings. She had left the books from her classes on the desk, but after a moment's hesitation decided to keep the Pelanor book in her pack.

The room was filling rather quickly, and Lara began to feel small. When she had looked into this room during her visit with Iris' parents she had felt the size of the room, but sitting here as the focus of attention, made it all the more intimidating. The number of senators was surprising. She had only really seen a few at her initial meeting and then when she came with Iris to meet Hyacinth. This room seats at least a hundred people.

All the senators were dressed in finery. None of them wore uniforms like the students at The Stone House, or the soldiers, but she noticed many of them had incorporated the bands into their clothing somehow. An older woman around Lara's age wore a slim fitting dress in a shiny satin that boasted four rings of silvery blue around the hem as it swished around her calves. A man in a dapper jacket of soft crushed velvet had three bands on the cuff of his right sleeve.

The crowd was talking animatedly, and she often caught them pointing toward her, sitting alone on display for them. The constant murmur of voices that she couldn't quite make out, wore on her already frazzled nerves. Just as she thought she might have to get up and pace, she heard a small shift in the room. Looking up, she saw that Axel had entered. There was obvious reverence from all the Senators. He was their founder, and it showed on their faces that they held him in high regard. She felt a bit more confident about her chances since he was on her side here.

The room was set up simply, but grandly. Lara was placed on this plain chair on the stage in the front of the three-story room. Behind her was a high panel glass window, from floor to vaulted ceiling with a beautiful view of the waterwall. But she had her back to it. Instead, she faced rows of senators. They had four rows of comfortable soft chairs for all of them to lounge in. This was obviously a room they were used to sitting in at length.

The first semi-circular row had seventeen chairs, and the waterweavers began to fill them. Lara conjectured that this meant one was a seat for every possible waterweaver. One of those chairs might have been hers in another life. The second row was for the higher-level senators. Lara concluded this was based on rings. Detmer took a seat in the row directly behind the Waterweavers. The upper rows had senators with three rings.

Lara didn't notice anyone in the room with less than three bands aside from Kiera. She was set up at a table again to the far side of the room, and although she had smiled comfortingly at Lara, she had not come over to engage with her. Lara understood. This was definitely a much bigger deal than the initial short questioning had been.

As the room was almost full, Lara saw Chairman Gliron enter. He walked straight through the room, not speaking to anyone, and came directly to stand before her.

"Chairman Gliron," Lara said, slowly standing.

"Hello again, Missy. You didn't quite settle in the way we had hoped, huh?" Lara was relieved to hear a hint of amusement in his voice.

"No, Sir. I don't believe I did."

"You will have a chance in a few moments to state your case after Headmaster Shauna states hers. After each of you have made your statements, the Senators will deliberate and we will give a ruling. We will know soon your fate."

The Chairman turned slowly, leaving Lara quite alone in the center of the stage. Everyone was mostly settled as the Chairman moved to his podium.

"I call this tribunal to order. The accused is Lara Soleil. The accuser, Senator and Waterweaver and Headmistress of the Great Stone House, Shauna Merrick. The Chair invites Weaver Shauna up to state her case."

Shauna stood at the front of the room and faced everyone, her back to Lara. "This woman has broken into one of the most sacred spaces in Azural. She entered our Oculus. Not only did she enter the room, but she stole from us. From you, me, and all the Azurans. She has taken a stone for herself. She has stonegrafted."

There was a hushed intake of breath from the back few rows, where obviously they hadn't yet known.

Shauna grabbed Lara with her left arm and pulled her up next to her. Lara could almost see the satisfaction in her eyes as she pulled Lara's sleeve up to reveal the tattoos to the room at large. "She has become a waterweaver, after flouting our rules and skipping trials. Trials that all of you, all of us, had to go through. After she flat out skipped these, she has taken the stone and NOW?" Shauna paused, letting the anger foment. "Now she plans to take it and leave our Realm!"

This had the crowd's energy heightened. The Senators were talking with those next to them. Even from the dais, Lara could hear many of them.

"But no waterweaver is allowed to leave us. They are here to protect us."

"Who does she think she is?"

Shauna cleared her throat loudly, and the crowd settled a bit, but the murmuring continued. "I have called this meeting of the Senators of our great realm so that we can decide how to handle this situation. For I am at a loss. Short of death, this stone is now grafted on Lara. My initial thought is that we must jail her somehow, but I will leave it to this body to decide. We cannot trust her to stay here."

Chairman Gliron moved forward, "Thank you Weaver Shauna, you make take a seat." He reached over and took Lara's hand gently from Shauna.

"The Chair calls on Lara Soleil." He gave her hand a slight comforting squeeze and then moved aside.

Lara squared her shoulders and stood before the crowd. She started in the back row. Slowly turning her head so that she could take in the people of the room. And that is the thing. They were just people. As she moved to the next row, she realized she had more in common with these people than different. She was so tired of everyone looking at the differences, when so much was the same. Why did they look on her as an outsider, as an interloper, as an other?

In the second to final row, she found the familiar face of Hyacinth and Detmer. These friendly faces were a balm to her aching heart. She knew that there were those in this room who supported her, maybe she could reach more of these strangers.

As she finally came to the bottom, where she knew the faces the best, she slowed her pace. Each face here was someone who, just a few weeks ago, had been an awe-inspiring, practically made-up thing. These waterweavers had intimidated her and felt untouchable.

And now she was one of them.

When she finally landed on Axel's face, his knowing eyes gave her the final push to speak her truth to the leaders of Azural.

"When I left my home in the Wastes because our water well had run dry, I thought I was on a mission to save them. I had planned to do my best to bring water back to them. But I also thought it was a chance for me to find out who I was. Who could I be now that my children have grown and moved on. I came here hoping that I could prove myself a strong, reliable person and worthy of the Water magic that would save my home.

"But I realized something when I was in the room with those stones. Many of you have been there, you will know what I mean. The weight of trying to understand what the stones are looking for felt incomprehensible. I was overwhelmed with what I was trying to get across. I turned inward and started really looking inside myself. As I started circling that pedestal of magic that could save my loved ones, the truth hit home for me. I realized that to be true to myself I also need to be true to those I love. I had been trying to define myself separately from my family, but my family is a part of who I am, and they always will be. The stones understood this honesty and truth. The magic saw me as worthy." Lara looked down at her shoulder, still on display for the Senators. "This stone chose me."

The Senators were quiet, and it gave Lara hope. She needed to convince them to let her go home.

"Your rules are made up. They are constructs built from the founders thoughts on what was right. But we all need to be open to listening to new truths. When presented with new information, we need to reconsider.

"I have met so many people since I left home, and I see commonality in all of us. From Brown traders on the Wheel Road, to Senators and food workers at the Stone House, to youth from Blue and other color realms and yes, even Weavers - I have found friends.

"The Blue realm needs to remember like I did in that Oculus, that Azural cannot define itself without the rest of Chroma. Azural is a part of the larger whole. It is time for you all to realize that the water in Azural needs to be shared. It doesn't make you any less who you are to embrace those around you. In fact, I believe it makes us all stronger.

"I hope that you can all see past your current rules to the truths beyond them. I hope you can see that all I want is to refill the Hope River and bring water home to my family. I am not here to take something of yours. Where do you think the stones came from? I am trying to bring something back that was ours already." She sat carefully in her chair, holding her head high and began looking over the crowd to see if she could gauge their thoughts.

Axel stood slowly. His body was obviously wracked with the pain of age. The Chairman looked stricken for a moment, this was obviously not planned, but he quickly recovered. "The Chair gives the floor to Weaver Axel."

Axel made his way up the few stairs to reach the dais. His steps were slow, but with his head was held high, there was gravity to his countenance.

"I have stepped back over the years to let the new generations lead, but there are times when my years of wisdom need to chime in. Over sixty years ago, my friends and I made the biggest discovery of modern times, and..." he paused and looked at each person in the room individually making sure they were paying him close attention, his head moved up row after row, "...the biggest mistake in modern times. We broke our world. It is time to admit that and work to fix it."

He walked slowly directly across the center to Lara. He grabbed her hand firmly and gave it a tiny tug. She stood up next to him. "This woman is here to fix the very problem that has been plaguing me for the last few decades. My friends and I made choices without thinking of the consequences. We Azurans have closed ourselves off from the rest of the world, ignoring the problems that we are causing. I closed us off." He turned to look at Shauna directly. "No color weaver leaves Azural. All unused blue stones live in the chamber sitting dormant on that useless pedestal. Meanwhile, Lara's home and so many countless more have gone dry. They are losing their resources because we hold them captive. And not just us - Red, Green, Yellow, Purple, we are all responsible." His voice was sounding more powerful as he continued speaking. "You know who is not responsible? Lara. She came here with the clearest of intentions and has worked harder than any of us to make this happen. She is here to save her home, her family, her town, her world. Our world. And here we sit in judgment, as if we have the ability to decide if that is her right?"

He let go of Lara's hand and slowly walked back to his seat. As he sat down, he spoke in a hushed tone, however, all the attentive ears in the room heard clearly. "We overstep."

As Axel sat, the room again buzzed with animated conversation. The Chair came to the front and called the room to order. "Order please, Order. This is an important decision. I truly believe this is one of the key moments we have had in Azural during my role as Chair. I want us all to take a break to deliberate on the decision we are about to vote on. I will clarify our vote now, and you may then take the time during break to speak to each other, which you are all seeming want to do, or just go and mediate in the garden over this momentous choice. The vote is: on one hand, we find Lara Soliel guilty of breaking our laws and confine her here with a lifelong prison sentence; or on the other hand, we admit the need to adjust our laws, to forgive her for breaking them, and allow Lara to leave for her home. I, myself, plan to go on a walk in the gardens. This is not a simple decision. I suggest none of you make it too quickly. We will meet again in this chamber when the sun hits The Midway."

The chairman gestured toward the window and Lara saw in the pane a circle of metal placed centered in the large paned wall of glass. The interior of the round Midway was tinted dark blue. From her place on the dais she could see that the sun's path would lead it to be right centered in the circle within an hour.

And with that, the room erupted into loud conversations and shuffling as many left the room or started speaking in raised voices. Lara sat in her little chair feeling a strange sense of being small, while also being the biggest problem these people had ever dealt with. She was a bit amazed at how one person can really change the world. New ideas were hard to swallow, and they certainly seemed to put people out.

She thought again of Stella bobbing her head in support and was reminded that the youth might just change this world for the better if these, set in their ways, curmudgeons wouldn't listen. She caught herself, because some of these curmudgeons were her biggest supporters. Her eyes met Axel as he sat in his chair, answering the questions of people coming to speak with him.

This was going to be the longest hour of her life she thought, and decided to turn her chair so she could look out on the waterwall rather than this tank of decision makers who held her home's future in their hands. Lara sat and watched the sun slowly move toward the Midway circle in the glass.

# The Vote

Chairman Gliron stood next to Lara looking at the sun. When the last bit reached the circle casting a full blue light across the dais he turned back to the Senators. "The sun has reached The Midway, I am calling it to a vote."

Lara liked the ease of this man. He was obviously respected by all the Senators, which seemed so extraordinary to Lara now that she had seen how much they disagreed strongly on the topic of her and her future.

"I will remind you that this decision will be final, so please do not vote lightly." He turned toward her, "Lara, we always allow the accused that are found guilty the chance to bring their claim back to the Hall once a year, so if you are found guilty, you may come back here on every 8th day of Summer. You will have a chance to state your case again at that time." He paused for a moment, looking suddenly sad and tired, "Should you need to."

And then he stated with a solemnity that told Lara he understood how much this meant to her future, "All those in favor of Lara being held for her breaking of the rules and taking an Azuran stone without having earned her five rings, please stand."

Lara watched as Shauna, Senator Rombauer, and a few others jumped up immediately, as if they were happy to fate her home to despair. But her heart just took another hit after hit as more and more of the Senators slowly stood. She saw Bariano from her first questioning stand, and she realized that his love for the rules overran his ability to see the larger problem. She saw almost all of those standing on the higher tier with their three bands come to their feet, and she thought about all the years they had put into reaching the right for the stone that she had skipped over. Some of them might have been great waterweavers, but were never given the chance to get near the stones because of this Realms rules.

The tipping point was reached and as she looked at all the Senators standing, her eyes filled with tears. They couldn't see past their own hollow expectations of the world. They were locked behind this wall, not only physically, but mentally and psychologically. She would never be able to convince them.

But then she looked at Detmer, who looked up at the standing senators with as much pain on his face as she felt. She looked at Penny, who looked up at her neighbor standing over her with sadness. She looked at Axel and found he was looking straight at her. For the first time, she leaned into the soul's gaze. She needed his support right now.

It was amazingly similar to what she felt from Fleck. The emotion was raw in both of them as they hurt from this decision. But he had a feeling she did not - hope. There was a flicker of shared image, a memory of himself standing on the shores of the Hope River before Azural had become the Blue Realm. He looked so young, and so heartbroken. Blue magic was thrumming around him. He was encased by swirling blue light and thin spirals of water that spun and spun. She could feel his pain as he stood looking down the path away from Azural, watching the young woman in pink walk away. The betrayal of his trust in their bond lasting forever cut at his heart and he pushed all of that emotion into the river. He pulled the water from the bed in a swift and powerful motion, pushing to his right and the water followed his lead. The waterwall formed in a resounding rush that shook the world beneath his feet. Rather than feeling exhausted from the effort, he was exhilarated. He was capable of so much; he was powerful and he didn't need anyone that didn't understand him. He used magic to form a bubble around himself and he walked under the pounding water as it fell from the waterwall he had just created. He didn't need Becca, and he didn't need anyone else out there. On the other side of the water, he looked out on the city and envisioned what it could become, and he looked up at the waterwall and felt proud of his accomplishment.

Suddenly Axel's voice rumbled inside her head, *Now Lara, undo what I have done.*

Axel broke the bond and Lara looked at him, stunned. He smiled a small, encouraging smile and gave her a slight nod.

She was so preoccupied with Axel that she almost didn't register that the Chairman was speaking, "...and so with that final count the decision is that Lara has been found guilty of breaking the rules of Azural's Great Stone Hall and will be held until the Eighth day of Summer of next year."

Lara's stomach turned as it hit her that although they believed Truth and Honesty to be core tenets of leading a good life, they only saw the truth through their own eyes. Each person in this room believed in what they said with their whole selves. They weren't going to change their minds. They had a clear understanding and belief that doing the right thing for Azural was the most important thing, and they couldn't look past their waterwall, closing everyone else out. They felt stronger and better for it, and they felt justified in any choice they made through the lens of order and fairness to only the people of Azural.

She could share the problems of the Wastes as much as she wanted. They didn't see it as their problem. She could explain how working with those different from you makes you stronger, not weaker, but even if they listened, they wouldn't hear.

It was really difficult to make people actually hear you; to take in new information and let it change them. These people would never understand what it is to depend on your community and go without. They sat here in their chamber; indeed, they were the most powerful people in the whole Blue Realm, and they felt the need to tell her what she was allowed to do.

Lara couldn't look at the people sitting in their ordered rows anymore. She was getting too frustrated and knew she needed to calm down. They would never support her if she acted out. She turned to look out the large windows.

The Waterwall towered over the city of Azural. She watched the water as it cascaded down for a moment, thinking it could settle her, but she realized that she wasn't calming down- the settled feeling in her was actually a little scary. Lara knew she couldn't just sit here any longer.

The water was here being held back and the riverbed on the other side was dry because it was simply pulled right back into this never-ending rotation of water.

For what? To protect these people?

From what? People like her. Her family and friends? The other color realms?

If her travels had taught her anything, it was that all of us had more in common than we had differences. She turned back to the Senators sitting in their large, cushioned seats and stepped forward.

She didn't care that it wasn't her turn to speak. She was done with the trappings of politics. She felt her magic hum through her, radiating from the stone, settling into her heart and hardening her resolve.

"I didn't come here to Azural to cause trouble. I came here for your help. Instead, you sit in your hallowed halls, thinking you know what is best for a world you don't even understand. You don't know what it is like to struggle to feed your children. You don't know what it is like to not see a blue sky for months, let alone years. You don't know what it is like to worry that your loved ones might have run out of water completely at this point." Each sentence she said built up her power. The emotion coursing through her was fighting to break free, but she held it in.

"My daughters are at home right now, waiting for me. Waiting with my husband, my friends, my neighbors, with the hope that I might be able to keep our home and loved ones alive." She paused to reel in her emotion. Her power was growing. "Alive," she choked out. "I finally have a way to save them, and you think to hold me here because you worry that I am not following your expectations?" Lara sucked in a breath to control the pulsing thrum of her blood in her veins. Not only did she feel the power, but she could also see it - blue sparks of light floating around her, zigging and zagging through the air.

# Waterwall

"The fact is that you stole these stones from us, from our land. I am just returning one. I am done with your hoops and rules. I am leaving." She shouldered her pack and began to walk toward the door but found herself suddenly unable to move. Looking down, she saw her legs being encased in water. The force of it pushed inward against her keeping her still.

She followed the shimmering blue light to find Shauna casting the magic, her face set with resolve. "You aren't leaving here Lara. It has been decided. We will be taking you to your cell." Shauna nodded to the guards who stood on either side of her, and Lara felt the water around her legs being pushing her toward the side door.

Lara lashed out with her own magic without thinking, pushing a frustrated blast at Shauna. Shauna easily split Lara's magic stream from her hand and controlled the water Lara had sent toward her. She simply turned it back, adding it to the force pushing Lara's feet.

Lara realized that she had to pull herself together. She was letting Shauna control the situation. As Axel had warned her, she needed to be in control of her emotions to use her full power.

Rather than be baited by Shauna and fighting against the push of the water, Lara turned inward. She focused on the emotions that had brought her here.

Her responsibility toward her family and town. She imagined James and Sheila in their backyard. She pictured Sally in her workshop, and Anna behind the bar. She imagined what Peter might look like in a field of yellow flowers with the sun on his face, and a closeup of Brie, since she had no idea where she might be. Brie's trusting eyes shining intensely, pushing Lara on. They all believed in her as much as she believed in them.

She remembered one of her favorite moments from the kids' childhood. James had been cooking a stew in the kitchen and all the children had surrounded them in the kitchen. Brie danced around, speaking loudly about her adventures in the afternoon. Peter was crawling on the floor with Sheila pretending to be a goat, too. Anna was working on her numbers while reminding Brie to watch out for Peter under foot. And Sally was propped up on Lara's knee, asking Brie if she had seen any dragons or unicorns in her adorable baby voice.

The peace she had felt in that moment grounded her instantly. She felt the magic grow inside her, but she held it there.

Next, she thought of the trust her town had put in her; she thought of the town hall and specifically Jada. Her friend had told her, as though it was a fact, that she would see her soon. Jada had believed in Lara, much more than Lara had ever believed in herself. And Lara remembered a conversation they had years ago. Jada had come to her by the stream, heartbroken and upset after her childhood crush, Sandy, had left town for the Red Realm. They had been there for each other, trusting in the advice and friendship they held.

She pulled the magic tighter as it grew from the belief in that trust she had built over the years. Fleck peeked out and perched on her shoulders, and she felt her magic increase. The magic coiled around her arm so tightly that she felt it constricting her muscle.

Finally, she turned to the obvious emotion. The one that had brought her here in the first place. The one that had plagued her for her whole life. It had always been a burden, yet what had defined who she was. She had felt it as a little girl, when her mother asked her to do the mending. She had felt it as a friend, when Jada had broken her arm. She had felt it as a wife, when James had asked her to run to market. She had felt it as a mother, when her children couldn't sleep. She had felt it daily from large and small sources. It defined her.

Responsibility.

She almost hurt from the magic held in tightly. She realized she wasn't moving anymore and looked up to see Shauna focused more forcefully and the surrounding water moving upward. Shauna looked concerned and Lara realized that her whole body was glowing blue with her own magic. She had surrounded herself with it. It was not just in her arm as she had seen from other waterweavers. The glow was everywhere, all the way down to her toes.

But wait, she realized she had seen this once before. Axel had glowed the same way before building the Waterwall.

Lara looked at Shauna, really looked, and initiated her first Gaze. Lara pushed past the light thoughts in the front of Shauna's mind and forced her way in, wanting to understand how anyone could put rules before real truth. She needed to understand. She saw Shauna as a young girl of about seven, sitting cross legged as Axel and Sansa came into the room. Her eyes were filled with wonder as they placed the rule book in front of her. She had been learning to read in the Great Stone House's library since she could toddle around. Her mother was a cook there. Her mother had told her she was going to be capable of big things, that she would be a weaver one day. That she would make all of Azural proud and keep them safe.

Lara had seen enough. Shauna was locked in a way of thinking that she couldn't break free from. She hadn't listened to reason, and there was no chance she would change her mind now. She looked beyond Shauna to the windows and the waterwall.

"Enough games." Lara shouted, and she felt the magic explode out of her. She focused her energy on Shauna, and the windows behind her. As the force blasted Shauna down and Lara felt her feet free of their shackles, she began to run toward the windows, her magic continuing out in front of her, pushing everything that was in her way to the side. As she came upon the windows, the water magic cracked the glass and the large pane shattered.

Lara looked behind her for a moment and locked eyes with Shauna first, laying on the ground, then moved to see Axel. He was standing now, with his magic holding Shauna and the whole of the seating area behind a wall of water, Fallon and Penny joining in. She felt a moment of guilt for leaving such chaos behind, but then Axel nodded at Lara and she turned her magic toward the stream leading to the waterwall. She pushed water from her hands toward the stream to propelled herself along.

As she made her way down the Azural River, seeing the waterwall with all of its gushing glory just heightened her frustration with all that had gone wrong. The people in charge here still had so much to learn about the outside world. With Lara gone, they would just continue to hide behind this wall.

And then she remembered Axel showing her when the waterwall went up. Axel had taught her that she was capable of everything he was. In their weeks of training, she had balanced out his power with her own. Again and again, he had told her, "Now, undo what I have done."

His voice echoed in her mind. This had been his intention all along.

The waterwall needed to come down.

She needed to restore order to the whole world, and it needed to start here and now. She walked along the path to the bridge under the waterwall and craned her neck to look up at the water. Water that should have been filling the Hope River. Water that should have been keeping her home hydrated and clean should have been weaving its way throughout the world along the Wheel Road and throughout all the Realms.

She pictured the map on the back of Nessa's wagon. The order and rules of nature had been broken and needed to be restored, and she could start by bringing this waterwall down. The thundering of the falling water drowned out all sounds other than itself, and she began to breathe in the moisture and feel the hydration with all of her senses. As she exited the bridge on the far side, she began to taste the cool droplets as she pulled them in. She continued to glow, surrounded by the blue magic pouring from the stone.

The magic built and built, as she watched the spirals of blue light and tendrils of water spin, she focused on a single powerful emotion, her responsibility to all of those in the Wastes, not just her family, not just her friends, not just her own community. The whole world of Chroma needed water. Blue was not the only place it was necessary to survive. She thought of that young girl in pink from Axel's memory, walking away down the path. She thought of relationships and her new friends lost behind the wall.

She felt the power start shaking her it was so great.

Lara closed her eyes, taking in the sound of the water. The emotion was true, the stone reacted and with a small nod, she opened her eyes and began to draw the water from the waterfall down into the riverbed, heading toward the Wheel Road. The magic in the waterwall snapped and the top of the wall began to collapse downward from the center. Waves of water gushed toward her, but Lara just joined in with them, working to control the water and keep it in the dry riverbed. Waves crashed and churned around her and she joined them in relishing this sense of freedom. She was finally heading home.

Her lessons with Axel must have been intentional. He had prepared her magic for just this thing. She flowed with the water, pulling it quickly and precisely toward the Blue Realm turnoff. Turning to look back, she saw the waterwall slowly sink as more and more of the water funneled back into the original riverbed.

She gave a moment of thought to what she had left behind and the bridges she had just burnt, for it was unlikely she would be welcomed into Azural again. But she laughed at her own thoughts. They hadn't really welcomed her with open arms the first time she arrived, either.

She still had many friends there. Maybe with the waterwall down, the Blue Realm might learn to look beyond their borders. The world was a big place. And more people needed sustenance from this water than Azural needing their wall to hide behind. Fleck reached out and pushed her head toward the river before them. Sending her images of home and family.

# Waterweaver

Lara was not waiting till she got home to save it. The riverbed behind her home had been lying dormant for too long, and she knew that their tributary was fed from the larger river that ran along the Wheel Road. She stood at the river directly across from the Spoke to Blue and looked at the water flowing.

She was still not confident enough in her powers to just send water along full force. She might flood her hometown without even realizing it.

She was nearing Purple; the violets popping up along the path when she felt the change in the environment. It amazed her that she could feel it, almost like her pulse. She was much more aware of the water in the river. Considering that she had been surrounded by water in Azural, it was no wonder that when there was less of it, she could feel it more strongly.

"Ok, Fleck. Here goes nothing." Lara lifted her arms and focused on Sheila. She pictured the goat's water dish empty in the dry cracked dirt behind their home. She pictured the trickle of water in the wide riverbed. She wanted to fill that water dish. Sheila was thirsty. The Blue flowed from her arm and the water flowed just a bit stronger. "I think that is enough. We can do more when we get there." Fleck looked at the water, then back up at her and she felt his agreement with her actions. Then he sped down the road toward home. Laughing, she joined him. She couldn't wait to get back.

A few days later, as she arrived at the wooden bridge and the turn off to Calambria she realized that the path was still broken. The water she had brought along filled half the riverbed and she scrabbled down to the muddy side of the stream. The gravel was just as dangerous as ever on the path from the Wheel Road and Lara and Fleck had to slow their pace. The slow pace gave her time to worry. Had she taken too long? Would she be able to bring the water back? Were her kids okay?

Almost as soon as she left the pebbled path and her feet found firm footing, she heard a call out to her, "Mom!" Anna was there running with her arms wide. Lara met her halfway and held her tight. Anna was laughing and Lara just cried. She didn't want to let go, so Anna just held tight too and started telling her about the last few days. Lara felt the words rumble quietly through Anna's chest, along with hearing them in her right ear.

"The water had started flowing two days ago, and we all knew you had done it. Sally and I have been taking turns watching for you."

Finally, Lara broke the hug and looked at her. "I've missed you so much. I have so much to tell you. So much happened. I don't even know where to begin."

"You can tell us when we are all together. Come on, Sally will want to see you, and I am sure Dad does too." Anna pulled Lara along the path. They didn't turn down her lane toward home though, instead they headed toward the town square. People saw them going by and dropped what they were doing to join them. When they arrived at the center of town, there was already a crowd.

People were asking her all sorts of questions, but she couldn't keep them straight. Each question felt too big to answer in a sentence.

Anna just shoved her way through to the fountain in the center of the square. It had been dry since before Anna was born and it had turned into a platform for speeches. She jumped up onto the top, where the statue of a wish dragon sat curled. "Enough with all the questions. She just got back. Come on up here, Mom."

Lara climbed up next to Anna. She smiled and looked around her. "I think that actions will speak louder than words here." First, she looked at the faces in the crowd. She saw Sally making her way through the crowd to her left. She saw James pushing his way past the people on the right.

Jada was up front already with a grin and a twinkle in her eye. She looked around at the grime on the homes, and up at the deep grey sky. Inspired, she closed her eyes and felt for the water.

The clouds overhead rumbled, and she thought of these people with her now. Her friends and family had trusted her to bring them the water they needed, and she had done it. The river was running beside town now, and they would survive, but she brought more than that. She owed them more than that. She reached inside herself and found the responsibility she felt for each of these people. She didn't just want them to survive, she wanted them to thrive.

She heard an intake of breath from the crowd and opening her eyes saw the now familiar blue mist had already surrounded her. She sent it upwards and pulled it down, and with it came the rain.

Her neighbors looked up at her with awe, and she felt a bit like a stranger to them. Then she met Sally's eyes, and she saw nothing but trust and love there. Sally wasn't scared, she wasn't awed. This was the mother she had always known. Lara felt her heart contract with love as she tried to balance it and control the power she was sending out. The rain fell harder, and the people cheered.

Children began jumping in puddles and Lara saw Granny Winslow just standing with her arms wide and her face up contentedly, letting the water run down her cheeks.

As the water continued to fall Lara began to split the magic, pulling water, but also pushing the droplets in the clouds. Her goal was clear in her mind. She needed to bring the blue skies back. The clouds slowly rolled across the sky over the mountains toward the south, and she saw the first glimmer of bright blue above. Granny Winslow was the first in the crowd to see, and soon they all pointed.

As the deep dark clouds above gave way to light puffy white ones, the townspeople, Lara's loved ones and family, silently stared. She brought her attention from the skies to their faces. Tears streamed down delighted smiles.

Lara climbed from her perch on the dragon's back and came down to hug Sally and James. Anna joined in.

Eventually, they reached their fill of hugs and pulled away from each other. Lara took a deep breath and turned, again focusing on her emotions. She poured the truth in her heart toward the wish dragon statue and the blue magic weaved its way through the fountain, slowly filling it with water until finally the water poured from the dragon's mouth hitting the black stones below.

The truth was that Lara was home. She had made it, and they were saved. She threw an arm around Anna on her right and Sally on her left and squeezed them close, marveling at the content she felt from a job well done.

$$\text{꒱꒱꒱}$$

Lara sat in her favorite chair by the window in the kitchen. She looked out at the blue sky contentedly. Fleck was out there perched on a fence post chittering away at Sheila, while the goat just stood there staring at him with her large eyes. Those two had become close, and Fleck spent most of the mornings telling Sheila about his adventures. She was patient and attentive, and it was adorable. Lara watched as Fleck moved around the yard at a furious, quick pace and then turned to wait patiently as Sheila slowly followed along.

James was similar to Sheila in that way. Lara told him all about what she had seen and done, new stories coming to mind over dinner or while they were reading and he would listen to her share supportively, then go back to reading or eating. She appreciated his solid, no-nonsense acceptance of her new abilities.

She looked around the house. Again, it felt empty without the kids. But the clouds were gone, and the sun was shining through the clean windows. She felt happy, but still antsy. She stood abruptly and grabbed her sack next to the door. "I'm going out for a bit," she called to James.

Walking down the lane to Jada's, she could see the differences everywhere. The houses were no longer covered in muck. The rain had washed them clean. And everything just looked better with the blue skies overhead. She saw more neighbors out in their yards than she remembered since childhood. Happy waves came from everyone.

She had spent every evening the first week back at the town hall telling her story and answering questions. Everyone wanted to know the details. But her story was told, and now there was so much to do. The town had hope again.

Jada was in her front yard with a shovel. She had been breaking up the mud to the left of her doorway.

"Hey Lara," she called, "I was about to head to the market. Is that where you are headed?"

"I just needed to do something, wasn't sure what, so I'll join you."

They stopped by Sally's place on the way. "Why don't you join us?" Lara had asked, but Sally and Fiero were busy, she said. The people in town were busier than ever. Hope had sparked newfound energies, which had sparked new needs. Walter had ordered a yoke for his cow. Almost everyone wanted shoes repaired. Fiero and her would be busy for weeks.

"Love you Mom, bye." Sally had called as Lara walked out the door.

"Love you." Lara called back, her heart singing.

The tavern was bustling. Anna was talking to a table of six who looked hungry. Lara recognized them as Wilmer's kids, all about Anna's age. They all looked so grown up. They had been helping Farmer Oswald in his field, she heard them telling Anna.

As Anna turned toward the bar, her face lit up at the sight of her mama. Lara would never forget that look. She felt her heart warm, and she took note to store this emotion away. Nothing felt quite as good as a daughter still loving you on the flip side of the hard years. Lara gave her a quick hug, and they took Anna up on the offer of some vegetable soup.

Sitting at the bar, Lara was again bombarded with the feeling that everything was good. The townsfolk were happy, her daughters were happy. She looked at Jada and saw that Jada was smiling at her a bit mischievously. She felt like her friend saw right into her soul.

"Everyone is happier." Lara said.

"Yes…" Jada answered, drawing it out to encourage Lara to continue.

"I have magic, the power to make it rain, and fill your cup with water." Lara did just that.

"But…" Jada prompted.

"But I still feel antsy."

"And what are you going to do about it?"

Lara felt the twinkle in her eye as she looked at Jada. "Maybe I'll just go and get me another stone?"

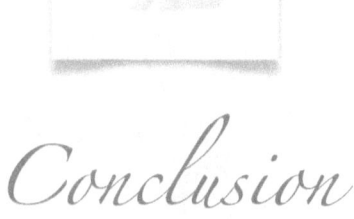

# Conclusion

The tiny creature had left the broken shell to go on with its amazing adventures, leaving its birthplace behind.

The white of the shell sat lightly on the green grasses with lovely wildflowers of pinks and reds, oranges and purples waving in the light breeze beside it. The blue sky above was home to the yellow sun shining down and warming the eggshell pieces along with the sturdy tree that had grown so quickly above it. The brown roots reaching into the healthy black dirt cupped the shell, protecting it and its treasures.

Inside the shell where the tiny dragon had grown, the seven magic stones sat. Their rainbow of resources seeping into the world around, making it beautiful and whole. A little slice of what the world was supposed to be. Balanced. Complete. Magical.

Maya Gouliard

# The End

# Sneak Peek at Terraweaver

## Preface

The sun beat down on layers of packed earth, highlighting a multitude of shades in lines from burnt sienna to a bright dusty orange. The old man stood sturdy and strong against the wind, appearing as one with the ground and canyon walls. But the dragon towering beside him, although looking comfortable and at home in the setting, stood out against all the color around him: as if he were more than all this grand wonder of nature. His white fur flowed in the wind, as if it were trying to pull him up into the skies.

They both looked out at the expanse of the canyon before them, each of them deep in his own contemplation. A comfortable silence sat between the two, a comfort that came from years of deep connection.

Without a word, they both started walking into the burnt orange hues of the sunset toward their home. It had been a long time since anything had changed for them, their mornings, evenings, and nights held the same disquiet, that nothing would ever change, when they both felt deeply that it must.

## Home

Lara pushed open the back door, carrying the basket with their laundry. It was only a few items. She had gotten into the routine of every morning gathering the few pieces from the day before, right after breakfast. She enjoyed the peace of the early morning yard. Sheila the goat was always a bit happier to see her first thing. Lara reached down to pat her bony head and then slid her hand down one of the goat's long soft ears. The velvet smoothness always made her just feel a bit more at peace.

Sheila pushed her head into Lara's knee forcefully. "Oh, something I should know?" Lara asked with a glimmer of laughter. She looked over and sure enough the water bowl was empty.

Lara walked over to the laundry line she and James had strung up between the house and the trunk of their dead tree. Branches had been cut down for firewood years ago, but the thick trunk of the once sturdy ash tree still stood. Considering that most trees in the Wastes had long since started keeling over, this one's roots must have been deep and strong.

Once she had set the basket down, she turned to Sheila. "Shall we play a bit?" she asked. Ever since returning from Azural, she had tried very hard to be responsible and in control with her waterweaving powers. The magic was always there, she could feel the water rush by in the river no matter where she was in town. She knew how full the well in the town square was at all times. She found that she could even tell if any of her neighbors were dehydrated. The water practically sang to her. She felt a tickle of it from the clouds high in the sky, it pulsed through the blood in her veins.

But she didn't want to be too different. She knew that all of her fellow townspeople loved her still, but now they looked at her askance and with hooded eyes more often than not. Her power had been on full display that first day back in Calambria. Pulling waters from the skies to make it rain, filling the almost dry Hope River again, these were not acts of just anyone. The sparkling blue magic had surrounded her that day on the Wish Dragon fountain in town, and she found that the image had stuck in their minds.

She was no longer simply their neighbor Lara, the girl they had played with as children in the dirt field behind the schoolhouse. The woman they had trusted to teach their children after the teacher had left town. The friend they had worked with when they were repairing the fence to keep the wolves out. No, she could no longer just be that old Lara to them now. She was something more. She was something bigger. It was a bit disconcerting from her end.

But in her back yard, it was different. Sheila didn't care. The goat just wanted her water dish —and her belly- full. Lara closed her eyes for a moment and let the glimmer of fun seep into her responsibility to this nanny goat. For years Sheila had supplied them with milk that many in the town had desperately needed. This goat had supplied the milk that created the cheese that Lara kept as her special treat each day. As much as the goat needed them, they needed her. Lara opened her eyes and marveled at the magic accumulating around her upper right shoulder. She had been a waterweaver for months now, but it was still amazing. The light emanated around in ribbons of thin blue from the stone grafted to her arm. The magical light caught the morning sun, and the sparkle reminded Lara of the ocean in Azural, the sun hitting the peaks of the waves, and then just as quickly disappearing only to have a glitter hit from another place. Lara's sparkle jumped along as the ribbons slowly moved.

She smiled at Sheila and playfully whirled as she shot the ribbon of light toward the river. She couldn't see the river from their yard, but she knew it was there. She had walked the path a thousand times, but she also could just feel the water. She sent the magic in a high arc so that it would land directly into the center of the river. The magical light dissipated as it floated away, but a ghostlike effect lingered for a few moments as the magic moved away from her.

She turned to Sheila again, looking at the water bowl next to her. She tried to gauge how much she was scooping up from the river. Could she control it enough to fill the bowl? She pulled what she thought she needed and leaped again, although it was unnecessary, and pulled the magic back toward the bowl. She used her right arm to create an arc in the air as if she were painting the water across the sky and pointed at the bowl at Sheila's feet. The arc of water followed the path she laid out and landed in the bowl, filling it.

Lara stopped it before it overflowed and sent the rest of the water back in a stream across the sky. Lara looked contentedly at the blue magic arches in the air. She stood silently as she watched the glittering magic slowly filter back down to the ground, settling in.

Sheila was not watching the blue, she was lapping up the water. By the time that Lara watched the last of the magic disappear into the ground, she saw that Sheila's bowl was empty and the baleful eyes looked up at Lara entreating her for more.

"All right, but no more games, I have to get this laundry hung." This time Lara just pulled the water she felt in the air around her, gathering it up and wringing it out above the bowl. A hint of blue hovered along her shoulder, but barely enough to notice unless one was looking. The goat didn't care if it was a big fanfare or not; she just loved to drink her fresh water.

Lara knew that her powers gave her the ability to dry these clothes by simply sucking the water from them, but she loved the way the clothes smelled after drying in the sun. It had been so long since they had the option to sun dry clothes. For most of her years as a mother, the sun had been hidden behind thick dark clouds. Now, the blue skies boasted a bright sun.

Strangely, the sun didn't help to warm the town of Calambria. Lara wondered at the elements and their connection to the magic stones. Was it yellow that pulled the sun's warmth down to them? The water stone's magic was abundant here in Calambria now that she had returned it. What would happen if they brought all of the stones home?

Lara threw yesterday's blouse over the rope and pulled at the corners. Then she ran a hand down the center of the wet fabric. The fabric, cool and rough, had been mended more times than she could count. That was the last of it.

She turned to head back inside with her empty basket loosely held by the handle in her left hand. She was almost at the door when her entire vision was flashed with a bright splash of pink.

Oh no. *What did you do now?* She didn't have to reach out to contact Fleck, because the flash of pink had linked them tightly. Her answer came two-fold: first, she saw a quick image of the living room, all the books on the floor; second, she heard James's shout, "Lara! He has done it again!"

Rushing in, she saw the sight of the books with her own eyes. She turned her back to it to see James. He stood in the center of the single room they used for both kitchen and living room, his hair disheveled.

"I was over here washing the dishes when all of a sudden there was a blast of air. I'm not sure what he was trying to get at, but the books all flew off the shelf." He looked like he was still a bit in shock. Then suddenly he laughed. Lara noted that his eyes were looking past her, so she turned around.

There atop a fairy tale book sat Fleck looking pleased as punch. He stared in wide eyed adoration of the full-size dragon in the image. "Of course!" James said. "He remembered the story from the other day. Aren't you just the smartest little baby dragon that ever existed?" James cooed.

Lara rolled her eyes. Of course, James would forgive anything. He loved animals so much. Lara, on the other hand, was getting just a little tired of the flashes of chaotic light that were hitting her and was starting to give her a nagging headache.

"Fleck. You could have just asked me. You know, sent a picture of the book or something. You didn't have to just blast it down."

James sat down next to Fleck on the floor as Lara began picking up the books. "Once upon a time, the Great Dragon Selephor ruled over the skies of Chroma. His flight path took him across the land." James voice always relaxed Lara. He had a way of keeping things succinct and clear in his tone. She rarely misunderstood what he was saying. He had a way with his own words, but even reading someone else's he was melodious.

Since returning to Calambria, Lara had gathered all of the storybooks she could find on the Pelanor. Hoping for hints about what to expect for this little one. They read them over and over again. Curled up on James' lap, Fleck didn't look much like the dragon in the drawing of this children's tale. He looked more like Granny Winslow's cat, but with much longer of a soft nose and a bit longer of a body, like a fox.

The only book she had that had confirmed Fleck was a Pelanor, or Wish Dragon, or Guardian Dragon, was the leather-bound book of Siegel's Journals. He had written it ages ago, and she had been lucky to find it in the Library of Azural. And been lucky it was in her pack the day she had been arrested.

The journals were all over the place in their lack of organization, so reading them for information was a bit of a hunt. She still hadn't learned anything about these flashes of color she was getting every single time that Fleck used any magic. Actually, she hadn't found anything about the psychic link connecting to a human. He had referenced the link they have with other Pelanor a few times though. He had conjectured that it was how they all communicated, through telepathic images.

As she finished placing the last book on the shelf, James stopped short of the end of the tale. Lara looked over and Fleck was fast asleep in his lap. She scooped him up and set him on the cushion by the fire. He was still so young, and although he was no human, she was constantly reminded of her own children. The bursts of energy, the enthusiasm, and the need for a good old nap.

James smiled as he slowly stood up. "Well, back to the dishes."

"I can do them if you like. I finished the laundry." Lara said.

"No need. Weren't you going to go into town to check on Jada, Farmer Oswald, and then go by Sally and Fiero's?"

"You wanna come?" Lara asked.

"No. I am almost done reading my book. And besides, someone better stay with this troublemaker. Tell Sally and Fiero hello for me. I'll see them tomorrow for dinner. Remind them I am making chowder. It's Sally's favorite." He said, heading back to the sink.

# About the Author

Maya Gouliard is a late-blooming fantasy author who discovered her writing voice after raising her children. Her debut novel "Waterweaver" draws deeply from her own life experiences, transforming personal challenges into magical realms where color holds power and motherhood strengthens the adventures. When not crafting fantasy worlds filled with baby dragons and everyday magic, Maya hosts her podcast, "I've Always Got Time to Talk," where she highlights how an inquisitive mind paves the path to wisdom. Her intimate understanding of family bonds and resilience infuses her writing with authentic emotion that resonates with readers of all ages. Maya's journey from mother to storyteller embodies the same transformative spirit that defines her characters.

https://calmillusion.square.site
https://linktr.ee/mayagouliard
https://substack.com/mayagouliard

Maya Gouliard

## Also by Maya Gouliard

### Terraweaver

Book Two of the Chroma Series
Follow along on Fleck and Lara's next adventure.

### Our Journey into Unschooling

A short memoir about the choices made to move to child-led education.

www.ingramcontent.com/pod-product-compliance
Lightning Source LLC
Chambersburg PA
CBHW021008260626
47169CB00006B/2005